Christopher Brookes

A Single Hair

Book One

The Langbourne Trilogy

Grosvenor House
Publishing Limited

Christopher Brookes is hereby identified as author of this
work in accordance with Section 77 of the Copyright, Designs
and Patents Act 1988

The book cover picture is copyright to Christopher Brookes

This book is published by
Grosvenor House Publishing Ltd
28-30 High Street, Guildford, Surrey, GU1 3EL.
www.grosvenorhousepublishing.co.uk

A CIP record for this book
is available from the British Library

ISBN 978-1-78148-798-3

Christopher Brookes was born in Hillingdon and attended Ealing Art College where he studied Fine Art. A singer songwriter, he has worked as a fashion and toy designer and for the last twenty three years has lived in South West France designing and building a Perigordian style Chateau. Married he now lives in Mid Wales.

A Single Hair is his debut novel and the first of The Langbourne Trilogy.

For 'Fritty'
"Love never dies"

PART ONE

Chapter 1

January 6th 1987

The Sulpha Crested Cockatoo was perched high in the branches of a gum tree that towered over the dense green canopy below when it stopped preening. It had seen something. Slowly and very deliberately it put its head on one side and fixed an inquisitive black eye on the other side of the valley where, in slow motion from the high road that skirted the far cliff, a shiny red car prescribed a perfect parabola as it fell into the gorge below. It was out of sight before the sound of its crashing descent and the terrified screams of its three occupants ricocheted back from the surrounding valley walls to the motionless watching bird.

Almost a thousand feet below that vantage point, underneath the mangled remains of the upturned car with a front wheel still slowly turning, arterial blood oozed down an arm, round and through the metal watch strap and along the index finger before dripping into the stream just a few inches below. The wristwatch appeared undamaged but it had stopped.

The time was exactly 11.47am.

Eighteen miles away Highway Ranger William Rodgers was on his way home when he spotted his wife's Holden parked outside the store at Bentwood Creek. He pulled in, climbed the three steps to the veranda and gratefully entered the coolness of the little shop. He took off his Ray-Bans, tucked them into the top pocket of his tunic and, taking off his wide brimmed hat, wiped the sweat from his forehead with the inside of his arm. The storekeeper looked up from his newspaper.

"G'day Bill, hot enough for ya? You wanna beer?" Bill didn't reply right away but cast his eyes round the self service store.

"No ta Hadley I'll be late for lunch. Where's Sandra?"

"Oh yeah I almost forgot, your wife's car wouldn't start, she got a lift with that couple from Launceston. You know the Harrises, they live next door to your folks. They're down on their half term hols and were on their way to pay you a visit with some stuff from your Ma. I think I heard them say they were taking the valley route to yours. I've called Dodds at the garage but he can't look at the car until later on this afternoon. You got his number Bill?"

"Yeah I'll ring him, thanks. Well, better go. See ya later Hadley."

"Righto Bill."

Twenty minutes later Bill drew slowly up to the broken barrier on the canyon road. He got out and holding onto the twisted barrier peered over the edge. In the sweltering midday sun, way down below the forest canopy where a little silver stream tumbled and twisted, something glinted. He raised his field glasses from the loop round his neck, adjusted the focus and carefully scanned the location, then he ran back to his patrol car and radioed in with the location and asked for the Special Rescue Squad.

An hour later the helicopter team from Hobart winched up each of the victims in a cradle and lowered them to the road near the waiting ambulance. Each was in a body bag. Bill knelt by the nearest and with trembling hands and a great sense of foreboding drew down the zip. For perhaps ten seconds and without comprehension his eyes travelled the ravaged, contorted face before a wave of darkness eclipsed his vision and he passed out.

Chapter 2

Felicity sat in front of her dressing table reflecting on recent events as she applied her lipstick. She lifted out a necklace in her jewellery box and saw beneath a tiny pressed rose that Harrington had given her when he proposed. She gently touched a petal before continuing wistfully with her make-up, occasionally stopping to lift her hair and remembering with some amusement when she last wore it like that.

She rose from the table and let the towel wrapped around her slip to the floor as she gazed critically at the many dresses in the wardrobe. She slid the hangers back and forth, occasionally half pulling out a dress and holding it against her before eventually choosing one and slipping it on. She wondered if she had the nerve to wear it without underwear. She walked demurely back and forth in front of the full length mirror calculating the acceptability of her breasts gently swaying beneath the beautiful Versaci gown. Despite having given birth, a rigid diet and even more draconian exercise program had returned her body to the head turning graceful curves that had been the first distant attraction for many a would be suitor before her marriage. She was, however, one of nature's rarities, an arrestingly beautiful woman with a figure to die for yet with a guileless engaging personality. She seemed to be unaware of her instant effect over men for they all fell in love with her, old and young alike. Even the Lotharios were totally smitten and in severe danger of reforming. But throughout she treated all the same with a wide-eyed and innocent interest as she appeared to hang on every word, making each and everyone to whom she gave her attention, feel strangely and intimately special as though they were sharing secrets peculiar to them. In a crowded room conversation would falter and heads turn as she walked past, each distracted by both her graceful carriage and enigmatic smile.

She returned to her dressing table and gazed at the beautiful woman reflected there. The mane of dark blonde hair tumbled softly to her shoulders where impossibly delicate straps captured the palest blue silk evening dress. Beneath the delicate wings of her eyebrows, lights danced in the blue grey eyes with their thick curling lashes as she noticed in the mirror the tall athletic figure of her husband behind her, leaning casually against the door frame. She picked up a diamond earring and, sweeping her hair to one side, threaded it in.

"Now, how long have you been standing there Harrington?" He grinned, walked towards her, placed a warm hand on her shoulder and whispered.

"Just long enough to notice that you have forgotten something." Puzzled she turned round and looked up at the handsome man with his unruly dark brown hair as he leant over her. She raised an eyebrow.

"And what might that be I wonder?" From behind his back Harrington produced the lace edged ivory coloured underwear she had left laid out on her bed. Felicity giggled, and blushing tried to snatch them from him. He evaded her and carefully folded them into his jacket pocket.

"No, you've obviously made up your mind not to wear any, so you won't need these. Bet that would get a few of our male guests a bit hot under the collar if they knew." Felicity looked shocked.

"You wouldn't!" He paused clearly contemplating the possibility, before very slowly shaking his head. Felicity laughed at him in the mirror and attached the other earring. "OK, You win. Shall I do your tie?" Harrington considered that for a moment, then turned and strode towards the door.

"No, sweetheart, I'll have a go. I'll have to learn sometime, after all you might not always be here. Five minutes, then we had better go down, the music has started, and unless I'm very much mistaken that sounded suspiciously like a bottle of champagne being opened. We don't want them to get drunk before we do or we'll have to listen to all their stories again." He laughed, looped his tie over his shoulder and hurried out to his own room along the corridor. Felicity brushed her hair, and poked at it with her fingers, noticing that a lock of hair annoyingly refused to be coaxed back into her fringe. She tried again for several very frustrating minutes.

"Ready darling?" Startled, she glanced at her watch, pursed her lips and pushing the stool back, stood up, briefly looked at her reflection in a long gilded mirror and hurried out. Harrington, looking very elegant in his black dinner suit, was waiting outside her room. "Darling, you look stunning!"

"Thank you, Harrington, and you-" she reached up and straightened his bow tie, "-look pretty good yourself, now." He smiled down at her, offering his arm. She acquiesced with the slightest of curtsies and as she moved closer to him suddenly smelt the spicy fragrance of his aftershave. She broke free and ran back towards her room. "Sorry won't be a sec, forgot my perfume."

She sat down at her dressing table and reaching for her Dior atomiser glanced once more into the mirror. The wayward lock of hair was still there. Frowning she paused for a moment, then on impulse picked up a small pair of nail scissors. She winced as, in her haste to cut off the lock, she had also pulled out one or two roots, then standing up she dropped the hair into the little wicker bin below the table and hurried out to link arms once more with her husband.

Harrington rarely looked at the ancestral portraits that adorned the plum coloured walls as they descended the immense curved marble staircase, but to Felicity, despite having lived in Langbourne House for almost five years, they were still fascinating. An unparalleled insight into the family from its Norman roots through to the present day. Almost wiped out by the Black Death in 1349 the Blaine family somehow survived and by the time Henry Blaine inherited the estate in 1685, it had grown to almost 3,000 acres with seventeen tied cottages, a mill, two farms and an extensive forest full of game with a small hunting lodge at its western margin. The Elizabethan era also proved to be a profitable time for the Blaine dynasty. In partnership with other merchant families in the county they commissioned several trading ships which revived their earlier fortunes. Originally built by the River Lang, on the remains of an old Norman keep, Langbourne Manor survived until 1827 when it was largely destroyed by a fire that started in the adjoining chapel. Sir William Blaine then built Langbourne House in its present form and restored the old chapel and family vaults despite the extensive damage and crippling cost. A scholarly man, he indulged his love of books and antiquities and added a northwest wing designed by Sir Nigel de Lacey to house them. His legacy, the Langbourne library, was sold to the nation to meet inheritance taxes in the early 1930's but a number of fine first editions were retained and they formed the nucleus of a smaller library in the same wing.

Harrington's father, an only child, was born just before the outbreak of the Second World War in 1939. Since his mother never really regained the buoyant health she enjoyed before confinement, Stephen Blaine was left much to his own devices. He would spend hours at a time marvelling at the artefacts that six generations of Blaines had garnered from the four corners of the earth. Two enormous elephant tusks sentinelled the tall ornate double doors to the collection. There could be found fearsome African masks, assegai and curiously beautiful black wooden statues that he later found out to be ebony, inlaid with ivory. High above the Victorian mahogany display cabinets with their fascinating Oriental contents, and witness to the skill of the taxidermist, more than a dozen wild beasts snarled silently down at him. Glass cabinets on fine plinths housed a variety of model ships. In one, a ship of the line, a marvel of shrouds and miniscule blocks and there, in another, an elegant tea clipper rounding the horn with scuppers awash sails taut as a drum. If he closed his eyes Stephen could almost hear the wind humming through the rigging, the deck vibrating beneath his feet. There were old iron-bound sea chests and brass-banded telescopes and a cabinet full of the most exquisite butterflies. Row after row of African Blues, Red Admirals, Peacocks interlaced with Western Blue Beauties, Janette Foresters, a rare Gaudy Commodore pinned in 1777 and hundreds more. But his favourite place, where if you'd lost him you would be sure to find him, was the annex. For there, with the pungent smell of polished wood and leather, was the library.

In everyday life Stephen was something of a disappointment to his father. He was shy, often preferring his own company to that of his contemporaries, and when occasion allowed him no escape, little to say for himself. For whilst he might appear to be paying attention, it was evident from the confused expression and heightened colour when asked a question, that his young mind was clearly elsewhere. Several relatives, notably uncles, attempted by occasionally taking him to the races or the theatre, to awaken other interests but to no avail. For Stephen was in love with books. Indeed so much so, that even when lads of his age were showing a healthy interest in the opposite sex, Stephen was to be found poring over an early illustrated edition of Darwin's Survival of the Species, or enthralled by the adventures of Defoe's Robinson Crusoe. When Stephen's father died prematurely potentially there loomed a crisis. For, because of his obsession with the contents of Langbourne library, there was a distinct possibility that the Blaine dynasty would end with him. However fate was to lend a hand, for on his twenty-sixth birthday, one of the guests, a distinguished man in his forties, rather bored with the small talk in the lounge excused himself and started to explore the house. In due course he came to the little museum and after spending half an hour peering with great interest at its artefacts he pushed open the annex doors and wandered into the library.

"Good gracious!" He exclaimed. One must suppose that to someone who was not familiar with the library, to suddenly discover such a treasure trove of books, it might indeed come as something of a shock. He repeated his exclamation and moved down the aisles of books his eyes everywhere at once. Then he paused, and with trembling hands gently drew a worn leather bound book from its shelf and turned the cover. He was lost in the wonder of it when a voice from the far end of the room brought him back.

"Homer's Illiad, first edition, Have you read it?" The guest, now clasping the book to his breast, slowly turned and smiling nodded his head at the young man looking at him over several piles of books from a desk at the far end of the room.

"Remarkable, quite simply remarkable. Did you know the Illiad was written more than 800 years BC? Ah yes, the Siege of Troy, fascinating. Oh by the way, I'm Professor Armstrong, Julian Armstrong and who might I ask are you?"

"The custodian of this great pile, Stephen Blaine, how do you do." Then with the understatement of the day. "Do you like books?" They looked at each other for a moment, then simultaneously burst out laughing

A week later the professor returned with his niece, a not unattractive young woman called Elizabeth, about Stephen's age and explained that if he had no objection might she start cataloguing his collection for a reference work he was writing about private rare book collections. Delighted that someone was interested in his books, Stephen readily agreed and in Elizabeth he found an instant rapport. To him she was intelligent, serious and despite her plain attire and lack of make-up, when animatedly discussing a passage or verse, very appealing. For above all she had a genuine love of books. Like him she loved the smell of them, the feel of them the look and the weight of them and of the books she had no knowledge she loved the surprise in them. In her he had found a kindred spirit. Within a week he realised he couldn't do without her and within a month plucked up the courage to tell her so. And so it came to pass that Stephen and Elizabeth tied the knot in the little chapel next to the house, much, it has to be said, to the great but agreeable surprise of his small circle of friends. However there was to be another surprise for it appeared that taken together their great all consuming love of the printed word eventually led them to establish a modest publishing business in Berwick Street, London. Success was slow in coming but with a number of astute takeovers, within ten years, Langbournes had become one of the country's leading publishers. By the time their only son Harrington was twenty, it was practically an institution.

Felicity paused at the last portrait as they continued their descent. It was a portrait of Stephen and Elizabeth, six months before they died in a light aircraft crash. She is sitting in a leather chair with a book open on her lap, he on the armrest with his arm lightly resting round her shoulder. They are smiling. They are in the library.

"Harrington, my dear chap, and Felicity, how lovely you look," The professor, now in his sixties, took hold of her hands. He looked up at Felicity from beneath his bushy grey eyebrows, his pale eyes moist. "I saw you looking at that portrait of Stephen and Lizzie." he gazed across to the gilt frame for a long moment, then sighed. "Miss them you know, they would have loved this tonight. Well at least they are together." he paused for a moment, then, with his eyes twinkling, looked up, "Now remind me, Felicity, how old is that little lad of yours?"

"Two, Professor, your great grand nephew Michael was two years old yesterday." The professor beamed at them both, then squeezed and let go of her hands.

"Is that what he is? Yes, I suppose he must be. My great grand nephew. How about that. Or is it great, great nephew? Do you know I never could work it out. Well what does it matter, he's one or the other and none the worse for it, eh? Two you say? Now isn't that wonderful. One loses track of time -" Suddenly he straightened up a little as a waiter carrying a tray of champagne approached. Chivalrously he passed Felicity and Harrington a flute each before helping himself. Then, without another word, he raised his glass in a silent toast to them, smiled and melted back into the party.

"Oh, look, there's Annie," exclaimed Felicity, "rumour has it that she is expecting a baby."

"I wonder whose," whispered Harrington provocatively.

"Harrington!" She spun round to face him. Harrington held up his hands and smiled.

"Just joking sweetheart. There's Max, I'll catch up with you later." He turned on his heel and strode towards a blonde headed young man, standing uneasily on his own just inside the pillared entrance to the banqueting room.

Max was feeling very uncomfortable. Although he had been born on the estate and spent all his life there, he never felt quite at ease at any of the house functions to which he was usually invited, and especially this one since Harrington insisted that he wore a bow tie. He was much happier when they were walking the estate. Country matters and its husbandry was his territory, the social scene with its small talk, air of detachment and slight decadence most definitely was not. He watched reproachfully as Harrington moved leisurely from one group of guests to another sharing a pleasantry or simply joining in the laughter.

"Max, good to see you here and wearing a bow tie. I know how much you hate them and it was optional."

"What!" Max's jaw dropped," But you said-" He stopped abruptly noting that Harrington was laughing. "Oh, right, another leg pull, eh?" Max smiled grimly and in a gesture of defiance detached his tie and undid the top button of his dress shirt.

"Oh by the way Max, I didn't forget your birthday yesterday, I just thought you might like to have your present tonight. Actually it's in this foyer, but you'll have to find it." Grinning, Harrington turned away, but not before he'd noticed Max's puzzled expression. "And no more clues."

Max, more than a little intrigued, made his way to where a waiter stood with a tray full of drinks at the foot of the stairs. Refreshing his glass Max climbed several steps and leaning on the rail surveyed the room with its happy throng, wondering just where Harrington might have concealed his gift. Many of the guests he had seen before, but there were one or two new faces of which a tall willowy brunette immediately caught his attention. She was standing slightly to one side of a group and seemed faintly bored. Her black dress, with its plunge neck-line seemed a second skin from his vantage point and, when she moved fully into view, he noticed with a slight quickening of his pulse that it was impossibly short. He wondered, as she moved silkily towards the long corridor that led to the museum, if she was with anyone. He nonchalantly followed, occasionally stopping to talk to a guest but all the while discreetly watching her progress. Finally she passed between the great doors with its flanking elephant tusks and was lost to view. He hurried after her until he to reached the doors and then slowly ambled into the room. She was now standing in the doorway leading to the library. She entered, looking casually along the row of books, occasionally brushing them with outstretched fingers as she passed. Max drew nearer, but apparently unaware of his presence she suddenly reached up to retrieve a book from a higher shelf. The little black dress rode up and Max could see her soft fulsome curves and an edge of black lace beneath. She reached up again even higher for the elusive volume. Max strode forward, aware as he did so that even more of her undergarment was on view.

"Allow me." He easily retrieved the book and turning handed it to her. She took it from him and coolly appraised him. She liked what she saw, the thick blonde hair, the strong tanned face and the slim muscular build. Max noticed that she made no attempt to ease down her dress that had ridden up high enough for him to see the soft curve of her sex beneath the lacy knickers. He raised his eyes to hers. Was she silently laughing at him? He reddened slightly, but held her gaze.

"Hi, I'm Max——" she put her finger to his lips, then shaking her head and looping her fingers behind his belt buckle drew him behind the row of shelves and out of view.

"There you are Harrington. Did you find Max? You didn't forget to get him a present did you? You know it was his birthday yesterday."

"Of course I didn't, Sweetheart, In fact I think he's opening it right now." Harrington sauntered off trying to keep a straight face and leaving a slightly puzzled Felicity wondering what he'd been up to.

To the south side of Langbourne House there is on the first floor, flanked by two wings, a sheltered open terrace with a fine stone balustrade. From this lofty vantage point Felicity looked down to a cobbled courtyard illuminated on either side by lamps regularly spaced along the stable walls. At the far end an impressive arched gateway divided the two storey buildings where the staff resided. Beyond that arch with its great cast iron gates an English park with its towering trees, lake, elegant mausoleum and the meandering silver ribbon that was the River Lang, stretched away in the moonlight, towards the darker shadow of the distant woods.

"Beautiful, isn't it," She glanced at Harrington as like her he leant on the balustrade contemplating the panoramic view.

"Oh yes, Harrington," she breathed, "it's enchanting and have you ever seen so many stars?" She moved closer to him, threaded her arm through his and in silence they gazed at the glittering night sky.

"That was such a lovely party Harrington, thank you." Harrington, looked down at the woman he loved, his heart full of tenderness and drew her closer. Eventually, turning he strode round the few toys that Michael had been playing with the day before, to a little table at the back of the terrace and started pouring out some champagne.

"Champagne darl -" Harrington stopped mid sentence, for looking back he saw that Felicity had picked up her skirts and was sitting on the balustrade with her hands clasped round a knee. He felt a stab of fear. "Come on sweetheart, you know I don't like you sitting up there."

"Oh Harrington, don't be such a fuss pot," she chided. "The trouble with you, is that you can't stand heights. Look, there's nothing to it." Felicity rose swiftly to her feet and with out-stretched arms and a seductive sway of her hips, started to walk along the balustrade coping. Horrified, Harrington dropped the glass he was holding and rushed across the terrace towards her. In his blind panic, he didn't see underfoot his son's small plastic football. He stepped on it, staggered and in trying to regain his balance pitched forward and collided heavily with Felicity. The next terrible moment would haunt him forever as seemingly in slow motion she shrieked and over-balanced. Harrington made a desperate lunge and with one hand frantically grasped the hem of her gown. As the material parted he staggered back. Half turning and screaming, her arms reaching out to him and with eyes staring, wide with terror, she fell more than thirty feet to the dark cobbled courtyard below.

Harrington scrambled frantically to his feet and with his heart pounding, drenched in sweat and sick to his stomach he threw himself across the balustrade and stared down hoping for a miracle. There she lay in the darkness below, her torn dress faintly luminescent and her face pallid in the moonlight. Her golden hair floating on a dark pool of blood spreading slowly around her. Shockingly she was still looking up at him. In the terrifying stillness he watched paralysed as the lights faded in her eyes and death stilled her trembling limbs.

Mercifully, at the same time footsteps and voices could be heard hurriedly approaching the tragic scene, Harrington fainted still clutching the torn fragment of her dress.

Chapter 3

Snow had been falling for several days at Langbourne, softly cloaking the landscape in a blanket of silence. In the far field a hare loped and beyond several red deer foraged in the margins of the wood. Harrington stood in his dressing gown at the study window sadly surveying the winter landscape. His lined, unshaven face was that of a man who had lost hope. He was consumed by overwhelming despair. He could neither eat nor sleep yet needed to do both. When complete exhaustion finally forced him to his bed it made little difference for whenever he closed his eyes the nightmare returned. He would wake trembling, bathed in sweat and on realising that it was not a hideous dream weep uncontrollably.

The physical toll was of particular concern to his old friend and doctor Ralph Bellamy. He had known Harrington from university days but was at a loss how to help him. His prescriptions remained largely untouched and any advice was met with a disinterested silence. Aware that Harrington was close to a massive breakdown he redoubled his efforts. He encouraged the resident cook at Langbourne to serve up all Harrington's favourite food dishes. He frequently invited himself to dinner in the hope that company and some conviviality might encourage his grieving friend to take some sustenance and whilst it proved partially successful it became progressively evident to Ralph that it was not enough and that Harrington, clearly suffering from a broken heart, might well pine away.

"You know Harrington," he said at dinner again one evening, "how would you like to come and stay with me for a week or two? I thought I might spend a few days at the villa. Do you good to escape from this winter weather. Monte Carlo is quite warm at this time of year, we could do some sailing, try the casino perhaps or just share a good bottle of red wine and look out over the bay. What do you say?" He looked expectantly across at the preoccupied figure across the table absently pushing his food around. Harrington didn't answer. It was doubtful that he was even listening. Ralph sighed, took up his napkin, dabbed at the corners of his mouth and leaning back in his chair looked speculatively at his friend. He watched him attentively for perhaps a minute, then gently shaking his head extracted a cigarette from its silver case, lit it, closed his eyes and inhaled deeply. They sat like that for a while, only the ticking of the clock invading the silence.

"I'll have one of those if you don't mind." Ralph Bellamy's eyes flew open and he burst into a violent fit of coughing. Finally with his handkerchief much in evidence and with tears streaming down his cheeks he stared across at Harrington.

"But you don't smoke, Harrington," he exclaimed hoarsely. Harrington pulled a face, pushed back his chair and walking round the table helped himself to a cigarette.

"Well I do now."

Bewilderingly from that point on Harrington started to recover. It was gradual at first but within two weeks he was eating moderately, taking walks and even reading the morning newspapers. His colour returned and he started to regain some of the weight he'd lost since the accident. Bellamy, delighted at his friend's unexpected progress, smiled wryly whenever Harrington lit up. He thought it somewhat ironic that he, a doctor, having failed so spectacularly with all the conventional medicines should have achieved such a remarkable turnaround with something that he spent most of his professional life advising against, despite his own addiction, and the rest treating its life threatening effects. From that day onward, in the corner of Ralph Bellamy's black medicine case amongst the pills and potions could be found a packet of cigarettes.

He remembered her sitting at the dressing table, laughing at him in the oval mirror. She was putting in an earring. He could not recall what they said but he did remember thinking what an extraordinarily beautiful woman she was and how happy they were. For both of them it had quite literally been love at first sight. He had been twenty-one, she nineteen.

Harrington looked round the room with its soft feminine furnishings and aware that his heart was beating a little faster, walked slowly towards the open doorway of her en suite bathroom. On the back of the door he discovered her bath robe and on impulse buried his face in its folds. The perfume again, only stronger. For a fleeting moment she was with him once more and in Harrington a terrible sadness welled up and he sobbed bitterly. Blindly he stumbled back towards the dressing table where he snatched up several tissues and dried his eyes. Slumped in her chair Harrington gazed into the mirror, seeing not his own visage but that of his dead wife. At last he dragged his eyes away and threw the damp tissues at the little bin beside the table, but in his agitation, missed. As he stooped down to pick them up Harrington's heart skipped a beat as he noticed a lock of golden hair in the bin. Almost afraid to touch it, with infinite care he picked it out and with it lying in the palm of his hand felt his throat constrict and the tears roll softly down his cheeks. Fumbling amongst the pots and jars of the dressing table Harrington picked up and emptied a tiny Victorian pill box. With shaking fingers, he placed the lock of hair within and gently closing it tucked the precious box in the top pocket of his jacket. Although, as he stood up, he was still trembling with emotion, he felt strangely comforted by its presence.

Chapter 5

Speeding towards London the motorway was its usual busy self. As they crossed into Middlesex and the sleet turned to rain, Harrington leaned back in the leather seat and noticed in the pouch below the driver division a newspaper. Reaching forward he plucked it out and turned to the front page. He noticed it was that morning's and with a half smile, nodded, appreciative of Max's thoughtfulness. The Times that morning had several leading stories on its front page. But the one to which it devoted more than half the page concerned the worsening situation between India and Pakistan. Harrington quickly scanned the text shaking his head and was about to turn to an inside page when he noticed an article bottom right enigmatically entitled 'Clones or Twins?' carrying identical photographs of two boys aged perhaps five or six. The accompanying article from the paper's legal correspondent sketched in the background, but what caught Harrington's eye was a quote from a certain Professor Ewen McGregor, a leading stem cell research scientist, who at the start of his evidence, late the previous day, had stated that 'human cloning was possible from the smallest DNA sample such as that found in a single hair.'

Harrington felt the hairs rise on the back of his neck. Twice more he read the professor's assertion and involuntarily placed his hand over the pocket shielding the little Victorian pill box. According to the Times the professor would be completing his evidence today. Harrington glanced at his watch, Number One Court would be sitting by ten o'clock. On impulse Harrington leaned forward and rapped sharply on the division glass before sliding it open a few inches.

"Old Bailey Max, and step on it, you've got less than twenty-five minutes." As luck would have it an ambulance, behind which they had been pacing for several miles, started accelerating, its lights flashing and siren wailing as it carved a route through the slow moving traffic. Max adroitly followed. At five minutes to ten they drew up outside the court and Harrington hurried up the steps and made his way to the public gallery of Number One court. After a security check Harrington took his place just as the Court rose in deference to the bench and watched as Lord Chief Justice Melbury took his place. The prosecution recalled Professor McGregor to the stand and after acknowledging he was still under oath he continued to expand on the detail of his testimony adjourned from the day before.

From the public gallery Harrington listened attentively to the tall, slightly stooping professor as, for almost an hour, he explained in depth and, wherever possible in simple layman's terms, the intricacies and difficulties of cloning techniques. He presaged his observations by explaining that whilst the technique of removing the nucleus from a donor egg and replacing it with DNA cells from another source was the shared procedure for both reproductive and therapeutic cloning, his own research only involved the latter. Ethically he was against human cloning but accepted that the successful cloning that resulted in Dolly the sheep had raised the issue in the public forum and expressed a hope, that given that there had been so much misinformation written, it was important to present clearly and in the simplest scientific terms what was actually involved in order that informed discussion could follow. The professor continued by explaining in detail the exact techniques involved and to many the surprise that once the DNA had been introduced into the egg, cell division - the first stage of an embryo - was activated by electrical fusion. A startled Harrington had a momentary vision of Michelangelo's painting in the Sistine Chapel where God gives Adam the spark of life. At this juncture Lord Melbury interrupted the professor and to the amusement of both bench and gallery asked him that given the egg could be tricked by an electrical charge into thinking that it had been fertilised naturally did this now mean that men were defunct? The professor smiled, and peering over his glasses at the judge, who was clearly enjoying his own observation, shook his head and suggested that the male of the species was most unlikely to go out of fashion - after all who would change a flat tyre? There was more laughter all round as Lord Melbury responded by thanking the professor and expressing his relief. Eventually the professor returned to his theme and expanded at length on the risks and success rates of cloning, together with an insight into the research and percentage probabilities of identical twins carrying exactly the same DNA profile. He was succinct, thorough and consummately professional. Undoubtedly his unparalleled knowledge and concise delivery left little room for argument by council for the defence, who, after deferring, refrained from cross examination. Thanked by the Judge, McGregor left the stand and resumed his place immediately behind counsel for the prosecution. Twenty minutes later, following submissions by QC for the defence, the Judge adjourned for lunch.

Harrington hurried from the public gallery and called Max to return with the limousine. As luck would have it, Max, who had managed to find a parking meter just a few streets away, arrived just as McGregor descended the Court steps and hailed a taxi. Harrington stood by the limousine and pointed out McGregor to Max.

"I want you to follow him Max. I want to know everything he does, where he goes, what he does, who he meets; everything." Max nodded and released the handbrake. "Oh and Max," he looked up as Harrington reached through the window and rested his hand on his shoulder, "don't lose him."

When Ewen Archibald McGregor was a month short of his sixteenth birthday his best friend died. A passenger in his father's Land Rover, Ryan McQueen's short life ended under the wheels of a goods train when, in driving rain, they stalled on an unmanned railway crossing.

Ewen was standing looking pensively down from his bedroom window at the rivers of water flooding along both curbs, when a police car drew up next door. He watched puzzled as a man, an inspector judging by his hat, emerged together with a police woman and were quickly lost to view as, with heads bent against the driving rain, they hurriedly gained the shelter of the McQueen's front porch next door. Ewen waited and watched patiently behind the rain splattered sash window for more than ten minutes before he descended the bare wooden staircase and found as usual his parents sitting by the coal fire watching television. He moved quietly behind their sofa and peeked through the heavy curtains at the bay window.

"Police next door Dad."

"Oh aye. What White's?"

"No, Ryan's." He waited, but his father was intently watching a game show. "One was a police inspector and other a woman," he added.

"Oh aye." but it was obvious he was not really listening. So with his hands in his pockets Ewen skirted the sofa to the door.

"Didn't he go to the Ranger's match?" his mother said without taking her eyes from the television.

"Yeah," Ewen turned, "went with his Dad. A surprise birthday present."

"Ah that's nice dear," sensing his anxiety she looked round at him and smiled. "It'll be something and nothing Ewen. You know, Boys."

"Yeah, but he was with his Dad." But his mother wasn't listening, she was back with the show. Ewen nodded glumly, mooched out and slowly climbed the stairs to keep his vigil. Twenty minutes later he came thundering down the stairs again.

"Ambulance next door!" He shouted to his parents as he wrenched open the front door and stuck his head out. Two medics with a collapsible stretcher and a case left the ambulance, its blue flashing light ricocheting off the terrace windows opposite, and walked the short distance to the front door. A few minutes later they emerged wheeling the stretcher. The policewoman was holding an umbrella over a still, blanketed form, above whom one of the medics was holding a drip bag. Ewen wasn't sure but he thought it was Ryan's Mam.

"Go and sit with your Dad, laddie." He turned to see his mother buttoning up her coat and reaching for an umbrella. As the front door closed behind her Ewen ran into the front room and peered past the curtain. He could see his Mam talking earnestly to the policewoman, then she went in next door as the ambulance drove off. About five minutes later a car, that Ewen recognised as belonging to Ryan's older married brother, drew up and he and his wife hurried in. Another five minutes passed and Ewen's mother returned grim faced. She took off her mac, shook it, replaced it on its peg, and walked slowly into the front room. Ewen, still standing by the window, exchanged troubled glances with his father as he waited tensely for his mother to speak. She looked down at her hands as though trying to marshall her thoughts.

"There's been an accident." Her bottom lip trembled, she looked up almost pleadingly to her husband. She couldn't look at Ewen, but then he already knew.

"It's Ryan ain't it Mam?" She hung her head for a moment then suddenly sat down and burst into tears. Ewen's Dad sat down beside her and put his arm round her shoulder. From somewhere she found a handkerchief to wipe her eyes and clasping her hands in her lap, she looked sorrowfully at her son.

"His Dad too Ewen, a train hit their car on a crossing." Ewen's eyes widened with disbelief, then suddenly his face crumpled and he ran sobbing up to his room.

From behind the wheel of his car the memories of that night nearly forty years ago flooded back as McGregor watched the last few carriages clatter across the road and the barriers rise. As he put the car in gear and rumbled over the rails he reflected on the many things that had happened since, not least his meteoric rise to the top of his select profession. After the death of Ryan, McGregor's personality changed. He became introspective but at the same time focused more on what he wanted to do with his life. Strangely enough Ryan was to play a major part in that decision, for it came almost as a physical shock when McGregor discovered that his young friend carried a donor card. In all the time they had spent together he had never mentioned it, nor apparently to his mother, who, although troubled by the idea, nevertheless, since he was a minor, still gave her consent for the use of his organs.

Years later, in his twenties, McGregor went to Medical School to study as a doctor with a view to becoming a surgeon. In quieter reflective moments he didn't have the slightest doubt that Ryan would have approved of that and some thirty years later, in lasting memory of his closest friend, his charitable foundation, a trust for ethical research, was named after him. The Ryan Trust had become an internationally renowned foundation whose profile had been raised when it was mistakenly reported that it was involved in human cloning. With the world's media in close attendance and with a number of television interviews the professor, who headed the Trust, firmly put his considerable reputation on the line by repudiating any such connection and demanding that his accusers provided proof to back their allegations. At the same time McGregor went into considerable detail of all the scientific work that the Trust encompassed, including the human stem cell research that was solely concerned with the possibility of providing organs for transplant surgery. He also eloquently put the case justifying such research citing the world wide shortage of suitable donors and the social and humanitarian dilemmas facing the families and doctors involved.

Once again he was transported back to those days and the plans he and his friend discussed as they walked the canal towpath with their fishing rods. The future seemed so simple then, everything possible.

"Oh Ryan laddie," and just for a moment McGregor, with a tightening of his throat and close to tears, was sixteen once more.

For the third time in a quarter of an hour, Max surfed the radio for something more interesting than the seamless pop music. He decided that, if his own experience of the last few days was anything to go on, you would have to be pretty dedicated to be a private detective and as he munched yet another bar of chocolate realised why they were so fat. Eventually McGregor exited the club where he had been lunching and with Max shadowing him returned to the Trust's headquarters. Max puffed out his cheeks, unwrapped another bar of chocolate, and leaning forward switched on the radio again.

After three days Max, using his car phone, telephoned Harrington from outside the flat in Queen Anne Street with little of interest to report other than, when posing as a delivery driver, a neighbour told him that McGregor was usually there on Wednesday evenings. Exasperated, he told Max to stay vigilant and to keep following the professor and hung up.

Harrington got up from his desk, stretched, walked across to the window and stared with unseeing eyes across the courtyard to the park beyond. His mind was racing, he was impatient to get on. He needed something on the professor. Half a dozen ideas crowded his mind but he rejected them all out of hand. Then he had a thought. He reached for his address book and picking up the phone dialled a London number only to be greeted by an answering machine.

"Tess, it's Harrington. Can you ring me as soon as you get back. It's urgent."

There is, on the corner of Elmtree Close, a small delicatessen that sells almost everything from just about anywhere and it was from there that evening, carrying a bottle of Reisling, a baguette and some Brie, that Theresa Rawlings splashed across the road in the lee of her umbrella to the four-story block of flats opposite. She shook out her umbrella before climbing the common part stairs to her top floor flat. Once inside she kicked off her wet high heeled shoes, peeled off her rain splattered mac, flicked the replay of the answer machine and hurried to the bathroom leaving the door open so that she could hear her messages. She washed her hands and was examining her face in the oval mirror over the sink when Harrington's message filtered down the hall. "Now there's a surprise," she whispered and with a parting, slightly mocking grin at her glamorous reflection, sauntered into the lounge, picked up the phone and dialled Langbourne House.

"Harrington, it's Theresa. How are you? I've been on an extended visit to my brother in Jo'berg so I've only just heard about Felicity's dreadful accident. I meant to ring, but, well you know when something like that happens the last thing you need is the world on the phone. Your true friends will always be there for you, I'm sure you know that and as one of them I just want to say that I am so, so sorry, you must be absolutely devastated. It's so, so horrible."

"Hello Tess. Thank you for that. Yes it's a nightmare, I can't begin to explain, it happened just a few hours after you left the party. We were just having a drink on the terrace ..." Harrington trailed off. There was a moment of difficult silence then he seemed to get a grip of himself. "Look I've got something I would like you to do for me. There's a chap that's been trying to stitch me up over a business deal and to put it bluntly I need to warn him off. He's a public figure and not to put too fine a point on it the last thing he can afford is a scandal." Harrington hesitated unsure how to continue. Theresa stepped into the breach.

"So you want me to pick him up?"

"Well, er yes." Theresa thought about it for a moment. When Harrington so briefly courted and then married Felicity she had been devastated. Whilst Harrington only thought of her as an occasional escort, to Theresa those brief encounters meant a great deal more. For if the truth were known she was secretly in love with him and because of that there was nothing she wouldn't do for him. Had she not proved that at the party? However after Harrington's marriage she accepted that whatever chance there might have been was lost and within six months was married herself to an oil rig engineer. Arnold was good to her, but deep down she wasn't sure if she loved him and his long working absences confirmed it. Despite the responsibility of a baby daughter she finally moved out of their Brentwood semi and into the tiny flat in Wandsworth. She took whatever work she could get and Harrington always called her whenever he needed someone glamorous and discreet to act as a hostess for his many business dinners. This request from Harrington was a slight departure for her but he'd been good to her and helped her out when her marriage broke up and she was practically destitute so she wasn't about to refuse him when it was evident he was in a bit of a bind. She lit a cigarette and exhaled.

"OK. So tell me where and when." Harrington told her where McGregor's London flat was and that he would be there Wednesday evening,

"What do you want me to do, record it?" A surprised Harrington pondered that for a moment.

"Do you know I hadn't thought of that. Yes that is a good idea. Actually I have the flat under surveillance and was looking for photos. But both would certainly button it up. Don't worry the photos are for my eyes only. I'll destroy them and the negatives after. Yes, thanks for that Tess. Let me know which evening and I'll alert my man. You still using the same bank account?" She told him she was. "Good shall we say five hundred then?" Before she could answer there was only the dialling tone. She quietly put the phone down and stared out of the window into the darkness of the deserted wet street.

"Story of my life," she whispered sadly to the empty room.

Wednesday evening, two days later, wearing a revealing dress beneath an open fur coat Theresa sat in her car several parking bays down from the Queen Anne Street apartment. She had been sitting there for more than two hours and was starting to regret the extra coffee she'd drunk before setting off. She decided to give it another fifteen minutes, then she would have to go and find a loo. She lit another cigarette and lowered her window an inch.

She had just turned on the ignition and was indicating to pull out when McGregor's Jaguar passed her and parked beyond the car in front. She switched off the engine and picking up her handbag was about to open the door, when she noticed that the professor was not alone. At the same time a long black limousine silently drew up opposite. A match flared in the limousine and for just a moment illuminated the profile of the driver. Theresa shrank back in her seat and the darker shadows. It was the man she'd met at Harrington's party. Undecided, but choosing discretion over valour she quietly drove back to her flat and telephoned Harrington.

A week later, around ten-thirty in the morning, that same man was shown up to Harrington's study.

"Max, come in and take a seat. Coffee?" Max nodded and from a large silver tray he poured and handed him a cup and waved an inviting hand towards the sugar and milk jug. Max helped himself to sugar and, re-seated, looked round the room thoughtfully stirring his coffee as he did so. He noticed that Harrington had installed a new computer on a table that practically stretched the length of the room to the left of the door and the window. On the opposite wall there was a large map of the world.

"Right Max, let's see what you've got." Max put down his cup unzipped a document folder, took out the contents and, moving his chair closer to the table, handed the documents across to Harrington.

"I've listed all his movements during the last ten days. His routine was pretty much established by the third day. He arrives at the Foundation offices about 9.30 and usually leaves alone to dine at his club, Denhams, around 1 o'clock. On Mondays, Wednesdays and Thursdays from two till five he is at his Harley Street practice. Most evenings he returns to his home in Chesney Walk .Once, sometimes twice a week he visits a club, Walsinghams and if late stays at a flat, which is registered to the Ryan Trust, in Queen Anne Street, from where I rang you last Monday. On Fridays he drives with his wife and twin boys, they look to be about fourteen or fifteen, to their country house at Hethersett just south of Norwich. Apart from going to church Sunday morning they mostly spend the time walking or working in the gardens which look to be about an acre, largely walled. The professor seems to be a keen gardener spending most of Saturday in the grounds. There were no visitors. Each Saturday his wife takes the boys shopping in the direction of Norwich and are gone for about three hours. Sunday mornings they go to church. They travel back to Chesney Walk Sunday evening, arriving at 9.30. In the envelope you will find photographs of all the places he visited, the offices, his houses, his wife and boys, his regular associates and who he talked to at the clubs as far as the zoom lens would allow. Most of the people he talked with were professional men of a similar age and, judging by their attire, mostly medical." Max paused and taking a last sip of cold coffee leaned back as Harrington leafed through the list and photographs. He frowned and rocking back in his chair, gnawed his lip.

"You've done a good job Max, but there's not much here," he murmured. "Pillar of society, a family man." Harrington looked across at Max, raised his eyebrows and started to shuffle the documents into some order. Max reached into his inside pocket and pulling out a small manila envelope, tapped it against his knee.

"And this," he said simply. Harrington looked up as Max slid the envelope across the leather insert of the desk.

"What's this?" Max raised his eyebrows and gave him a lop sided grin. Harrington opened it and keeping his eyes on Max, slid out the contents, and looked down at the photograph he'd drawn out. The photograph, taken at night, was of a young man on his haunches talking through the window to the driver of a car. The photo, which included the rear of the car, clearly showed the illuminated licence plate of Professor McGregor's XJ6. Harrington's jaw dropped and he looked up. "Where was this taken Max?" Max indicated that Harrington should turn the photograph over. On the back was written the time and the place.

'Old Compton Street, 11.20pm.' Harrington looked at Max. "Compton Street, isn't that in Soho?" Max nodded. Harrington got up and poured a small whisky from a drinks' cabinet to the right of the window. Suddenly he turned round to face Max. "It is what I think it is, isn't it? That is a pick up?" Max stretched and got to his feet.

"Yup, a minute later that lad got in the passenger seat and McGregor drove to the flat in Queen Anne Street. The boy left at 2.45 am."

"Too bad you didn't get a photo of him leaving," growled Harrington as he sat back down at the desk, picked up the photograph and studied it afresh. Smiling, Max slid another manila envelope across the desk.

"Oh, but I did."

Chapter 6

Ralph Bellamy was just writing out a prescription for yet another of his many patients who had arrived with all the symptoms of the virulent strain of flu that was going around, when reception rang through to say he had an urgent call. He asked them to hold it for a few minutes.

"One after meals and drink plenty of fluids. I'm afraid you'll be out of action for the rest of the week Mrs Mandelson. Make an appointment on your way out for Monday of next week, and we'll see how you are then." He smiled at the middle aged woman as she wrapped her scarf round her face and taking the scribbled note walked wearily out into the corridor. He pushed the door to and picked up the phone

"Yes, Bellamy. Harrington, how are you? Good, good. What's that? Denhams? Yes I'm a member, it's mostly medical clientele you know. Yes, Yes, uh, huh, Ewen McGregor, yes, I'm on nodding terms with him. Well, I suppose so. When did you want to meet him? Next Monday, well I guess so, yes alright, Monday it is then. One o'clock, fine. See you there then. No, no, not at all. Okay, cheerio then."

When Bellamy got to the club the following Monday Harrington was already at the bar.

"Ralph, good to see you, what would you like?" They shook hands and Bellamy glanced at the optics. "A Glen Morangie if I may and with all this flu about better make that a double." He rubbed his hands together as the bartender squeezed two good measures into the heavy tumbler. He took a warming gulp and then another.

"Right, old boy, what's this all about?"

"Just business Ralph," said Harrington into his drink, and then turning to him, "McGregor heads a charitable Trust and I've decided to make a sizeable donation. Good for the Trust and there are tax advantages for Langbournes." Bellamy looked keenly at Harrington, but noting the cool expression decided not to pursue it.

"Well have you in mind any particular -" Harrington interrupted him.

"Just introduce me as a wealthy business man interested in making a donation -" Harrington broke off and whispered, "actually he's just walked in, invite him over for a drink." Bellamy turned and watched as an attendant took the Professor's coat.

"Ewen," Bellamy called across the lounge, "come and join us, like you to meet someone." McGregor hesitated, glanced at his watch, then strode towards them taking the hand Bellamy offered.

"Nice to see you again, Ralph isn't it?" Bellamy beamed.

"It is, haven't seen you for a while, how are you? Let me introduce you to my good friend Harrington Blaine, he's in publishing you know. Ewen, Harrington, Harrington, Ewen." The two men looked each other in the eye and shook hands firmly. Between them Bellamy clapped each lightly on the shoulder. "Now what will you have Ewen?" The Professor indicated a single malt to the barman and leaning against the bar looked at Harrington.

"Did Ralph say you were in publishing? Anyone I know?" Ralph interjected.

"'Course you do Ewen. Langbournes, family business founded by Harrington's father." McGregor peered down at his drink, then looked up at Harrington.

"Langbournes, yes that name rings a bell, now where have I seen that? Not Berwick Street is it?" Harrington grinned at him and in acknowledgement raised his glass. Bellamy drained his glass and started to button up his coat.

"Sorry chaps I have to be off, early appointment. Now Ewen, stay and talk to Harrington and tell him about your work, he was saying only just before you came in that he was looking to make a sizeable donation this year to a good cause, that or give it to the tax man. What about your charitable Trust Ewen? Anyway, see you again sometime. My best to your dear lady. Catch up with you later Harrington, give us a ring soon, come round for dinner. Bye." McGregor and Harrington watched Bellamy leave, then turning looked at each other and with a smile shook their heads and finished their drinks.

"'Nother?"

"No thanks Ewen, better be off." Harrington pulled his card from his pocket and gave it to McGregor. "Ring me later this week. Why don't you come over to dinner on Thursday, it's Langbourne House near Bicester. I really would like to know more about your Trust and I'm serious about a donation. What do you say?"

"That's very nice of you Harrington. I'll check with

my secretary, but off hand that sounds fine. Why don't I ring you tomorrow evening?"

"Great, well that's settled then." They shook hands and whilst McGregor ambled off in the direction of the restaurant, Harrington paid the barman and left shortly after.

Harrington descended the great staircase just as McGregor arrived. Brooks took the professor's coat and scarf and McGregor advanced to the middle of the circular foyer and looked round admiringly. He moved to the foot of the staircase drawn to the portrait of Stephen and Elizabeth Blaine. He studied it for a moment, looked at Harrington and then back to the portrait.

"Your father?" Harrington smiled. "You look just like him, very much so."

"Like a clone?" Startled, McGregor spun round only to find his host grinning at him. Harrington jerked his head in the direction of the dining room. "Hungry? Mrs. Whiting wants the menu to be a surprise, but -" Harrington leaned towards McGregor and whispered conspiratorially, "I'll put money on it, the main course is a mouth watering steak and kidney pie." McGregor chuckled and followed him into the panelled room with its magnificent banded rosewood dining table. Two places had been set at the far end, and whilst they waited Harrington poured McGregor a glass of red wine and indicated a leather chesterfield adjacent to the huge marble fireplace. They sipped their drinks in silence for a few moments looking into the blazing fire.

"Tell me Professor, what was the outcome of that court case the other week? Old Bailey wasn't it? Didn't I read somewhere that you were an expert witness? Drop more wine?"

"Yes, thank you. Not proved actually, but then it is a difficult subject and in all cases, if there is the slightest doubt, the judge is obliged to remind the jury of that. So a verdict not proven, or whatever your English equivalent is, was I believe returned."

"But surely Professor no two DNA samples can be the same, can they?"

"In normal circumstances, no, not even in twins, but these were identical twins. Most of the arguments centred on that probability. Some research has been carried out but even that was not conclusive, since the donor egg has some DNA residue." Harrington leaned forward.

"But what do you really think, Professor, is human cloning possible? You are recognised as perhaps the leading expert, could you do it? And what about the gender, can that be predetermined? I seem to remember reading that you are on record as saying that cloning is possible from as small a sample of DNA as that found in a single human hair." The professor, smiled wryly.

"Yes, I did say that, but actually it's not really my interest. All my research centres around therapeutic cloning where instead of implanting the embryo back into a woman, which is reproductive cloning, we extract stem cells from it, enabling us to grow human organs in the laboratory. The beauty of these organs is that they can be used in the DNA donor as a sort of repair kit, without the most common problem of rejection occurring. But in answer to your specific question, yes, it is relatively easy to extract the DNA from a human hair and use the cells to create a new nucleus and inject those into an egg that has had its own nucleus removed. With regard to the gender that is simply a matter of PGD - pre-implantation genetic diagnosis of an embryo and selecting the one with a Y chromosome for a male or an X for a female. Of course, as I said before, it's not my interest as human cloning is not only, in my opinion morally unthinkable, it is also, as it happens, illegal."

"At the moment perhaps," said Harrington, "but -" He looked round as a servant carried in a large silver tureen. "Ah, dinner is served. Shall we?"

An hour later the professor held up his hand declining a second serving of the succulent wild strawberries that Harrington pressed on him.

"Excellent dinner, Harrington, but I couldn't eat another thing."

"Actually, neither could I, shall we retire to my study, I've got some excellent port decanted, and I wouldn't mind a cigar. How about you?"

"The port yes, but not the cigar if you don't mind, unfortunately I gave up smoking almost twenty years ago. But, please, smoke if you wish, just remember to waft a bit in my direction." They laughed and strode into the study. Harrington poured them both a good measure of vintage port and raised his glass to McGregor.

"Well Professor, here's to the - ," Harrington, his glass poised in the air, looked up at the ceiling then smiling back at the professor continued, "-here's to the unexpected." Puzzled, the professor hesitated before sipping his port and glanced uncertainly at Harrington, who opening a drawer, took out a brown manila envelope and slid it across the desk. The professor put down his port and picking up the envelope, looked quizzically at his host. Harrington, settling back in his chair, looked back unwaveringly through the haze of his cigar smoke. Now, there had been times during the evening, and not always in conversation, when the professor had felt decidedly uneasy in Harrington's company. This was just such an occasion and as, at his host's gestured invitation, he started to open the envelope he had the strongest suspicion that he was not going to be altogether happy with its contents.

For perhaps a minute, the professor looked intently at the photograph of his car and the young man alongside. He turned it over, noting the location, then returning it to its envelope, he replaced it on the desk, and removing his glasses started cleaning them with a handkerchief. The professor's mind was racing, despite his anger, he realised that he must remain calm, but try as he might he could not see the end on game here. Harrington was obviously wealthy, so it was unlikely to be money that he was after, he himself was well connected but not that well politically, so he could see no connection there. So what could it be? As he replaced his glasses and pocketed his handkerchief Harrington pushed a tiny pill box towards him. The professor reached forward and opened it to discover a lock of hair. So that was it! The professor shot to his feet. Shaking with rage he leaned forward and looking Harrington furiously in the eye, thumped the desk.

"No! I won't do it! You must be mad! That photograph is proof of nothing. It is obvious I was merely asking for directions. How dare you think you can blackmail me!" Harrington unmoved by the tirade remained seated and looked coolly at the professor through the smoke of his cigar before taking another envelope from the same drawer and passing that across. For a moment it looked as though the professor was going to storm from the room. He half turned to do so, but then paused and turning back angrily snatched up and opened the envelope. A moment later the professor, his heart pounding and feeling sick to his stomach, slumped into his chair.

"Yes, Professor, the unexpected. Now it could be worse, these photographs could be on the Editor's desk of the News of the World even as we speak. After all you're a well known figure they could even make the front page." The professor looked up absolutely horrified.

"You wouldn't?" It was a statement more than a question, but he could see the answer in the unsmiling eyes and the set of Harrington's jaw.

"Right let's get down to business, shall we," said Harrington briskly. He picked up the envelope, returned it to the drawer, locked it and pocketed the key. "You will, Professor, switch the embryo of a couple undergoing invitro fertilisation for one carrying the DNA extracted from this hair, and that will be an embryo with an X chromosome I might add. You will also take appropriate surgical steps to see that she is unable to conceive in the future. In return, you shall, at a later date and should the procedures prove successful, have the negatives, which are in my safe-keeping, and I will make a sizeable donation as promised to your Trust. You will of course return to me the rest of the lock of hair in its box, as it has great sentimental value and then, quite frankly, I see no reason why we should ever meet again. Afterwards you will carry on with your 'therapeutic cloning' research as though nothing has happened and I shall do the same, for, as far as I am concerned this meeting, this evening, never happened. But it is not negotiable. Refuse and I will ruin you."

The professor retrieved his handkerchief and wiped the dampness from his brow. For a moment he considered refusing. Never in his life had he done anything illegal. He was by nature highly principled and entirely dedicated to his profession. Whilst he accepted his weakness he had always been a firm believer that it was better to own up, no matter what the cost, than be a victim of blackmail. But then he had never been in that position until now. What should he do? His mind was everywhere at once trying to rationalize the implications of what was happening to him. What would happen to his life's work, the stem-cell research, the Trust? What should he do? His mind racing he tried to gather his thoughts and make some sense of it all. He thought of Ryan his inspirational boyhood friend and the countless friends and professionals that looked up to him. What should he do? With Harrington gazing unsympathetically at him he couldn't think rationally under the pressure of having to give an answer. He felt rising panic until he thought of his wife and their two boys. With his heart beating ever faster he realised that he couldn't put them through the ruin and disgrace of such a scandal and the inescapable public humiliation. Whatever he'd done, they didn't deserve that. His shoulders sagged.

"So that's agreed then?" The professor nodded miserably and put his head in his hands.

Chapter 7

That night, Harrington slept badly. At three o'clock he was wide awake. He lay in the darkness pondering the events of the last few days. He actually felt some sympathy for the professor, but accepted that there were inevitably going to be casualties and that he was satisfied that the end justified the means. What he did recognize however, was that he was very much in uncharted waters. Whilst he was now convinced that the cloning would eventually take place what bothered him most was the unknown to follow. Perhaps for the first time, the magnitude of what he was trying to do hit Harrington. Could it really be possible to experience the love and companionship of the same beautiful woman he so tragically lost? He pondered the age gap and its implications, then throwing back the covers, he went to his bathroom and stood in front of the full length mirror. He studied his body's reflection and tried to imagine it in twenty years. Nodding, he made a mental note to purchase a total gym machine.

Harrington sank to his haunches and without looking at anything in particular thoughtfully rubbed his chin. Meet again, he mused, I'll be in my mid forties. But so what, she fell for him before and what's another eighteen or nineteen years between true lovers. He also realised that nineteen years would coincide with their son's twenty-first birthday. He smiled as the symmetry of his plan unfolded. He met Felicity at his twenty-first, so why not meet her again in the same way, at the same place? Langbourne. Why couldn't he with all his money and determination, make it happen? He had the beginning and the end pencilled in, but what about the 'inbetween'? That wouldn't be particularly straight-forward. He could have her physically cloned, but what about her life? A person's interests, personality and tastes are not purely genetic; there are cultural, educational, environmental and not least, parental influences. Ah yes, parental, now that would need very careful selection. Distracted, Harrington ran his fingers repeatedly through his hair. His eyes were shut and he puffed out his cheeks as dozens of half-formed ideas and doubts jostled for attention. Wearily he rose to his feet and wandered back to his bedroom, slipped on his dressing gown and sat on the edge of his bed. He swallowed hard as his mind raced over some of the more serious implications of what he was attempting. Although the intricacies of planning and executing complicated business deals were the stuff of his daily life, his mouth went dry as he contemplated the monumental task of trying to manipulate the day to day circumstances of someone else's existence.

Full of indecision Harrington bowed his head. Suddenly he got up, fetched the key to her bedroom and walked resolutely down the hall. Entering the room he realised the impossibility of the whole idea. He resolved there and then to remove all traces of Felicity from his life and started to pull her belongings, left untouched since her death, out of cupboards and closets. Within no time the bed was covered with her clothes. Dozens of her dresses, coats, skirts, blouses and jumpers piled high and slowly collapsing. Then another great pile of trousers, jeans and jackets. Occasionally he would pause over an item of her clothing and with a lump in his throat dwell momentarily on the memories invoked, before shaking his head and adding it to the growing pile on the bed. Her underwear he left in their drawers but those he stacked in the centre of the room and finally piled her shoes, boots and trainers next to them. Then he took out all her suitcases and travel bags from a cupboard with a view to packing some of her clothes away. But something caught his attention. Right at the back, almost hidden in the shadows, he drew out a small battered suitcase. Obviously not empty, he knelt down on the bedroom carpet and flipped open the catches.

Harrington quietly leafed through the various papers he found there. Exam certificates, rosettes, newspaper cuttings and college sketch books. As he looked through those he realised how little he actually knew about her life in Tasmania. He gazed pensively out of the window into the blackness of the night. They had talked about making a trip back there together. When drawn on the subject Felicity evocatively painted a picture of a land far removed from the open parkland and woodlands that typified their surroundings at Langbourne. He remembered how animated she was. Her eyes sparkled as she described the flocks of sulpha crested cockatoos high in the gum trees. Of family trips to the white sands of the island coast, of cycling for hours with a friend in the summer sun to bathe exhausted in a cool lagoon fed by an enchanting waterfall. With his heart brimming, he was about to replace the sketch books when he noticed underneath a sheet of protective brown paper a number of small books. He picked one out and then another and another. Excitedly he realised that there, spread out before him were Felicity's diaries. He sat cross-legged on the carpet and started to read about the unknown life, thoughts and desires of the young girl that was to become the woman he fell in love with and married. The diaries spanned the twelve years from her seventh birthday until she left for England following the tragic death of her parents in a terrible road accident.

Several hours later as Harrington turned the final page of the last diary, he wiped away the tears that hitherto unnoticed were running down his cheeks and breathed deeply. The terrible pain of her loss and his part in her death welled up and he sobbed uncontrollably. Gradually he composed himself and realised that he could not live without her and so he resolved there and then to continue, rightly or wrongly, with his original plan. He couldn't be totally sure that the diaries contained every last detail of her formative years but with a quickening of his heart he began to think of the wealth of authentic information he had found. Like the lock of hair, he felt that Felicity had meant him to find the diaries. It was almost as though she was reaching out from her grave, trying to make him aware that her only way back was through him.

Harrington carefully replaced the diaries in the case. As he sorted through Felicity's papers once more his mind was racing ahead, trying to grapple with the order and logistics. First a couple would have to be found that could give her the stable family background that so much of this depended on. How would he do that, where would they live? Would that have to be Tasmania? Could he find a house similar to - Harrington stopped abruptly and concentrated on the letter he had been holding for the last five minutes. It was from solicitors in Hobart, Tasmania advising Felicity that under the terms of her parents will she was the sole beneficiary. There were certain bequests and legal jargon that Harrington skimmed through until he read 'and our property known as Windermere House, Launceston and its contents....' Harrington closed his eyes for a moment, then, his eyes shining he looked up.

"Thank you Darling," he whispered. He knew nothing could stop him now.

Chapter 8

Professor Ewen McGregor glanced at his watch, took a last gulp of his cold coffee, shuffled the papers on his desk and tidied them into a folder. Putting the folder into his brief case, he donned his overcoat and glancing back at his desk to check that the various computers and printers were silent, switched off the lights and closed the door. Satisfied that there was no one else in the building he made his way along the corridor to the research laboratories and entering switched on the banks of neon tubes. In the far corner of the room he unlocked a cupboard and taking out a tray placed it on the stainless table alongside. From an inside pocket he took out a little Victorian pill box and for the next few hours he worked on the exacting task of extracting the DNA from the hair within. Normally a strand of hair in itself would be insufficient for the task but amongst those he had taken from the pillbox were several with the roots attached and essential to the success of the procedure.

Eventually he retraced his steps along the corridor and descended to the ground floor, where before leaving the lift, he straightened his tie and buttoned up his coat. He walked thoughtfully through the deserted foyer, towards the double doors of the entrance.

"Night Professor." Startled he turned back to the reception desk.

"Oh, yes, goodnight Mrs Marshall. Sorry miles away. You still here?"

"Meeting my husband at Mario's round the corner in twenty minutes, so rather than go home to come back, I thought I'd stay here, do a bit of long overdue filing until it was time." The professor looked down at the attractive well groomed young woman sitting there smiling up at him. "But then you are working pretty late yourself Professor." He nodded ruefully,

"Yes, afraid so, office work, urgent report. They all want them yesterday. I think I've got what I need, but I'll keep the keys with me, in case I need to come back. Well, I'll see you tomorrow, Mrs Marshall, goodnight." He walked slowly towards the plate glass double doors of the entrance. He had the uncomfortable feeling that he had forgotten to do something quite elementary. Mrs Marshall glanced at the retreating professor and back to her switchboard security monitor and wondered why the laboratory lights were on.

McGregor closed the front door behind him and struggled out of his coat. Helen his wife took it from him and hooked it on the hallstand

"You look tired Ewen, busy day?" He smiled weakly at her and started up the stairs. "Dinner is almost ready. Hungry?"

"Actually I am, won't be long dear." He carried on upstairs to his bedroom and, taking the papers from his case, switched on the lamp and picked up the phone.

"Harrington? McGregor here. I have the list. Do you want to go through it with me?"

"No, just fax it through, I don't have time right now." McGregor pursed his lips. This was not what he wanted. The list was confidential and he'd far rather discuss the details of each couple over the phone and when one had been selected pass across their secret code.

"Well, I'll send them another time when you are free then." Without waiting for a response McGregor cradled the phone and smiled wryly to himself. The phone rang almost immediately.

"Now in which newspaper would you like to read about yourself?"

"I don't know what you mean -."

"Don't fuck with me Professor. You're not telling me anything. I'm telling you! You got that? I said have you got that?" The professor said nothing but he was absolutely furious at being spoken to like that. There was silence on the phone but the tension was very tangible. "Right, well I'll take that as an affirmative. So let us start again Professor. Fax me the list." The phone went dead. Still seething, McGregor went down stairs to his study and fed the fax machine.

"Yes I'll be right along dear. No I didn't forget. Give me two minutes." He angrily swept his hands though his hair. Actually he wasn't very hungry.

Harrington ate a ploughman's as he sat in front of the fax machine oblivious to the crumbs that settled in his lap and speckled the floor as he watched the machine methodically print out the list sent by McGregor. He glanced briefly at each page, then took them over to his desk and laid them out side by side. Each page contained a photo of the couple and a written description of their main physical characteristics. This was important since where possible the consultant always tried to match the couple to the donor. He would not, for example, mix races and he would also recognise the inherent danger in mismatching backgrounds and IQ. The rest was largely unimportant as it would be dependent on upbringing.

It was obvious to Harrington that McGregor had assimilated and applied all the information that Harrington had sent him, gleaned from Felicity's diaries about her parents. There are at any one time more than 7000 couples awaiting or undertaking fertility treatment, so to reduce that list to 19 represented a considerable amount of work and the fact was not lost on Harrington, who felt rather bad about the telephone threats he had uttered to McGregor. For, if the truth was known, he quite liked the mild mannered professor, but for all that realised he could not let sentiment get in the way of the task before him. However he would telephone him later to thank him.

He held a photograph of Felicity's parents in their late twenties that he had discovered in the suitcase and compared them with the couples spread out on the desk. One photo immediately caught his eye. In fact, noting that the woman had blond hair, it was a pretty good match generally. He collected up the others and put them to one side, and lighting a cigarette sat down and started to read the accompanying file.

Paul and Rose Beresford lived in Steeple Morden about a dozen miles south west of Cambridge where they were supply teachers. For almost five years they had tried for a baby but without success, despite the best advice from their local doctor and all the usual rituals and help from well meaning friends. Eventually it started to put a strain on their largely happy marriage, so they decided to seek clinical advice and each underwent the full gamut of tests. Those tests confirmed that whilst Paul's sperm count was on the low side there was no apparent reason why pregnancy had not been achieved, since they were young and healthy, but because they felt they could wait no longer both agreed to the IVF treatment. Glancing at his calendar, Harrington noted that Rose Beresford was already taking the necessary cocktail of fertility drugs to enable the retrieval of healthy mature eggs, and was expected at the Ishmael Clinic on the 14th March for the trans-vaginal oocyte retrieval procedure. The eggs are kept for about two days in a laboratory and monitored by an embryologist who at the optimum moment implants the sperm. When the eggs have started to divide they are considered to be of pre-implantation status, and three to five days later as an embryo they are introduced through the vagina and implanted in the uterus.

Harrington calculated that McGregor had about ten days maximum to complete his work, obtain some of Rose's eggs, substitute Felicity's DNA, get them to embryonic stage, select one with the X chromosome and carry out the implantation. He reached for the phone.

McGregor was, through his Foundation, a well known and familiar figure at the Ishmael Clinic. He regularly visited the laboratories and was an expert consultant to the clinicians and embryologists who worked there. Indeed the Ryan Foundation initiated a number of innovative techniques there that were subsequently adopted by most other clinics in their IVF procedures, particularly around chromosome screening for genetic faults. Whilst in recent years the professor found himself increasingly involved in the administration and politics of the Foundation, he was determined to remain personally involved in the research and application and was frequently to be found in various laboratories at the cutting edge of stem cell research from discarded embryos, which was the driving vehicle for cell and tissue reproduction, essential to organ regeneration and replacement.

That Thursday, embryologist Julian Bruce, his face masked, was fussing over some laboratory dishes, when McGregor in a white coat entered the laboratory.

"Hello Julian, how's it going?" Julian looked up and waved a surgically gloved hand at the professor.

"Hi Professor, fine, how are you? With you in a second." McGregor waited near the door as the young man replaced the lids and lifted the tray of dishes to the adjacent incubator. He watched while he adjusted the temperature and wrote a few notes on the attached clip board.

"That's good timing, I was about to go for lunch, care to join me?" McGregor waited while Julian snapped off latex gloves, chucked them in the pedal bin and slipped off his white mask.

"Yes I'd enjoy that, but why don't you let me buy you a lunch at the club, they always keep a table for me? They do a very nice cod roe."

"Oh no, not more eggs." Their laughter echoed down the corridor as Julian locked the laboratory and moments later deposited the key with the receptionist and signed the book.

Two and a half hours later McGregor presented himself to reception at the clinic and asked to see the senior administrator. She rang through, spoke briefly and replacing the receiver showed the professor into a spacious office along the corridor. A thick set, slightly balding man in a badly creased suit looked up and clambered to his feet.

"Ewen, how nice to see you, how is Helen? Sorry I've not been in touch but I'm....." he waved a hand apologetically in the direction of his desk piled high with papers and files.

"Oh think nothing of it Charles. Usually in the same boat myself. Yes Helen's well, taking a brief holiday. Long weekend in Dorset with her Aunt, do her good, a bit of country air and a few days rest from the twins."

"Right, that's nice, how old are they now, fifteen?"

"Yup, bit of a handful; they're on a school camp in Yorkshire."

McGregor settled himself in the chair offered and beamed at the friend he'd known for almost twenty years. Charles looked round to a table with a few bottles and glasses on a tray behind him.

"A wee dram laddie?"

"No thanks, bit early for me. Actually, I'm here to offer my services." He paused, whilst Charles fumbled in his jacket pockets, found a packet of cigarettes, extracted one and lit it. "Yes, I was lunching with Julian Bruce today, catching up on the latest gossip, when he was taken quite poorly. At first I thought it was something he had eaten, but then it couldn't be as we'd both ordered the same. Anyway to cut a long story short, I got him home and called his doctor, who has indeed diagnosed acute food poisoning, and confined Julian to his bed for at least a week perhaps ten days."

Charles puffed out his cheeks, stubbed out his cigarette and ran his fingers through what was left of his greying hair.

"Blast, that's unfortunate, he's doing a couple of IVFs at the end of next week with eggs retrieved tomorrow morning. We need the embryos to be ready for implantation for next Friday afternoon. Everything's arranged and we can't delay it. We're very short staffed right now, damn it."

"Yes I know Charles, so let me do those procedures for you, after all I feel a bit responsible, since it was my club -."

"No, no Ewen I couldn't possibly ask you to do that, it -."

"Of course you can Charles and I insist, the least I can do to help out an old friend. I know you'd do the same for me."

"Well if you are sure Ewen that would be a great help."

"Good, then that's settled. Who are the patients?" Charles shuffled through some papers on his desk and held up a page as he fished out his glasses from his top pocket and awkwardly hooked them on.

"Let me see…Ah yes, Beresford, Rose Beresford. She's the first tomorrow, and then Carolyn Martin, I'll get you their files from reception and an ID tag as you'll be needing the keys to the laboratory."

"That's great, I'll read up their files tonight and I'll see you tomorrow. Don't worry, it will all be fine."

Chapter 9

Rose Beresford sat anxiously in the waiting room of the private clinic. She glanced at her watch, sighed and picking up yet another magazine, absently leafed through the pages, occasionally pausing and looking apprehensively at the door whenever she heard voices in the corridor beyond. After another interminable ten minutes, lost in thought she looked out of the window at the rain soaked landscape. So this was it, she thought. The culmination of all those tests and the fertility drugs. She pensively chewed her lip and closing her eyes prayed that it had all been worth it. She knew how much it meant to Paul; to both of them.

"Mrs Beresford?" Startled, for she had not heard the door open, Rose dropped the magazine from her lap. Retrieving it she looked up into the smiling blue eyes of a doctor holding the door open. Colouring slightly, she stood up and picking up her handbag nervously started to follow him. He turned back to her.

"I'm sorry, I haven't introduced myself," he put out his hand and held hers, "My name is McGregor, Professor McGregor, I shall be carrying out your retrieval procedure this afternoon. I'm afraid your regular doctor, Mr Bruce, was taken ill yesterday, so the clinic, rather than cancel your appointment, asked me to stand in. There is however a minor complication, the scan has shown that you have a small cyst on one of your fallopian tubes. After I have retrieved your eggs I think you should let me remove that so that it doesn't cause you a problem should you wish to conceive naturally in the future." Rose bit her lip and clasped her handbag to her body.

"Well I know we would like to have more children one day. But exactly what is involved when you remove the cyst? Will I have a scar? Does that mean I will have to stay in?"

"Yes, but just for a few days. The procedure itself is a very simple one using laparoscopic surgery; you'll probably know that as key-hole surgery, but while you are under I will of course have done the egg retrieval and you most certainly will be perfectly well for the embryo implantation next Friday." McGregor looked kindly down at the anxious face of Rose. Seeing the questions there, he put a comforting arm around her shoulder and with his head bent close to hers whispered, "Don't worry Mrs Beresford I've carried out this sort of procedure many times before and the incision is less than a centimetre. In a few weeks I doubt if you will be able to even see the scar. Shall I give you a few minutes to think about it?"

The following Friday McGregor stood by the wall mounted incubator with its two embryos in glass culture dishes and looked across at a sedated Rose lying on the operating table. During the last few weeks he had imagined this moment and whether or not he would have the courage, even at this late stage, to change his mind and walk away. He even debated the pros and cons of going to the police and confessing that he was being blackmailed, in the hopes that he might at least salvage some dignity as the whistleblower. But he knew if he did, Harrington could quite easily wriggle out of it. After all what exactly did he have on him. Some hair. Well that could belong to anybody, and as his dead wife might well have been cremated then that particular trail would probably lead nowhere. Yes he could prove that they had met, indeed that they had spent an evening together at Langbourne, but no doubt Harrington would quite simply put himself forward as a philanthropist discussing a donation to the Ryan Trust and that would be backed up by Bellamy. No, the truth was, he didn't really have anything on Harrington, but Harrington certainly had something on him. The professor's mouth went dry as he thought of the retribution Harrington could wreak with those photographs. No at the end of the day, unlike his blackmailer, he had everything to lose. A resigned McGregor stretched his fingers in the surgical gloves, hooked up his mask, opened the incubator and reluctantly took out one of the culture dishes.

Several hours later Rose was in the recovery room and McGregor was in the scrub room preparing himself for Mrs Martin's IVF procedure when the door swung open and Julian Bruce hurried in.

"Ewen, my dear chap. I cannot thank you enough for stepping in and carrying out Mrs Beresford's implant. Everything go all right?" McGregor stared at him.

"Yes fine. However when I reviewed her scan before her retrieval procedure last week I noticed a small cyst on her right fallopian tube. Easily missed. Anyway Mrs Beresford agreed to its removal, which I carried out after her procedure. Apart from that her implant today went as smooth as silk. But enough of that, how about you?"

Julian looked across, his wet hands held high as he turned off the tap with the inside of his elbow.

"I'm OK thanks. Can't believe I missed that cyst though. Mind you it has been pretty hectic the last few weeks. Anyway, food poisoning. Phew must have been something I ate at your club. Did you order the same as me, I can't remember. Anyway you were there when my doctor told me what I was suffering from. He reckoned I would be at least a week recovering. But I'm fine now and glad to be back. Thanks for all you've done, but I'll take over now." He turned to the nurse, "OK let's go and find Mrs Martin shall we?" As he pushed through the theatre doors he looked back, "I'll catch up with you later Ewen and thanks again."

As McGregor stripped off his latex gloves, binned them and left, a theatre nurse retrieved the remaining embryo culture dish from the incubator and carried it across to a waiting Julian Bruce.

Harrington leaned back in his chair and gazed at the map of Tasmania on the wall above the computers. He had contacted Australia House and was waiting for them to return his request for a list of current teacher vacancies. The diaries revealed that Felicity's parents had both been teachers in Tasmania and at the same school in Launceston which would probably explain her knowledgeable interest in so many varied subjects. Frequently Harrington was not only amused at her ability to engage friends and acquaintances on practically any topic, but was invariably surprised at how well informed she was. There was usually unanswerable logic to her assertions and frequently Harrington would come to the aid of an intellectually cornered guest by interjecting a question or changing the subject. However on the odd occasion that she did glance in his direction whilst holding forth there was always a glint of amusement there. Her fund of knowledge and particularly her love of the English language invariably meant she would beat him at crosswords and scrabble. The fact that he was a successful publisher held little sway and she would regularly tease him about that in their intimate literary contests. Harrington closed his eyes and for a moment she was there laughing with him, and for just an instant there was her perfume and the fragrance of her hair. She was gazing tenderly at him with those wonderful blue eyes and reaching up towards him but somehow out of focus and her outline blurring. Though unwilling to let her go, Harrington opened his eyes and stared without seeing at the map until it slowly came into focus and she was gone.

Earlier that month Harrington had bought a limited company and applied to Companies House to change the name to The Burlington Foundation. He then transferred £100,000 from an offshore account and registered the Foundation with the Charities commission using two nominees from Solicitors Nairsmith and Greene who regularly acted for his publishing group.

Australia House faxed him the list and as luck would have it there were five teaching vacancies, three in Hobart and two in Launceston. Launceston Grammar School had a vacancy in physics and also were looking for a suitably qualified mathematician to serve as Deputy Head. Harrington rang the school and asked if it would be possible to contact the Chairman of the Board of

Governors with respect to the vacancies. The school secretary thought that would be in order, but suggested in the first instance he emailed the school, or perhaps faxed them, and that she would personally see that it got to the Chairman the next day. She also informed him that he could download the school prospectus from their website and that she would also send a hard copy to the Foundation's address. He thanked her for the suggestion and rang off.

Harrington took his time writing the e-mail since the last thing he wanted was a refusal and the lost opportunity to put his proposal directly to the Chairman. He explained the ethos of the Trust and asked if the Board would be interested in appointing a younger well qualified teacher to the post of Deputy Head, particularly as the Trust would meet all the relocation costs, salary, private health and pension contributions. He copied in Paul Beresford's CV, and after re-reading it all, pressed 'send'.

Next Harrington turned his attention to writing to Beresford with the offer of employment as a Deputy Head in Tasmania. He leaned back in his chair and tried to imagine the sort of offer that would tempt him if he was a young struggling supply teacher. He thought it might be a good idea to learn a bit more about the island first so he started sifting through various websites, in addition to some travel brochures he had collected for whatever they had to offer on the subject. As he started to sift through the mountain of information he unearthed he began to realise why Felicity had so much wanted them to holiday there. From Hobart in the south to Launceston in the north; from the stunning cliffs of the west coast to the silver sand beaches of the east, this island of some 24,000 square miles looked quite enchanting. It was not lost on Harrington that much of what he was reading would have been well known to his late wife and, as he viewed some of the amazing photographs particularly of the conservation areas to the North near Launceston, he little doubted that Felicity would have walked there in her teenage years. For just a moment Harrington sat perfectly still as he realised that in a few years' time she would walk there again. As he reached for a cigarette he noticed his hand was shaking.

To his absolute delight within twelve hours the Launceston school secretary replied that, under instruction from the Chairman, the school was most pleased to offer the position of Deputy Head to Mr Beresford under the terms offered by the Burlington Foundation, and that a contract with all relevant paperwork would be sent in the next few days together with a list of available local accommodation.

Paul Beresford opened the front door of their rented apartment in St Mary's Road, Ealing and taking off his anorak looped it on a peg.

"Is that you Paul?" He grinned at the question that greeted him every evening as he returned from work.

"I'm not sure," he looked in the mirror of the hallstand. "Does Paul have streaked blonde and blue hair with pink eyes and a wart on the end of his nose?" He felt a soft jab in his side and turning put his arms round the pretty blond woman who had stolen up beside him. He nuzzled her neck and ran his hands over her dress feeling the softness of her body beneath. He started to ravel up the hem untill the coolness of her skin was his to caress. Laughing she pulled away and smoothing down her dress wagged a finger at him.

"Dinner's ready."

"Bugger it, can't I have dessert first?" He put his hands up, wriggled his fingers at her and with a growl chased her down the hallway and into the kitchen, where, with a giggle, she kept him at bay with a frying pan.

Rose had spent some time decorating the table. There was a small vase with red roses flanked by candles in modest holders, several glasses for each setting including flutes, pretty napkins and a bottle of champagne in ice. Paul walked slowly round the table. It wasn't their anniversary and certainly not either of their birthdays. Puzzled he looked at Rose who could barely conceal her glee as approaching him she took his hand and gently placed it on her stomach. It took several seconds to sink in but when it did Paul let out a whoop and putting his arms round her waist lifted Rose and spun her round.

"Darling, that's fantastic! But when did you know?"

"This morning I went to the clinic, and saw Dr. Bruce who confirmed that I was pregnant and was terribly pleased for us even though he had been too ill to carry out the IVF himself. I can't believe that was six weeks ago. So there we have it. Mind you Dr. Bruce did say we were really lucky that out first implant had taken, because the average success rate for that was only about twenty percent, which is why some couples try for absolutely ages. But obviously we are one of the lucky ones and it was meant to be. They want me to visit every week for the first few months to monitor progress, but otherwise I can carry on as normal like any other pregnancy." They embraced and kissed passionately before Rose broke away and busied herself at the stove, while an elated Paul popped the champagne and exuberantly overfilled the flutes. For the next ten minutes while the meal cooked they sipped champagne and chattered happily about the coming event. Eventually Paul sat at the little table in the cramped kitchen and with a sigh picked up the newspaper and turned to the situations vacant.

"I don't know," he mumbled as Rose placed an appetizing grilled chop with a green salad before him. "With an extra mouth to feed I've a good mind to try a rep's job. At least you get a decent car, salary and some appreciation. I'm really fed up teaching. Nothing but abuse from people who think you have a real soft number working from nine 'till four and with three month's holiday every year. They should try it. I bet they don't have three hours work marking homework and preparing lessons most nights. Let alone seminars and school clubs." They ate in silence for they were no strangers to the topic, but whilst Paul often talked about leaving the teaching profession, Rose knew that deep down he actually loved the work since he had a genuine empathy with children. Eventually Rose reached across and covered his hand with her own.

"You'll find the right school Paul. It would be such a shame to waste all that training and you are so well qualified. Something will turn up soon, you'll see," she gave his hand an encouraging squeeze. "Would you like some coffee?" He smiled up at her and nodded as she started to clear the table.

"Yes please Sweetheart, that would be lovely and thank you, that was a really marvellous meal. Well I suppose I'd better see how many bills the postman brought today." He sifted glumly through half a dozen until he came to a grey envelope. Thoughtfully Paul slit it open and unfolded its contents. It was from something called the Burlington Foundation.

Chapter 10

"Would you follow me Mr Beresford, Mr Blaine will see you now." He walked behind the receptionist along a carpeted corridor and was ushered into a panelled room with stunning panoramic views across the River Thames.

"May I take your coat, Mr Beresford?" smiling he handed her his coat and scarf and as the door closed behind her walked across to the plate glass windows and looked down at the river. The Cannon Street offices of Nairsmiths and Greene afforded a magnificent view of the Thames as it swept east towards London and Tower Bridge beyond and westward along Kings Reach to the bridges of Blackfriars and Waterloo.

"Impressive, isn't it?" Startled Paul turned round to face Harrington.

"Er, yes. It is. What a fantastic view."

"Yes isn't it. Please take a seat Mr Beresford. Would you like tea or coffee?"

"Coffee if I may, thank you." While Harrington rang through to reception, Paul studied the tall dark suited man. He judged him to be about thirty despite the trace of grey at the temples and around six feet two inches in height. Beneath smooth dark tapering eyebrows, the wide-set eyes were a deep brown and the nose, though long, was finely chiselled. The jaw firm with a broad mouth and even white teeth. In truth, a handsome man with a distinct air of authority about him. His train of thought was interrupted by the arrival of the coffee. Harrington poured him a cup and while Paul sipped his drink Harrington leaned back in his chair and looked through the dossier he had retrieved from a drawer.

"Right Paul - you don't mind my calling you Paul do you? - let's discuss the appointment. You will already have read the general aims and ethos of the Burlington Trust, and will know something about the vacancy on offer, the terms and conditions, and I think you will have had a chance to look through the school prospectus which I forwarded to you last week. This is, as you must be aware, an excellent opportunity for both you and your wife," Harrington paused and looked through his notes, "Do you have children Paul?"

"No Mr Blaine, but my wife is pregnant." Paul looked anxiously across the desk. "Do you think that will be a problem?" Harrington smiled reassuringly.

"Good heavens no, in fact the very opposite. I have always thought that family men in the long term make the best teachers for that very reason. No, no and congratulations. Are you hoping for a boy or a girl?"

"Actually we don't mind, but the doctor seems to think it's a girl. We won't know for another week. Not that one has any choice in these matters of course." Harrington smiled down at his papers.

"No of course not," he murmured evenly.

Chapter 11

For the umpteenth time Max walked down to the rear toilets of the 747. Not that he needed to relieve himself but quite simply because he could feel the cramp setting in. After about five minutes he returned to his place, thankful that he had an aisle seat and therefore didn't inconvenience his fellow passengers with his frequent sorties. At 0230 hours the Captain announced that due to a technical fault they were diverting to Adelaide and expected to land there around 0450 hours. He assured them it was not an emergency but quite simply a precaution. Max listened to the buzz of conversation the announcement aroused amongst the passengers. Cabin staff patiently answered questions and promised that everyone would have the opportunity to contact waiting friends and relatives at Sydney and arrangements would be made, if necessary, with respect to connecting internal flights. Max settled back in his seat, quite unperturbed by the announcement. He looked at the map of Australia, and calculated that as it was his intention to drive south from Sydney to Melbourne to catch the ferry to Devonport in Tasmania, there was little difference in driving to the port from Adelaide.

An hour after landing, having collected his luggage, he ate breakfast in the airport restaurant and then took a taxi to the nearest used car lot. After a good look round and drawing on his adequate mechanical knowledge as a chauffeur, he finally chose an old short-wheel based Land Rover that had belonged to a mining engineer who had recently returned to England at the end of his contract. As he settled up and insurance was arranged he asked the salesman if he knew of any caravans for sale. The salesman asked him what sort he had in mind as he had two single axle Bergmanns out back that might interest him. Again Max, mindful of its future use, carried out a careful inspection, finally selecting the larger four berth and after insisting that a sway bar was fitted and that it had a good spare, shook hands with the smiling vendor.

Several hours later, with the bar fitted, Max headed south-east along the coast road towards Mount Gambia. At the first gas station he filled up the tank and the two jerry cans strapped to the sides and glancing at the map calculated that with a safe towing speed of not much more than forty-five miles an hour it was going to take him about ten hours to get to the ferry terminal at Melbourne. As he settled behind the wheel and rejoined the coast road, he noticed that the Land Rover was without a radio. Ruefully with one hand he adjusted his Ray-Bans, wound down the window and with a warm pleasant breeze ruffling his hair, started whistling.

Twelve thousand miles away, Harrington switched off the master computer and checked his watch with one of the two clocks on the wall above. The one on the left was set to Greenwich Mean Time and registered 2030 hours, whilst the other was set to Australia's Oceanic Time zone and read 0630 hours. He wondered if Max had cleared customs yet.

Harrington could hardly believe how quickly the time had sped by since Paul Beresford's appointment was confirmed by the Launceston school governors, and all his contingency planning had kicked in. The school had agreed that Paul would take up his appointment at the beginning of February a month after Rose had given birth. Immediately following the Board's announcement Harrington met the Beresfords again and went through the details of the Trust's sponsorship particularly with reference to the accommodation they had secured for them. Under those rules the Beresfords could not alter the property without prior notification and agreement and in any event the Trust reserved at all times the right to carry out such repairs and alterations. The appointment to Deputy Head was also linked to the accommodation and was uniquely a continuous contract. In addition the Trust had already appointed a guardian who would primarily maintain the gardens but was also there for all the routine maintenance of both the property and grounds so that Paul could concentrate on the main interest of the Trust which was his teaching appointment. A car provided by the Trust would be at the disposal of the couple. Harrington also pointed out that the Burlington Trust was very much in the background but was there if they had any specific problems and first contact could be made through the guardian. Their relocation expenses would be met by the Trust and an international removers would be in touch with them nearer the time.

When he first broached the subject of Tasmania to Max, Harrington wondered just how much he should tell him. For whilst he had always trusted Max and not been disappointed, this was, he realised, rather different. He knew Max to be discreet and unquestionably loyal but Harrington also knew that future events would test those qualities to the limit. And therein lay the problem for Harrington. Should he tell Max at the outset about the cloning and risk Max refusing to have anything to do with it or should he just let events unfold and hope that Max would understand why he had not been completely transparent about what the job would entail because of his wish to protect the clone as she grew up. When Max was shown into his office Harrington had still not entirely made up his mind.

"Hello Max, sorry to drag you away from the shoot, but this is important and I will need an answer from you by the end of the week at the latest. Can I get you a beer?" Max settled into the chair across the desk and stretched out his legs.

"Yes, thanks, I could do with one, it has been hot work out there today. What's this all about, if you don't mind me asking?" Harrington poured Max a beer, set it before him and walking over to the computer table studied the large contour map of Australia pinned on the wall behind. He looked over his shoulder as Max gratefully sipped his drink.

"Ever been to Australia Max? Come and have a look. I was over there about eight years ago, backpacking for six months. Fantastic place almost sorry to leave it, but Dad insisted I took up my university place back here. Mostly stayed in South Australia, but made quite a few trips including Cairns in the north, up here, Sydney of course and even hitched to Alice Springs. Never got to Tasmania though. You probably know that Felicity came from there Max." Harrington paused as fleeting images of her crowded in on him. He cleared his throat and without looking at Max spoke to the map afraid that the brightness of his eyes would give him away.

"I have a very special job I want you to do for me Max. There's no one else that I trust as much as you and I think you know that." He turned round and walking back to his desk sat wearily down. For perhaps a minute he said nothing, then suddenly making up his mind, Harrington got up, walked round his desk, crossed the room and closed the door. He paused, then taking a deep breath turned and with both hands grasping the handle behind him, leaned back.

"Sit down will you Max, I'm going to tell you exactly what has been going on and what I need you to do."

Chapter 12

Bill Rodgers groaned as he got to his feet and taking off his straw hat, squinted up at the midday sun and mopped his brow. He stretched his back and replacing his hat glanced down at the flower bed he had been weeding and decided it was time for a beer. As he turned towards his veranda he paused and tried to remember if he had collected his post that morning. He guessed his forgetfulness must be a side effect of the medication he took, in fact he half recollected the doctor telling him that. He thought he might as well check if he had any mail, so rather awkwardly, as the circulation slowly returned to his legs after kneeling for so long, he shuffled down the long drive. As he got to the mail box nailed to the gate post he remembered that he had looked in it earlier. Shaking his head with exasperation, he flipped it open anyway.

"Excuse me." Bill, thinking he was alone, almost jumped out of his skin as Max spoke to him.

"Christ boy! You usually sneak up on a body like that?"

"Sorry I thought you knew I was here." Max tried his disarming smile as Bill glared balefully up at him from behind his gate.

"Yeah right," Bill angrily tipped up the brim of his hat for a better view of the slim blond man holding a map in one hand. "You lost then?"

"Well I guess so. They told me at the store to head on down the river road for about three miles, follow my nose and I would find Windermere House next to a farm." Max looked down at his map. "Are you the farm?"

"Pom, eh?"

"Beg your pardon."

"Pom I said. You're from the old country. England. That's right ain't it mate?" Max grinned at him and nodded.

"Yes got off the Melbourne ferry this morning in Devonport." Bill looked him up and down noting the sweaty patches on his shirt.

"Ya wanna tinny?" Max looked blankly back. "A beer! A tinny's a beer. I dunno, Poms. Well ya want one or not?" Max wiped the sweat from his brow with the inside of his arm and grinned.

"Great, I could murder one." Bill swung the gate open for him.

"Well, come on then, we're wastin good downin' time."

Bill pushed open the fly screen with his hip and backed on to the veranda with four cans of Fosters in each hand. He snapped out a couple and passed them over the plastic table to Max, who gratefully opened one and took a long pull of the ice cold beer. They drank in silence for several minutes fanned by a large slow moving ceiling fan. Bill was on his third tinny as Max started his second.

"Well I'm Bill, and you?"

"Max, Max Routledge. Pleased to meet you and thanks for these." Bill eyed him over his can and nodded.

"So ya lookin for Windamere eh?"

"Yes, do you know where it is?"

"Sure do mate, it's right behind you." They got up and walked to the end of the balcony, where, through the bamboo and gum trees that bordered Bill's garden, Max got his first look at the distant gable end of Windermere House. "Looks like it could do with a lick of paint, boy." Max nodded

"I think it needs a lot more than that Bill."

"You bought it then?" Max laughed and shook his head.

"No. I'm the gardener. Young English couple renting it. He's a teacher. My job is to get it ready for them by January. Reckon I'm going to have my work cut out." he added ruefully.

"Too right mate. Been empty for five or six years at least. Couple that lived there died, can't remember how, but it was about the same time as I got taken ill." Max turned to look at him, but Bill had his head back and was draining another tinny. "Well," He clambered to his feet, "I reckon you'll wanna go take a gander at it. You know where I am if you fancy another tinny." Abruptly, without waiting for an answer, Bill turned and went inside leaving the fly screen to thump behind him.

Max turned right out of Bill's drive and walked for about fifty yards to where he'd parked the Land Rover and caravan. He lifted out a small canvas bag and slinging it over his shoulder walked perhaps another fifty yards until he found a five bar gate hanging crookedly by one rusty hinge. Lifting, he dragged it open and walked up the remnants of a very overgrown drive with numerous saplings randomly growing in its crown until he came to the house.

The property was typically colonial in style with five stone steps leading up to a spacious veranda that skirted the weather-boarded house on the south and west. Max pressed his thumbnail into what looked the worst of the boarding, for it was in much need of paint, but to his surprise found the wood unyielding. Several large green lizards scuttled into crevices as he approached the front door. He searched in his shoulder bag, fished out a bunch of keys that he had by arrangement collected from a solicitor's office in Hobart earlier that day and eventually found a yale-like key that turned quite easily in the brass lock and the door creaked open.

As Max slowly walked through the house, noting the rooms on which he would have to enter a detailed report to Harrington, it felt as though the house was in waiting. Absolutely nothing moved. He felt like an intruder. It was almost as if the family that had lived there would walk in behind him at any moment. He glanced uneasily over his shoulder at the bright light of the open doorway, half expecting to find someone silhouetted there. He wouldn't have been surprised to find a cigar still burning in an ashtray or a kettle steaming on the old Rayburn in the back kitchen. He did find a dead bird surrounded by bits of glass in the living room and the broken window it had flown into. He looked at his watch it was almost ten to three in the afternoon. Slightly disturbed by the uncanny stillness of the house, Max walked across to the mantelpiece, wound up a mahogany cased clock sitting there and set the hands. As he turned back towards the hall the ticking of the clock seemed to be a signal, for by the time he had made the stairs, flies buzzed and small insects whirred once more.

There were three bedrooms upstairs and when he'd swept back the dust laden curtains he could see that they were quite spacious. The largest dual aspect bedroom looked out west and north and Max judged by its solid furniture and traditional wallpaper that it must have belonged to the parents. He found a smaller room filled with oddments of furniture and cases and beyond that another, somewhat larger, but with a lighter feel. He guessed this must have been a girl's room. He made another mental note to gather up any papers and personal possessions and ship them off to Harrington. He glanced at the board with its few cards, designs and photographs pinned there. With a slight shock he realised that one group photo showed Felicity laughing at someone standing behind her. At the precise moment he reached out to touch the photograph, the clock chimed downstairs. Max snatched his hand back and broke out in a sweat. For one hair-raising moment Max thought he heard distant laughter in a far corner of the house.

Harrington signed personally for the special delivery parcel before taking it straight up to his office, or mission control as Max called it. He placed it on his desk and after pouring himself a glass of wine, sat down and examined its contents. Max had obviously been quite assiduous in his collection of anything that had belonged to Felicity. If he had been in any doubt as to its worth, he included it anyway. There were several new sketch books, a quantity of newspaper cuttings and a great wad of letters. Those he would read later, but of particular interest were about half a dozen photo albums. He quickly and excitedly flicked through them. As he did so Harrington realised that the photographs would flesh out the two dimensional diaries.

Over the next few days he would carefully examine each one and download them. They would be an invaluable record of how Felicity lived, where she went, what she wore and what she surrounded herself with. The photographs would also fill in gaps in her development that were not recorded in her diaries. As Harrington sifted through them, one of the photos reminded him of another important matter to be organised. Picking up the phone he rang Paradise Motors to see if they could find him a red 1936, Drophead Bentley Coupe.

Max had also phoned to tell Harrington that he had found in the attic boxes of her clothes that probably went back to when she first started school together with her toys and books. Harrington told Max to box them up and ship them back to him. Two days later Max sent him the complete inventory of the property. A general assessment of the state of the structure, together with photographs of the house, outbuildings and various shots of the gardens, with its clogged pond and wilderness of weeds. In addition he furnished Harrington with a full plan of the interior of the house with a breakdown of the state of each room, including its furniture, floor coverings, walls, woodwork, windows, doors, wiring and general fittings, together with scores of photos of the same. After a week of sifting through everything Max had sent and comparing it with anything he could find in the albums and from descriptions in the diaries, Harrington was able to build up an accurate picture of how the property must have looked.

He sent Max old photographs of the gardens in their heyday, and whatever he had of the house exterior, with instructions to engage local artisans to start its renovations. He also asked Max, where furnishings were beyond cleaning, to send him bits of the materials so that he could match them. He would then arrange for the materials to be shipped back for Max to find upholsterers and curtain makers.

It soon became clear to both of them that Max should temporarily install a fax machine, as well as a computer and printer so that queries, materials and techniques could be instantly transferred to Harrington and decisions taken without the delay of the post, missing emails - the signal was poor, or the possible misinterpretation of the telephone. Within a week the phone line was reconnected to the house and a few days later, having taken the ferry back to Melbourne to buy the new equipment, Max was on line.

Several months later with windows repaired and the weather-boarding painted, a rejuvenated Windermere House started to emerge. The open planking of the verandas were sanded and varnished, roof tiles replaced, chimneys swept and re-pointed. Gutters cleaned, downspouts unblocked and the huge rain water collection tanks into which they flowed, emptied, cleaned and re-filtered. The whole of the internal plumbing system of the house was replaced, and so as to not alter the internal appearance of the house, hot-air central heating ducts were installed below the floors with discreet adjustable grills mounted in the skirting boards. Most of the furniture required no more than a good polishing, but for one item, the piano, more was required. Because the piano would play an important part in the daughter's upbringing it was deemed prudent to ship that to Sydney where it would be fully renovated with new hammers, felts and strings.

From a specialist security company in England Harrington accepted their quotation to supply and fit all the camera and surveillance equipment in the Tasmanian house. After an update from Max, six weeks later he discreetly arranged for them to travel to the property when all the local artisans had finished and their equipment had been delivered.

Working to a very precise design Harrington sent to Max, mini cameras and microphones were concealed in light fittings and behind two way mirrors in the second bedroom, hallways, lounge, living room and kitchen. There were also several wide-angled remote cameras positioned in the garden, so that the drive, and comings and goings to the house could be monitored, as well as the main lawn and gardens. The wiring was concealed in the loft and behind skirting boards. Several satellite dishes were fixed discreetly on the roof, one of which was for the television, with an additional receiver that would enable Harrington to remotely change television channels from his control room at Langbourne.

A month before Rose's confinement and two months before the Beresford's were due in Tasmania, Max found a secluded wood with a small clearing and a deserted, dilapidated two roomed house about three miles from Windermere House off the road south towards Hobart. After contacting the owner, a retired shop-keeper who lived in a little bungalow on the west coast and handing over a few hundred dollars in rent, Max towed the caravan and parked it alongside the little house. With a letter from the owner Max contacted the Hydro Board and telephone company and two weeks later a power line was branched from the poles that ran parallel to the main road beyond the trees to a new one at the edge of the clearing and a few days later a telephone line followed. Max cleared up the debris in and around the house, and using part of his caravan as an office transferred the computer, fax and printer from the renovated Windermere House and moved in.

A week later on the morning of December 18th, Rose Beresford entered a private clinic, and at 4.18 that afternoon, with Paul by her bedside, gave birth to a healthy baby girl. They named her Emily.

PART TWO

Chapter 1

January 26th 1994

At six o'clock in the morning in the brightening dawn light, Paul Beresford caught his first glimpse of the Tasmanian coastline through the porthole of their cabin. He looked over his shoulder to the bed where Rose slept with Emily cradled in her arms, before turning back to study the deepening line on the horizon. There were times when Paul could hardly believe their good luck. It seemed almost unreal, almost as though they were living out a story in a novel. Their extraordinary luck seemed to have changed from the moment Rose found out she was pregnant. He thought it the most bizarre coincidence that on the same day her pregnancy was confirmed he should get an offer out of the blue from the Burlington Trust. Up until then he had no idea that such Trusts existed to further teaching families like his. He wondered, as he continued to look through the porthole, whether perhaps he should have checked out the Trust; find out who else they had helped maybe. But when he met Mr Blaine and listened to him he seemed to answer all the questions that Paul had in his mind to ask. The financial arrangements were in order and all those promised by Mr Blaine on behalf of the

Trust had been honoured, but there was in the back of his mind an unidentified doubt. Whichever way he looked at the cards they always added up to twenty-one, but there was still a tiny nagging concern and that only surfaced when he asked the rhetorical question - Why? It all seemed too good to be true. He looked at Rose again as she slept peacefully with Emily, just five weeks old, in her arms. He wondered if he should have talked to her about his doubts, but the time never seemed right. As her pregnancy advanced he had never seen her happier and as he witnessed that he realised the chance had been lost. Well whatever it was, for better or worse, here they were. He looked down at his hands, his mind elsewhere as his eyes took in their fine lines and creases.

"Are we almost there?" He blinked up at her. "Hello, is anyone there?" he smiled tenderly at her as she leaned her body against his.

"Sorry, I was miles away, yes -" he looked at his watch, "I think we'll dock in about three quarters of an hour." From his sitting position he gently wrapped his arms around her naked bottom and buried his face between her nursing breasts. With his eyes shut he could faintly smell her milk.

"Mumsy." She pulled back from him slightly.

"What did you say?" He grinned up at her.

"Mumsy. You remember, Michael Caine in 'What's It All About Alfie?' He was complaining about his pregnant girlfriend going all Mumsy on him."

"Oh, complaining are we?"

"No of course not. Far from it. You've never been or looked sexier." She wriggled against him feeling his arousal then stepped back.

"Well?" Paul glanced anxiously at the sleeping baby.

"She'll be fine, I'll put her in the cot."

"No, it's not that Rose, don't you think it's a bit soon after..." he trailed off, "you know."

"Well, I think I'm the best judge of that, don't you?" As she gently lifted Emily off the bed and placed her in the cot alongside, Paul drew the little curtain across the porthole.

At exactly 0700 hours on Tuesday 26th January, the Spirit of Tasmania berthed at Devonport. They watched as deckhands fore and aft flung out ropes that were caught expertly by dockers who quickly hauled up the great braided mooring lines and looped them over the bollards. A line of cars, that reflected the eclectic tastes of the native Tasmanians, waited to pick up family and visitors. They were particularly in admiration of a magnificent open top red Bentley with its great chrome stone guarded headlamps, louvered bonnet and running boards. With Emily in a carrycot, and with two large suitcases they descended the gangway.

"Mr and Mrs Beresford?" They turned to look at the smiling blond man wearing a white T shirt and faded blue jeans.

"Yes. You must be Max. How do you do. I'm Paul and this is my wife Rose and this," Paul nodded towards the carry cot, "Is Emily, but you'll probably get to hear her later." They all laughed, shook hands and Max took one of the suitcases.

"Okay folks, well....." he bounced his eyebrows. "Walk this way." They laughed again and followed him until to their enormous surprise and glee he stopped at the Bentley and opened the great gleaming door.

"Wow! Where did you get this? What year is it? Is it yours?" Max held up his hands at the barrage of questions and holding up the key-ring shook his head.

"Nope it's yours. It's a 1936 four and a quarter litre Drophead Coupe. It's the car provided by the Trust."

"Gettaway! Jesus, it's absolutely beautiful. Can I drive it?"

"Sure can, I've got the Land Rover in front. We'll load the cases in that, then you just follow me. Oh yeah the gears; it's a right hand gate change. You'll get used to that in a couple of miles. OK, Wagons Ho!" From Devonport they set off south and after about thirty miles headed west towards Launceston and then south again on the Campbell Town road. Seven miles along they again turned west onto Evendale Road where, after about a mile and a half, they followed Max as he swung into the drive of Windermere House.

Both Paul and Rose thought the house and gardens quite enchanting. They settled Emily into the cot, draped the mosquito net over and noting that all their worldly possessions had preceded them and were neatly stacked along the hallway, set out to explore the house and grounds. Max answered their many questions and assured them that he would be working in the grounds most days should they have forgotten anything. Helpfully, pinned up in the hallway, he had provided them with a large contour map of the island together with a list of emergency telephone numbers including his own. The school number was also there so, after moving some of their belongings into the bedrooms, and with a cup of tea alongside, Paul rang them to confirm that he had arrived and as arranged he would take up his position for the post summer vacation term on Monday the 7th February. He chatted briefly with the secretary about their trip over and his first impressions of Tasmania before giving her their telephone number and address.

For the ensuing ten days, Paul and Rose, with Emily in her carrycot firmly strapped in the rear seat, leisurely drove to various parts of the island. They visited Launceston numerous times to send letters from the post office and make their own personal financial arrangements at the Bank. They shopped for summer clothes and extra baby-wear for Emily and visited the library. They took in the West coast near St Mary's and travelled to Hobart and onto the deportation prison of Port Arthur. They had read anything and everything they could about Tasmania before the move; much of it forwarded by the Trust, and now they had arrived it was all that they had hoped and more. In no time at all, as they explored the island with its stunning scenery and glorious climate, their life in England faded to a distant memory.

Chapter 2

Rose pressed the four candles into the icing of the birthday cake before returning it to the top shelf of the larder. She afforded herself a little smile, anticipating the glee on her daughter's face when she would blow out the candles and make her wish. 1997, Rose could hardly believe how quickly the last four years had passed. Paul was at last in a teaching post where his many talents were appreciated, and with Emily at playschool, she herself was about to take up some part-time work at the same school. Rose paused over her washing up, listening to the sound of the piano emanating from the drawing room down the hall.

Rose was quite used to Emily sitting at the piano and prodding at the keys. It evidently amused her for she would happily play for hours at a time. Suddenly Rose realized that it was no longer random note thumping. She paused and fixing her eyes on a butterfly slowly opening and closing its wings, the better to focus her hearing, she listened intently. She did so for several minutes and whilst she couldn't put her finger on it she realized that there was definitely something happening.

She walked quietly to the drawing room drying her hands as she did so and stood silently in the doorway. Emily, with her back to her, was sitting as usual on her knees on the piano stool. But this time she had before her some sheet music open and was looking from that to the piano keys and back as she played. Rose herself was not musical and was unable to read music, but like most people recognized when someone could. Hardly daring to breathe she advanced in to the room until unseen she was standing just behind her daughter. The manuscript was quite old, well thumbed and yellowing. She leaned closer in the dim light of the room shaded by the shutters from the afternoon sun until she could focus on the title. She quietly stole out of the room, but her heart was thumping, for her four year old daughter, who had never had a single piano lesson in her life, was teaching herself to play Happy Birthday.

When Emily wasn't playing the piano she would spend hours at the breakfast table with sheets of drawing paper and crayons. She loved to draw and obviously had a talent for it. Only the week before her birthday she had drawn, very skilfully for one so young, a little puppy. It was recognizably a golden Labrador and Rose asked her where she had seen it.

"Oh, that's Sandy, it's the puppy for my birthday." she said without looking up from the drawing of a cockatoo she was colouring. Rose decided not to question her further but mentioned it to Paul when he came home that evening.

"Did you say anything about giving Emily a puppy for her birthday, Darling?" Paul looked up, puzzled.

"No Rose, I don't know what you're talking about, perhaps it was Max."

She shrugged her shoulders at him and he returned his attention to the paper he was reading. She stared into the saucepan of vegetable soup and mechanically stirred the contents.

"She's even given it a name," she said out loud. Paul peered over the top of his newspaper.

"What's that? A name?" He frowned and once again with a slightly exasperated air returned to his reading.

"Oh, nothing," sighed Rose, but she continued to stare into the saucepan, as though seeking an answer there. "I'll ask Max."

When Rose had broached the subject of the dog no one was more taken aback than Max. Yes there was a little puppy that he'd had for several weeks at the caravan where he lived, but he had never mentioned it to little Emily since it was to be a surprise. They stood in the shade of the Catalpha, its huge heart shaped leaves barely moving in the afternoon haze. There was an awkward silence before Max glanced anxiously at Rose who was evidently waiting for him to say something.

"I'm sorry Mrs Beresford, I guess I should have asked you if it was okay to give her a puppy, but she's on her own and........" Max trailed off. Rose's gaze softened and she rested her hand lightly on his tanned forearm.

"It's alright Max, Mr Beresford agrees that under the circumstances she should have it, but we would appreciate it if in future if you could run your ideas past us first, particularly where Emily's concerned." Max reddened slightly.

"Yes of course, I'm sorry, I didn't think." Rose looked down at the planks and saw benches.

"Well I had better let you get on with your work. I suppose that is the kennel you're building?" He smiled ruefully and laughing, Rose turned away. She had perhaps stepped no more than a dozen paces when she turned back to where Max was starting to lightly hammer a nail in place.

"By the way she is going to call the dog Sandy." A startled Max faltered in mid-swing and hit his thumb.

Everything about Emily's birthday party went without a hitch until Max turned up apparently without a present. Up until then Emily had been excitedly opening her presents from several other children invited from the kindergarten she attended. But at the sight of Max arriving she leapt to her feet and ran up to him clapping her hands.

"Can I see him Max? Can I?" Max stared down at the excited little girl now clinging to his trouser leg.

"See what young lady?" He laughed, as he picked her up and she nestled in the crook of his arm.

"Sandy, my little puppy."

"Now who told you about that?" Her blue eyes clouded slightly then sage-like she said, "'Cos it's my fourth birthday, silly." Max could feel his mouth run dry, but he managed a smile and with a querulous glance at Paul and Rose, lowered Emily to the ground and taking her hand led her down the garden until they were lost to view.

Some fifty metres beyond the main lawn with its pond there is, hidden from the house, another smaller circular lawn, tucked amongst the Hibiscus and rose bushes and where, nestling at its margin, a little dog kennel that Max had placed there during the night. Flopped out and dozing half in and out of its little arched doorway lay a golden Labrador puppy. With a squeal of delight, Emily ran forward.

"Sandy, Sandy," she cried, and the puppy jumped to its feet and wagged its little tail so vigorously that, in turn, it seemed to wag the rest of him. Emily scooped him up and puffing slightly under his weight ran back towards the house and the party. Max watched her run off and reached for his mobile phone. He paused, wondering whether he should tell Harrington that the child knew she was going to get the dog before anyone told her, but decided against it and simply dialled through and left the briefest message.

"September 5th. Two legs picks up four legs."

Harrington was standing as usual before the window overlooking the courtyard when Max's message played back on the answer phone. He glanced down at the watch on his left wrist and then at another set to 'down under' time on his right. He also looked up to the two clocks on the wall above the computers with their different time zones to see if they matched. They did to the second. He gave a wry satisfied smile and then walked from the room.

It was 8.35am at Langbourne, 6.45pm at Windermere. Emily is four years old. Sandy, her dog, will never get to be that old, but only one person knows that and he was tunelessly whistling to himself as he descended a great spiral staircase more than twelve thousand miles away.

Chapter 3

Bill sat on the Bentwood rocking chair that had belonged to his father and from his vantage point of the elevated terrace looked out across his garden. It was raining. Not the sudden violent type that accompanies a thunder storm and runs off the hard sun-baked soil to giggle and gurgle into the ditches by the road, but a soft almost hesitant rain. Out of a seamless grey sky it settled like a heavy mist on the corrugated roof from where, in steady rivulets, it descended to fan out across the shingles of the sloping veranda to insistently drip from the fretted barge board. It gently soaked into the flowerbeds and lawn and almost instantly greened them. Bill sat there gently rocking the chair in comparative silence now that the rain had silenced the shrill clatter of the cicadas. He was deep in thought, well, as deep in thought as his medication would allow, for something had happened late that afternoon before the sun played hide and seek with the inbound clouds and lost. The little girl next door had called excitedly to him from where their gardens snuggled up to the same tall picket fence.

"Uncle Bill, Uncle Bill come and see." He had put down his pruning shears, limped toward the fence and peered over. She was holding in her arms a little golden puppy. "This is Sandy, Uncle Bill, isn't he beautiful? I got him for my birthday." Bill hadn't immediately answered because for a split second he saw two little blond girls each holding a tiny puppy. One with blue eyes full of happiness with a puppy licking her face, the other also with blue eyes, but these glistened with unshed tears, and the head of that puppy lolled. Bill blinked and as his eyes reopened he saw only the first. Instinctively Bill tried to cast his mind back to grapple with and identify that fleeting image, but years of anti-depressant drugs had scattered the stepping stones of memory so he returned almost empty handed. However there had been, long ago, another little girl with a puppy, but as for where and when?

"Do you want to hold him?" Emily's question jerked him back. He looked down at his dirt ingrained hands with their ragged nails and with a wry smile held them up for her to see. She nodded, accepting the refusal, and lowered the dog to the grass where it scampered off towards the house. With a wave to Bill she happily ran and skipped after it. Bill momentarily raised his hand in reply and paused.

"Yes, bye..." For a tantalising moment another name surfaced, brushed the tip of his tongue and then elusively dissolved, "...little ...." He stood stock still with his hand raised and just for a moment no bird sang, no fly buzzed, nothing moved. It was as though just for a split second the whole world held its breath, then a little wind gently sighed through the mimosa fronds and the spell was broken. Bill's hand continued up and touched the brim of his hat as he squinted up at the changing sky and turning walked slowly back towards his veranda. But he was not alone, for at that picket fence amongst the fragrance of the flowers and trees, a distantly familiar smell had slowly surfaced and as he breathed it stole in and nestled in the pit of his stomach, never to leave him. Slowly but inexorably it would, cell-like, divide and multiply until it would settle on him like a second clammy skin. Only then in the years to come would he recognize it for what it was. Fear.

Chapter 4

The night before Emily's birthday, Max sat outside his little caravan nursing a can of Fosters and gazing at his bandaged thumb. He was totally mystified by the revelation that Emily not only knew that she was to get a puppy for her birthday, but that she had both the breed right and quite astoundingly the name too. It had always been Harrington's plan that when Max gave the Labrador to Emily that he was to say that the puppy answered to the name Sandy. Well that wouldn't be necessary now he mused. Whichever way he looked at it, it all added up to a damn sight more than coincidence. One yes, but three. "No way." he muttered to himself and there was another thing. The piano playing. He didn't know that Emily was having piano lessons. He asked Mr Beresford when he'd taken the Bentley key back to him after adjusting the hand-brake and he could hear her playing. Paul had frowned at him as he took the keys.

"She's not," he said simply and went inside.

Max pondered all of that for perhaps five minutes before with a shake of his head he reached down and fondled the sleeping puppy at his feet. It stirred slightly, half wagged its tail and then with a shuddering contented sigh fell back asleep. Max stretched, got to his feet, his brain and his thumb sore with the day's events and climbed into the caravan wondering just how much of this Harrington knew. As he fell into a restless sleep the moon waxed and through the little fly-screened window cast a creeping shadow across his troubled brow.

Four miles away, as the crow flies, Rose too lay in bed. For a while she listened to Paul slumbering beside her, noting the cadence of his breathing. The soft inhalation followed by the shorter more rapid expulsion as he exhaled. She lay there quietly for perhaps ten minutes, but she couldn't sleep, so very gingerly she drew back the sheet, got out of bed and padded softly to the window and gazed out into the darkness. She needed to think. Of all things that had happened over the last two days, it was Max's comment that Emily was on her own that stuck in her mind. Inadvertently he had highlighted something that had initially both puzzled and bothered Rose for some time. They knew when they first visited the fertility clinic in England that the main reason she had not been able to conceive was almost certainly down to stress. All the tests showed that she ovulated normally and that Paul's sperm count was fine. Indeed as the doctor treating them pointed out it was more common than not that IVF patients were subsequently usually able to conceive naturally. Both she and Paul were keen on having another child, but more than nine months after the birth of Emily there was no sign of her periods restarting which meant she was not ovulating. However in the excitement of adjusting to their new life with Paul happy in his work, little Emily to bring up, it gradually slipped into the background. In compensation, the loss of her monthly cycle allowed them more spontaneity with their love-making until four years on she had completely forgot about it. However Max's casual reference to the fact that Emily was an only child decided her that she would raise the subject with her doctor. Happy that she had made a positive decision, she returned to her bed and very gently snuggled up to Paul as he slept and within in a few minutes fell into her own dreamless sleep.

A month later, with an introductory letter from her GP, she motored down to Hobart to keep her late afternoon appointment with the gynaecologist. Noting her recent history and her fertility treatment he made a thorough physical examination and the nurse took her for a scan. Finally before she left he asked her for the name of the doctor who carried out her IVF procedure in England. He explained that he would contact the clinic with a view to obtaining her records and on receipt of those would write to her Launceston GP. He showed her to the door and watched her until she turned the corridor, before resuming his seat. He twirled his pencil in one hand and occasionally tapped his teeth with it as he gazed out of the second floor window to the parkland below. Then he swung back and looked yet again at his examining notes and the scan taken. What puzzled him was not so much that her fallopian tubes had been surgically blocked, which was highly unusual in itself, but, evidently she was unaware that she had undergone that procedure. So before he contacted Mrs Beresford's doctor he thought he needed the answer to both questions. Why had the procedure been carried out and why was Mrs Beresford still in ignorance of that fact? He glanced at the name she had given him, checked his watch and reached for the phone.

"Good morning is that the Ishmael Clinic? Could I speak to Professor Ewen McGregor please. Yes, of course. My name is Rashiid, Doctor Rashiid and I'm ringing from Hobart in Tasmania about a Mrs Rose Beresford who undertook IVF treatment at your Clinic in late 1992. Oh I see, well why don't I fax a message and my contact details, and perhaps you will pass it on to the Professor. Is that Okay? Thank you, yes I'll do that. Bye."

When Julian Bruce entered the clinic about an hour later, he was handed the fax from Dr Rashiid by the receptionist.

"You know Professor McGregor don't you Dr Bruce? This fax has just come in, but I did explain to Dr Rashiid that the Professor was an occasional consultant here, but would try to contact him. Do you want to take it from here?"

"Yes that's alright Margaret, I'm actually having lunch with him tomorrow, I'll pass it on to him then."

They were well into their second cup of coffee after an excellent lunch, when Julian Bruce remembered the fax. He fished it out of an inside jacket pocket and passed it across to the professor.

"Sorry Ewen this came for you yesterday, I almost forgot. Rose Beresford, I remember her. Didn't you do her implantation procedure when I was taken ill?" If he hadn't been trying to catch the eye of the waiter while he said that he would most certainly have seen the professor visibly blanche. But by the time he had turned back McGregor was tucking the fax into his top pocket and was his usual urbane self, though in a hurry to be off.

"Too bad Julian, that was great, but got to dash had no idea it was so late. You'll settle up will you and I'll give you a ring next week, perhaps you and Maggie would like to dine with us? We haven't had a foursome for ages."

"Yes we'd like that Ewen, thank you. You alright?" He thought the professor looked more pallid than usual.

"Fine, twinge of heart-burn, nothing to worry about. Catch you later." Then he hurried out.

McGregor sat behind the wheel of his Jaguar in the car park, and re-read the fax. His mouth felt very dry. There was always going to be the risk that one day Rose Beresford would be examined by a gynaecologist, but after four years he had completely forgotten about it. Now this. He gnawed his bottom lip and then reluctantly reached for his mobile phone and rang Harrington.

That afternoon they met on the Embankment. To the casual passer-by they were doing no more than exchanging pleasantries as they gazed out over the river, but there was nothing pleasant about their exchanges. The professor was very agitated and it took all of Harrington's considerable self control not to lose his temper.

"The first thing Professor is to remain absolutely cool and the second is to shut up while I think." McGregor bit his lip and miserably dug his hands into his coat pockets. Eventually Harrington turned and looked evenly at him.

"This is what we do. This Doctor Rashiid, in response to a dossier sent to him, is going to make a report out to Rose's GP. So we have a choice as far as I can see. We either convince him with the dossier that there is a plausible reason why the fallopian tubes were operated on without the patient's permission, or if that fails we intercept and exchange the letter he sends to the GP. What do you think? You're a consultant there's bound to be something medically logical." The professor considered that for a moment.

"Well if it's a letter interception that would be relatively easy because the replacement would quite simply advise the GP that both fallopian tubes were in poor shape with multiple cysts, which was a contributory reason why she had the IVF in the first place. There would be absolutely no reason why she would not accept that. The only problem that might arise from that is if she decided to make a follow up call to Rashiid." He glanced at Harrington who seemed to be mulling that over.

"Okay, so that's a possibility, but what about the dossier? What would convince the Gynaecologist? We might be able to swap letters if the dossier doesn't convince him, but what else, apart from writing to the GP, is he likely to do?" The professor leaned on the coping of the embankment wall and looked out across the Thames.

"Well if he smelt foul play, quite a bit and there would be no covering that up since the Ishmael Clinic would have to protect its reputation and look for a scapegoat, and we all know who that is going to be," he said bitterly. "I'd be ruined. I should never have let you -"

"You did it to yourself you pervert." snapped Harrington angrily. "Now get a grip man for Christ's sake!" McGregor hung his head and made a conscious effort to pull himself together.

"Well I suppose I could tell the truth." Harrington whirled on him.

"I don't think so."

"No, hear me out. I could admit to the operation on the fallopian tubes. I can rewrite the dossier to intimate a progressive and irreversible degeneration of the tubes that only became apparent with the oocyte retrieval procedure, and as I stepped in to carry out the procedure at the last minute assumed the patient knew they were to be operated on."

"Yes....." Harrington seemed unsure. Suddenly the professor swung round to face him. His mind was working feverishly and his eyes darted from one thing to another.

"I've got it!" He shouted and Harrington made a shushing sound as he glanced quickly round. The professor lowered his voice.

"Wrong dossier," he whispered. Harrington looked puzzled. "Yes, don't you see, I surgically blocked the tubes because it was the wrong patient." He looked encouragingly at Harrington as his face clearly reflected the dawning possibilities.

"I see what you are getting at." The professor glanced over his shoulder and leaning closer continued.

"We reply to the Rashiid letter on the Clinic's headed notepaper with an admission that the fallopian tubes had been operated on by mistake due to a clerical mix up. He is then informed that an internal investigation has been put in motion and that its official findings will be forwarded to him. If it endorses the clerical mix up then the clinic would write to Mrs Beresford with an offer of compensation. I will be exonerated. Rashiid could do nothing but accept the findings, Mrs Beresford's loss will be ameliorated by her compensation which you will pay no doubt. But most importantly, no publicity. The only thing we might have to do is arrange to intercept any mail or telephone calls at the clinic's reception from either Mrs Beresford or Rashiid."

"I can arrange that," said Harrington. "We just need to get rid of the receptionist, who will probably be a temp anyway, and put in one of our own." He mused momentarily, then thought of Theresa. "I just happen to have someone in mind." He grinned at McGregor and squeezed his upper arm. "Oh just one more thing, did you bring it? "The professor looked blankly at him for a moment, then with a nervous glance left and right, nodded and drew out from an inside pocket a little Victorian pill box. Harrington carefully opened it to reveal its precious contents.

"Good, well I reckon that sorts it out. Now how about a drink? You look like you could do with one. I know I could." The professor was too relieved to say no.

At Langbourne that night Harrington sat down at his desk. Before him was a sheet of paper and he was writing. In fact he was drawing a sort of family tree. At its head he wrote his own name, then below that he drew an oblique line to the left and wrote Max and then an oblique line to the right and wrote McGregor. He studied it for a moment then from below the professor's name he drew the same oblique lines and wrote Rashiid and Rose. Below Max's another line and the name Theresa. He pursed his lips and getting up walked across to a board on the back of the door and pinned it up. His eyes narrowed, six people to a lesser or greater extent now knew something about his project. As he closed the door and locked the room behind him he had no idea that a seventh name should have been on that list. Bill Rodgers.

Chapter 5

2000

The first thing that greeted Bill without fail as he woke was the white plastic bottle of his anti-depressants. Without thinking, as he had done for the last fourteen years, he went into his automatic routine. He switched on the radio, unloaded a couple of pink pills from the plastic bottle, swallowed them, chased them down with some water and then lying back unclenched his buttocks and broke wind. Sometimes it amused even him and then he would look over his stomach at his unshaven reflection in the oak framed mirror on the wall at the foot of his bed.

"One day boy," he mused, "you're gonna shit yaself. Then what ya gonna do, Huh?" But today was different. Bill didn't know that as he woke up and he was still unaware of it as he habitually reached for the bottle that for the first time in fourteen years was empty on his bedside table. He had no idea that it was possible to satisfy the subliminal need of his habit if some elements of the paraphernalia were not actually there. If the dimensions of the same place, the same routine and the same time were maintained then it was not impossible. So on a spring Tuesday morning at 7.15am, mid-way through September, still half asleep, suspended in the limbo of those three coordinates, Bill reached out and switched on the radio. Drowsily reaching for the plastic medicine bottle, he shook out two imaginary pink pills, washed them down with real water, and lying back celebrated the ritual in his normal vulgar way, before turning over and going back to sleep. But part of the equation was now missing and the knock-on effect of that would be felt half a world away, because the real Bill Rodgers, so long in limbo, was starting to wake up.

More than twelve thousand miles away, sitting in his dressing gown, Harrington was reading the first page of Felicity's diaries. He had waited more than seven years for this moment, for it was only now, when she was two weeks short of her birthday, would parallel time really start for Emily. It was the shortest entry of any subsequent page. It read

'Sandy found dead.'

Harrington read it many times. Frequently he would get to his feet, light a cigarette and stare with unseeing eyes out of the lofty study window, knowing what it was like to have and to lose something you loved. In that short sentence, so much said and unsaid. Then, sitting at his desk, unshaven before a photograph of his beloved Felicity and with tears rolling down his cheeks, he picked up the phone and with trembling hands rang Max.

The following morning just as it got light Max, carrying a loop of wire in his hand, picked his way silently across the little dew laden lawn to Sandy's kennel. He felt sick to his stomach. He loved animals, they had been part and parcel of his life in England for as long as he could remember. There wasn't a day that one or other of his own Labradors wasn't racing ahead of him as he walked the woods of Langbourne starting up widgeon or legging it futilely after rabbits. When Harrington had called him to his office and first talked about Tasmania and told him what he was trying to do, Max had been more than sympathetic. He loved Harrington like a brother and at Felicity's demise had wept long and hard for him. Even when Harrington had explained that there would be some difficult things to be done and read him the passage from the diary, Max had agreed. More than anything he wanted Harrington to be happy. To find himself again, and there was nothing he wouldn't do for him. But that was eight years ago and what he read was eight years ago and somehow, casting his mind back to that fateful day in the study, it had seemed all too easy to agree. But this was now, and here he was creeping up on an innocent sleeping trusting dog that had not an ounce of malice in its body. Then, inadvertently, Max trod on a twig and it exploded like a rifle shot beneath his foot.

Sandy's eyes shot open, sleep banished in an instant and in that split second intuitively knew that Max meant him great harm. In a trice it had bounded from its resting place in front of its kennel and streaked across the lawn in headlong flight. Max made a despairing lunge towards the Labrador as it flashed past, and with one flailing hand tripped it up. But to no avail, it was instantly on its feet. Now fleeing for its life and with its name-tag tinkling against its collar it disappeared amongst the bushes and trees towards the adjoining picket fence almost a hundred feet away. Cursing Max stumbled to his feet and tried to follow, but by now Sandy was out of sight and running faster than he had ever done in his short life. As the picket fence loomed before him he had only one thought and that was to escape the garden. Without breaking stride and at breakneck speed, with its heart pounding the dog launched itself at the high fence with every muscle in its body and almost made it. In mid flight as his front paws cleared the picket he instinctively knew it was not quite high enough, so in a last desperate attempt Sandy twisted in mid air to try and swing his body clear. But in so doing his forward momentum was lost and as his head dipped over, one spike of the fence slipped unerringly through his collar. As the body twisted past, but with the head trapped, something had to give and Sandy died instantly as his neck snapped. Unseen from the Beresford's garden, the dog hung lifelessly from the picket fence. Max looked diligently for half an hour, before giving up. He secretly hoped that the dog had run off, but something deep inside told him otherwise.

The same morning Emily puffed out her cheeks and gave a very big sigh for such a small girl. She slowly swung her legs over the side of her bed and dropped the last few inches to the polished wood floor. She put on her Garfield socks and going to her chest of drawers rummaged through until she unearthed her Mr Grumpy knickers and slipped them on. She pulled up a pair of washed out denim jeans and half tucked in a plain white T shirt. She squirmed around on the floor trying to put her sneakers on without unlacing them and padded along to the bathroom. Finally descending the staircase she found her mother sipping tea and reading the gazette at the yellow pine kitchen table.

"Ah, you're up." She beamed as Emily pulled out a chair. "I'll get you some cereal." But Emily wasn't hungry.

"Have you seen Sandy this morning, Mummy?"

"No darling, I expect he's sleeping by his kennel as usual." Emily glanced uneasily out of the kitchen window.

"No, he's always by the kitchen door when I get up," she said in a small voice. Rose smiled tenderly at her little daughter and reaching across the table patted her hand.

"You have your breakfast, then we'll go and look for him. I expect he's got his head down a rabbit's burrow." Emily hung her head and looking at the bowl in front of her, said almost in a whisper,

"He's dead." Then she looked up at her mother with great glittering blue eyes. Rose felt a terrible sadness wash over her.

They buried Sandy in the corner of the garden beyond his kennel. No one said anything as Max tumbled in the earth over the still form, pushed in a wooden cross and hung there the little collar with its brass name-tag. Bill was in a state of shock, having found Sandy hanging from the fence. To free him he had to release his collar and as he took the weight of Sandy's lifeless form its head lolled against his shoulder. Bill froze, suddenly remembering the fleeting image all those years ago of a tearful little girl holding a lifeless dog.

"Bill?" He looked vacantly at Max, then the moment passed and he lifted Sandy over as Paul, Rose and Emily stood quietly by.

As they all trooped away from the burial, Max lengthened his stride until he was alongside Emily and pushed a little parcel into her hand. She didn't look up, but simply took it to the house and went up to her bedroom. She placed the parcel on her desk and reached beyond it for a biro, before unwrapping it. Then as the tears brimmed and tumbled she did what another seven year old girl, sitting in the same chair before that same desk had done almost twenty years ago, she turned to the first page and started to write her diaries.

Two weeks later Emily received a letter from Tina, a girl her own age, who lived in London. Tina wrote and said that she had heard from her Uncle Max that she'd lost her dog and just wanted to say how sorry she was and would she like to be her pen pal? When Emily wrote back, Theresa sifted it from her other mail and gave it to her daughter as she ate her breakfast, then, closing the door of the kitchen went into the lounge and telephoned Harrington.

Chapter 6

Most weekdays, usually to escape the unforgiving midday sun, Max would sit with Bill in the shade of his terrace. Sometimes they would look out in silence across Bill's patchy green lawn flanking the driveway to the stringy-barked eucalyptus that bordered the road and beyond to the pastel shades of the rising scrub hills. Other times, with a tinny in hand, they would jovially reminisce about this and that and occasionally theorize and, when they could be bothered, put the world to rights. Then, after an hour, Max would eye his watch, apologetically get to his feet, punch his cotton sun hat into a wearable shape and with a lop-sided grin at Bill amble off to continue his gardening duties next door. For his part Bill would sit there and wait until he'd reached the gate, and then, as Max turned and waved, raise his beer in a salute before exiting the terrace for his afternoon nap. However today, Max was a dozen strides towards the gate when, looking to his left, he stopped and turned back.

"Oh yes Bill, I almost forgot. That old paddock of yours, any chance I could use it for Emily's pony?"

"Sure, but I thought she stabled him up at her friend's farm."

"Well she did, but they're selling up and the new owners have got other plans."

Bill got to his feet and limped off the veranda.

"Yup, no problem at all, though you'll have to get rid of some thistles mind and the fence'll need fixing. My Dad used it for just about everything when he was alive. Horses, goats and even pigs. Must be more than ten years since. It'll need a bit of work, but come on let's have a look, you'll need a water butt and a bit of a stable for wintering. Ya know it'll be good to see it being used again." Bill looked quite animated. "And I'll tell you something else, that paddock's big enough to put up a couple of practice jumps. She trained that pony to jump yet?" Max laughed and shook his head as together they reached the field, and cast a critical eye over it.

"You're right Bill we could build a temporary stable and wind break in the lee of those trees and a shed to store hay. I think it would fit the bill, Bill." He grinned as Bill groaned and rolled his eyes. "So how about I rent it from you? What do you want for it?" Bill stroked his chin, he was going to enjoy this.

"Well," he paused and looked sideways at Max. "Let me see, there must be at least two acres. There's been a lot of interest in it recently, particularly today. Difficult to find a good paddock around here that's not in use. Worth a bit, might put it up for auction," he continued, managing to keep a straight face. He could feel Max tensing up, then he grinned and gave Max a slap on the back. "Gottcha! Right, just to keep it honest, you can have it for dollar a year if you bring your own tinnies lunch times." They both burst out laughing. That evening a contented Max emailed Harrington with the good news about the paddock.

Harrington spent most of his time in the control room. He glanced at the clock on the wall and getting up rounded his desk to the corner opposite, looped a towel round his neck and straddled the multi-gym. For the next ten minutes he pulled and stretched the wired weights until, sweating profusely, he swung off and towelled down. It was a rarely missed ritual he performed two hours apart, four times a day. He was determined to keep in shape and it was evident when he appraised himself in the mirror after showering that apart from slightly greying temples, he was doing just that. Satisfied, drying his hair, he returned to his desk and, after reading Max's email, opened one of the diaries.

When Emily found out that Jane's parents were selling up and moving to New South Wales it came as a double shock. Not only would she be losing her best friend but Gypsy her pony would be without a home. It really upset her and no matter how hard Rose tried to take her mind off the issue by encouraging her to do some baking or suggesting she played the piano for her, Emily would not be consoled. Eventually Rose asked around the school, where she was now teaching French full time, to see if anyone knew of any available stabling. Max, whilst repainting the weatherboarding alongside the kitchen, had overheard Rose on the phone discussing the problem with the mother of one of Emily's school friends. He felt a bit guilty about the pony since it was he, at the behest of Harrington, that had found Gypsy in the first place and encouraged Emily to start riding, so no one was more relieved than Max when Bill agreed to let them use his paddock.

Over the next few weeks, by working every hour he could and with a lot of encouragement from Bill, not to mention a few Max-bought tinnies, he managed not only to clear the paddock of its many thistles, construct a stable, hay store and repair the fencing, but also found the time to build and paint two novice jumps. With Bill's agreement Max kept the pony's new home a secret from the family.

That weekend with the horsebox in tow, Emily sat despondently alongside Max as they drove the Land Rover to collect the pony from her friend's farm. Under pressure and to buy a little more time to find somewhere more suitable, Rose had reluctantly agreed that Gypsy could be tethered temporarily on the little circular lawn at the far end of the garden. Whilst Emily was happy to have Gypsy so close she was also aware it was very unfair on the pony since it would have no space to wander and graze. As they drove back towards Windermere with Gypsy in tow they did so in silence. Max felt for Emily sitting so withdrawn alongside him and was very tempted to come clean about the pony's new home but he resisted the temptation. He had arranged, whilst they were collecting Gypsy, for Bill to break the news to Rose and Paul so that they too could be in the paddock for the pony's arrival.

As they travelled along the lane towards Windermere House Max casually turned through Bill's open gates. Emily looked at Max.

"Max, you've turned through the wrong gate, ours is the next one."

"Oh yes, so I have, silly me. Well I'll turn round in Bill's field over there and come back out." Emily, her blond hair tied back with a black bobble, settled grumpily back in her seat and stared at her hands whilst Max drove into the paddock and unexpectedly put the hand brake on. Emily looked up.

"Max, why have you? -" She stopped. Her parents were standing in front of the bonnet. Confused she glanced quickly towards Max but by then he was out of his seat and had disappeared. Then her door opened and a smiling Bill held out his hand to help her down. Still not quite sure what was happening, but with her heart beating a little faster, she allowed Bill to take her to her parents and together they all walked to the middle of the field just as Max arrived with Gypsy. Suddenly on seeing the stable and hay store Emily understood and with a squeal of sheer happiness broke free and tearfully hugged her pony's neck. "Oh Gypsy look, your new home!" Bill blew his nose and Rose, with Paul's arm around her waist, dabbed at the corners of her eyes with a dainty hanky as an ecstatic Emily led her pony around inspecting everything. It was then that Max realised why he loved his job so much.

Paul and Rose always insisted that Emily was not to ride her pony unsupervised. They were quite happy, knowing the gentle temperament of Gypsy, for her to groom and feed him and even muck out the stable on her own, but on no account was she to mount and ride him without an adult present and never ever without her riding hat on. So it was arranged that if either of them were unavailable Max would stand in and, as a backstop, Bill also offered.

That summer Emily spent every spare minute with her pony. She brushed Gypsy every day, washed and combed his mane and tail and was always there when the farrier came to shoe him. She spent hours polishing the bridle and waxing his saddle and straps and quite a few more sketching him. Gypsy always stood patiently by in his stable. To the casual passer-by he looked more interested in his manger of hay, but Emily was convinced, by the way his ears twitched and the look in his big brown eyes whenever he turned his head and looked back, that he understood every word she was saying.

Wearing a black T shirt over grubby beige jodhpurs and with her long blond hair escaping her brown riding hat Emily would regularly put Gypsy through his paces. Usually the attending adult would be Max since Emily's parents found much of their spare time taken up with either developing timetables, marking homework or supervising extra evening events at the school. In truth without Max it would have been practically impossible for Emily to follow her love of riding. It was always Max that helped her load Gypsy into the horsebox and drive her to a local gymkhana or a horse riding event. Not that it was a chore for him since he loved being in her company and no one was more pleased when she won her first rosette for the best turned out pony. Gradually, as she bonded with Gypsy and her jumping improved she would in those coming months add quite a few more to her collection. For his part, as he sat on one of the dozen bales of hay in the open store and watched the girl endlessly cantering round the paddock and expertly taking the jumps, Max was troubled. Earlier that week, during his routine phone update to Langbourne, Harrington had talked yet again about an entry in Felicity's diary concerning a riding accident which had resulted in her breaking a collar bone and giving up her hobby. Max understood what was on his mind but also realised that for the first time Harrington was faced with a very real dilemma. If Emily too had a similar riding accident there would be no guarantee of the outcome. There was a genuine possibility that she might suffer more than a broken bone. What if, God forbid, she were paralysed, or worse? Well in that scenario it would all be over anyway. If on the other hand there was no accident then the vital link to the diaries might well be broken and Harrington's grand scheme with it.

Max got to his feet, brushed the straw from his jeans and with folded arms watched Emily unerringly clear both jumps. Turning she reined up Gypsy, rubbed his neck and waved happily to Max. He mopped his brow and waved back.

"I know one thing," he muttered darkly to himself. "He'll get no help from me on this one."

Harrington was not happy. As he alternated between looking out of the window across the Langbourne estate and pacing back and forth in front of his desk, he was in genuine turmoil. Whenever he returned to look at that opened page of the diary he just could not see a way forward. He had run it past Max several times but had been greeted with protestation the first time and a stony silence for the second. He didn't blame Max, how could he, after all no one would want to deliberately endanger a young girl's life. Still he had expected a little more from Max, what exactly he didn't know. To be fair if he could answer that then obviously he wouldn't have needed Max's input because he would have already come up with the answer himself. Although he refused to admit it deep down he already knew there was no solution that would enable him to keep faith with the horse riding accident in the diary. It was, quite simply, too big a risk. There was quite literally too much at stake. Exasperated he decanted himself a large whisky and standing with it by the window, tried to assess the possible damage to his overall plan for Emily. Up until now everything written in Felicity's diaries had been accomplished. Emily's school reports indicated that she was an intelligent and talented pupil with a precocious ability as both an artist and musician. For a ten year old she showed unusual individuality in both and was already an inter-schools winner in her age group for piano and a regular exhibitor at local art shows. Harrington instinctively knew that at the very least the riding must stop in order that future events would re-align with the diaries so that she would spend more time developing those artistic talents. After all, it was clear that as a result of the considerable pain and the tedious recovery when breaking her arm, Felicity had lost any appetite to continue riding. But how to bring that about? Without Max on board he had absolutely no idea. As twilight drifted in and blurred his outline at the window, two things became apparent to Harrington as he gazed out at the autumn landscape; he was not as resourceful as he thought and for the first time he now realised just how much he depended on Max.

To Bill, seeing the paddock back in use after so many years, the next few weeks were some of the happiest he could remember. Frequently as he sat on his veranda in the late afternoon he could hear Emily urging her little pony on as its hooves beat a tattoo on the sun-baked earth. Occasionally there would be a momentary pause in the pounding, then a cheer as Gypsy cleared a fence and sometimes, following a rap on a pole and the hollow ring of it being dislodged, a bit of a scolding. At times like that and knowing Max would be perched on a hay bale in the shade of the store, Bill would carry out a couple of beers, a bottle of lemonade and, tucked into his hatband, a carrot. Whilst the three of them sat around chatting and quenching their thirst, Gypsy would slyly nuzzle up to Bill until he discovered the treat and to great hoots of laughter carry it off usually with the old straw hat attached. In truth the little pony was quite a character and, as Bill wryly put it, brought more than just flies to their impromptu meetings. They laughed a lot at that. For most of its time the little pony wandered happily around the paddock occasionally munching a tuft of grass and at other times just standing backed up against a fence post resting a hoof and with its tail occasionally swishing its flanks.

One Sunday afternoon with the family away visiting and Max up a ladder painting barge boards Bill decided it was time to sort out the very overgrown field beyond the paddock. It was in his mind that it would yield some useful additional grazing for the pony and a chance for the paddock to rest and rejuvenate. So for several hours with a scythe that his Dad used too many years ago to remember, he patiently set about cutting back the nettles, brambles, weeds and sword grass, heaping them up ready for burning. Eventually he set light to five different bonfires. The white and grey smoke billowed skywards for about ten minutes whilst Bill heaped on yet more of the field's detritus. Then from nowhere a slight breeze materialised and started to waft the smoke in a thickening haze towards Windermere House. Max shouted across towards the paddock as he descended the ladder coughing and spluttering.

"Bloody hell Bill, do you have to?"

"Sorry mate, there was no wind when I started. I'll try and put them out!"

"Never mind, I'll give you a hand." It was then that they heard Gypsy whinny and realised that the smoke had blanketed the paddock.

"Christ Bill the pony! We'll have to get her out." By now Max was running at break-neck speed down the drive to get round into Bill's and the paddock. He could just make out the stable and snatching a bridle from the peg outside ran with a handkerchief to his face into the thick smoke. Max could hear the pony neighing as it panicked and thundered blindly round in the acrid cloud. Unable to see and half choking he ran in what he thought was the right direction with even more urgency. Then he heard a loud crash as the stand and poles of one of the jumps collapsed and the terrible scream of a pony in agony that would live with him forever. Max got to the pony at the same time as Bill. As he looked down at the squealing pony valiantly struggling to get to its feet Max could see the broken fetlock with the bloody bone protruding. Bill was ashen. He grabbed Max's arm.

"I'll get my gun." Eyes wide, Max dropped to his knees and tried to comfort the thrashing pony as with eyes rolling and mouth foaming it continued in vain to get to its feet. With his heart pounding and sick to his stomach he placed his hands on the sweating quivering neck of the terrified animal, then closing his eyes, unable to speak, nodded miserably.

Rose took Max's call on her mobile and discreetly excused herself from her friend's dinner table. A few minutes later she returned and from the door way beckoned Paul, who quietly folding his napkin, placed it on the table and followed her into the hall. Returning, and careful not to catch his daughter's eye who was busy chatting with her school friend Lucy, he whispered earnestly to their hosts who on a pretext took their daughter from the room so that Emily's parents could be alone with her.

An hour later they returned to Windermere and despite pleadings from her parents, a red and swollen eyed Emily insisted on seeing her precious pony. Rose took her hand as they walked quietly into the paddock where they could see Max, his head down, standing on the far side next to a tarpaulin draped over a still form. Emily broke free from her mother and with a heart-breaking sob ran across the paddock and sank to her knees beside her beloved Gypsy. Eventually her shoulders stopped shaking and letting go of her pony's mane for the last time, got unsteadily to her feet. Looking round she saw Bill standing fearfully on his own near the stable and with her cheeks still wet with tears walked across and sought his hand. She looked up at him with her great glittering blue eyes,

"Thank you Uncle Bill for helping Gypsy," she whispered. With his heart too full to speak and close to breaking, Bill got down on one knee, put his arms out and drawing her gently to him, wept helplessly.

A week later beneath a sullen sky, Rose, Paul and Emily returned to the silent paddock and walked slowly across the soft turf to where Max and Bill were standing next to a simple wooden cross. A few days earlier Bill, still blaming himself for the tragic accident, with the help of a local farmer and his son, had buried Gypsy where he had fallen. Nothing was spoken as Bill beckoned Emily forward and together they lifted in beside the cross a pretty Rowan tree, spaded in the soil and tied it to a post driven in alongside. They all stood quietly for perhaps a minute, then started to walk away across the paddock, but not before Emily, turning, ran back and from beneath her coat drew out a little brass-buckled bridle which she kissed and gently hooked over the cross. She never rode again.

Chapter 7

2008

Ever since she could remember Emily felt uncomfortable walking through the upper landing. Whether it was to the bathroom or to descend the staircase she had the strangest impression that she was not alone. Frequently as she left her bedroom she would pause and momentarily glance over her shoulder and look down the hall. But always there was nothing, only the polished floor, the wainscoted plaster walls adorned with old hunting prints leading to the long gilt framed mirror with her own reflection looking enquiringly back. At the age of nine she stopped walking naked down the hall to the bathroom. By the time she was thirteen she also stopped walking down the hall with just her bra and panties on and always covered herself with a towelling robe. Then one day, with her parents out visiting for the day and with little to do, she wandered out into the hallway. She was fifteen, tall for her age, her blossoming figure would one day be willowy and already her hair was a luxuriant mass of ash blond that fell to her waist. As usual she looked over her shoulder and the great blue-grey eyes looked back at her from the long mirror at the other end of the hall. She had intended to go downstairs and ring Sally but instead she found herself walking slowly down the hall past her parents' bedroom and the box room until she stood in front of her reflection. She turned to her right, pushed open the box room door and the morning sun flooded in. She turned back to the mirror to where her sunlit form blazed back at her in sharp contrast to the dim hall behind and she looked steadily into her own eyes. There was something about the mirror. She leaned closer and closer until her nose almost touched the cool glass.

At exactly the same moment, sitting before his banks of computer screens, Harrington flicked the switch that turned on the camera in the upper hallway and with a hoarse cry leapt to his feet. Filling the screen looking straight back at him was a vast human eye. It took several moments for him to realize what he was seeing, then slowly, with the hairs on the nape of his neck charged with static, he lowered his tense body into the chair.

Emily stood back and with an unwavering gaze looked straight into the unseen camera behind the mirror. Mesmerized Harrington stared at the face before him, taking in the perfect oval shape, the slight upward tilt of the nose, the fullness of the beautiful mouth and the glorious hair that tumbled to her shoulders and beyond, but most of all the wonder of her eyes. No artist's palette could ever justify the blueness with its touch of grey. One moment they glittered and lights danced in them, then in another they changed to a fathomless translucence that drew him like a magnet. For just a moment he was drowning in them. For the first time since the tragic accident Harrington felt his body awake. All the love, of which he never spoke, whispered to his soul, and in his solitude, with his chest heaving and his heart brimming, welled up and flooded over him. Through the windows of his tears he gazed longingly at the young woman he would one day meet. Suddenly he tensed, for no longer standing still before him Emily moved closer and her eyes moved slowly round the periphery of the mirror and cold fingers closed around Harrington's heart. She was examining the gilt frame. Even before her long fingers reached out to touch it Harrington realized her intention and in a blind panic reached for the phone and punched in Max's mobile number. As he did so he frantically flicked on other cameras until he could see Max raking up leaves at the far end of the garden.

Unaware of the urgency Max let the phone in the pocket of his denim jacket ring several times before reluctantly ambling across to pick it up. Beside himself, with adrenalin pumping alarmingly, Harrington watched the two images of Max approaching the phone as Emily grasped the mirror frame.

"Max, for Christ's sake get to the house. She's trying to take down the hall mirror. Bang on the door. Shout help! But do anything to distract her and get her out of that hall. If she finds that camera it's over. Go on man move!" Even before that final exhortation Max was running helter-skelter through the shrubbery, leaping bushes and low walls.

Emily had just found the first of the six screws that held the mirror to the wall and was about to get her metal nail file to see if she could undo them, when she heard Max banging on the back door and calling urgently to her. She ran down the stairs to find Max sitting just inside the back door cradling his arm. Dismayed she ran across and knelt beside him.

"Max, what's wrong? Are you alright?" Max turned to look at her and winced.

"No I feel a bit faint actually. Could you get me some water. I've hurt my wrist. I don't think it's broken," he gingerly wriggled his fingers, "but it hurts like hell."

"Oh you poor thing, yes of course, I'll get you some aspirin as well." Emily hurried into the kitchen and in less than a minute returned with a glass and some pills. She slipped the aspirin into his mouth and tipped the glass gently to his lips. Max swallowed, aware as he did so of her close proximity. He could smell her perfume and feel her warm breath on his cheek. He closed his eyes.

"Shall I ring for the doctor?" Max's eyes shot open, the moment gone. He pushed himself into a more upright position.

"No, that's kind, but I'll be alright. Perhaps if you have a bandage."

"Yes, I'm sure we have, I'll go and see."

That afternoon, with his wrist bandaged, Max sat at the little terrace table on the patio, and allowed Emily to make a fuss of him. She expertly made and tossed a green salad, added a smaller bowl with tomatoes and onions sliced in olive oil and served it with bread. They washed it down with cream sodas and then strode round the garden munching apples. This was the first time for many months that Max had spent any real time in the company of Emily, and as they examined the many facets of the garden and chatted he found her quite enchanting. She talked about her music and the school orchestra and very animatedly about her art, of which Max knew very little. She shyly asked if he would like to see some of her drawings, and when he indicated he would, she ran back to the house and quickly returned with a large art folder which she untied and placed on the pond wall.

It was quite evident even to Max's untrained eye that she was good. He laughed at sketches of himself in the garden and marvelled at the detail she put into her drawings of the plants with butterflies and birds in abundance. She seemed to be able to capture the peculiarly human expressions of some of the animals and in turn some of the animal expressions of the humans. That really made him laugh. What did sober him up briefly, however, was a drawing of the fountain. When Max had restored the fountain all those years ago, the centrepiece, with its little mermaid and shell from which the water fountained, had been so badly damaged by frost and corrosion that he had been unable to get it repaired so he replaced it with a simple iron pipe. Eerily Emily's drawing showed the fountain with the mermaid in place. Max questioned her about that. She laughed guilelessly up at him,

"Artistic licence Max, I thought it would look more in balance, so I added it." Max smiled, but as she tidied up her drawings and put them back into the folder he glanced keenly at her. They were walking back to the house when the telephone rang.

"Max that was my friend Sally, she's going to pick me up and we're going to the beach. You'll be alright on your own, won't you?" She looked at his arm.

"I'll be fine, this will probably be right as rain tomorrow. You go, I'll just potter around." She smiled round the doorframe at him then disappeared inside. Twenty minutes later Sally arrived with her father and they all drove off. Max waited until he could no longer hear the motor then running to his car, returned with his canvas sack of tools and strode towards the house.

Chapter 8

Max spent most of his time on his own and most of that at Windermere doing the gardening and general house maintenance. But sometimes he would just sit with Bill, with whom he had a growing rapport, chew the fat and down a couple of tinnies. When he wasn't doing that he would probably be driving Emily to a friend's house for a party or sleepover and occasionally to a concert. Sometimes with her parents as well but more often than not just with Emily who accepted Max as one of the family and who would chat happily away in the front passenger seat about anything and everything. Other times, particularly as she grew older and entered her teens, she would confide in Max about her feelings, likes and dislikes; the latest Hollywood film, her favourite group, who of course Max had never heard of, in fact about all manner of things. Indeed Max would find himself drawn in about one topic or another and they would chat and laugh their way to their destination. In truth such outings were never a chore and he was more than happy to do them; indeed he felt himself to be one of the family having been there at the outset. For both Rose and Paul, Max was a Godsend for the reality of it was, with an ever increasing workload at the school as a result of a recurring illness to the Headmaster, there was precious little time available to spend with their daughter. So Max, Uncle Max as Emily referred to him in the beginning and then just plain Max as she reached her teens, became practically a surrogate parent to Emily and in an odd sort of way a confidante to them all.

Now whilst Max happily carried out these various functions and was frequently invited to share an evening meal with the Beresfords in reality he was quite lonely. Usually he filled that loneliness by working in the gardens of Windermere for he'd long ago given up driving into Launceston on a Friday or Saturday evening to a disco or club in search of a few beers and other adults. Quite simply in his early forties he was generally about twice the age of the company he found and in truth felt he had little in common with them. His music preferences were at least fifteen years behind the current cool and without knowing it were influenced mostly by the Beresford's love of musicals and Emily's classical piano playing. He would frequently, when driving out with Emily, find himself humming something which she would take up and harmonise to.

"Ah," she would say. "Debussy's Clair de Lune, you must have heard me practising it for my exams while you were in the garden. Lovely isn't it. I think Debussy is my favourite. He's so romantic." Then she would start miming the piece on an imaginary piano as driving along they sang it all over again.

And so the years passed at an ever increasing pace, with Max gardening, Rose and Paul teaching and Emily growing up. One late Autumn evening, Max was rounding up leaves from the considerable number of specimen trees that had been planted upwards of a hundred years earlier. He stretched his back and gazed up at the sixty-odd metre blue gum soaring dizzily skywards. He'd never seen such tall trees as those in Tasmania and when he asked Bill about them was amazed to find that the tree in the Beresford garden was a mere sapling to some on the Island.

"My word, well it's not exactly a tiddler at about two hundred feet," Bill said. "But there are maybe a hundred of the blighters on Tassie that have been measured over eighty meters and even one at ninety-eight." Maxed stared at him and whistled in amazement.

"Ninety-eight meters! Bloody hell Bill that's better than three hundred feet, maybe three hundred and twenty! To put that in perspective, Nelson's Column is only one hundred and seventy feet tall."

"Yup, puts us in our place, don't it? Not sure it's a gum though, might be a pine. Still three hundred odd feet it is. You know there's a Tall Trees group, spends all their time going round measuring them with lasers or something, though I reckons they have to climb up and drop-measure them to be accurate and eligible for inclusion in the register. Wouldn't catch me up one that's for sure." Bill cackled and took another pull of his beer. They chatted for maybe another quarter of an hour, then with the sun sinking and a bit of a nip in the air Max got to his feet.

"Right Bill, I'm off. I'll see you in the morning. I'm off for an early night, been a busy day, knackered after clearing all those leaves." He stretched and started to leave.

"Not doing anything special for your birthday then?" A surprised Max turned round.

"How did you know it was my birthday?"

"Noticed it was on my calendar, can't remember how it got there."

"Well, actually nothing Bill, getting too old for birthdays. Bed and a book I think."

"Too old. Rubbish! Now me that's different I'm over fifty, but if anyone asks I say I'm a QT."

"A cutie?" Max looked blankly at him.

"No, not that type of cutie, though a few girls thought I was at school, no QT. You know the letters Q and T. It stands for Queen's Telegram. Its easy Max. I'm fifty-eight, right? So I say I'm QT42. In other words I've got forty-two years to go before Maj sends me a telegram for being a hundred years young. Sounds better than saying I'm fifty-eight. So next year I'll be QT41. Looks like I'm getting younger with each birthday, see? Neat eh? It's a nice way of dealing with the ageism bit. Blimey it's not funny when you've got to explain it mind. But then I guess you ain't heard of QT before eh?" Bill stretched and scratched his shoulder. A grinning Max shook his head.

"No, but it's neat, I like that Bill, I'll remember but it's a few years before I'm a cutie. Sorry QT. Don't mind me I'm just bushed. I'll finish up next door, should be off in an hour. They're out tonight next door didn't say where they were going. What you up to?"

"Me? I dunno, have a bite, maybe watch a bit of telly, probably open and finish a bottle of whisky." Max screwed up his face.

"Don't think I could manage that." Bill looked at him sadly.

"You learn Max, you learn." Max waited, sensing that Bill had more to say. "Ya know it's been a strange sort of life. It's almost as though I've lost my way. I had a breakdown ya know, I dunno maybe twenty years ago, perhaps a bit more. I was married then. Her name was Sandra and she was killed in a car crash. To be honest I don't remember much about it, I think that's when I was taken ill and I moved up here back with my folks 'cos they didn't think I could manage on my own what with being ill like. My Dad absolutely worshipped her. Never stopped talking about her. Never talked about Ma like that. I think their marriage was just about done all but in name. They lived together but hardly ever spoke. But my Sandra he loved her like a daughter. Anyway after she died even I noticed the change in him, he just seemed to give up. Kept saying he wished it had been him. Dad was dead within six months. I reckon he died of a broken heart. Anyway we buried him in the graveyard of that church over there beyond the trees. I like it that I can see the spire from this veranda and know he's close. Funny thing was, after we buried him, Ma never stopped talking about him. Often in the afternoon you would find her in Dad's old rocking chair talking away like he was still there. She probably thought he was. For several months every morning I would find a cold cup of tea alongside the extra plate and cereal bowl she'd laid out for his breakfast. Then she started to get real forgetful, you know, going off, leaving things cooking on the stove, that sort of thing. I'd come down some mornings and she'd look at me and ask me who I was. The Doc reckoned she was in the early stages of dementia. Dear old Ma." Bill shifted in his seat and stared down at his boots. "I suppose in their own way they loved each other really, just forgot how to say it. Ma didn't last the year, massive heart attack. Shouldn't say it but it was a blessing really, she weren't going to get any better that's for sure. The Doctor reckoned it was brought on when she had a lucid moment and finally realised Dad had gone. She died ten years ago yesterday you know. They're out there buried side by side. I know that's what they would have wanted." Bill gazed out at the church spire his eyes bright.

"I'm sure you're right Bill. I know what it was like when my Dad died. I never knew my Mum." Bill took out his handkerchief, and blew his nose noisily. He glanced over at Max, then shaking his head stuffed his handkerchief back in a trouser pocket.

"Yeah it's very hard Max, but at least we're still here to remember them and we should remember them because if we don't what was the point of their lives? It's just I miss 'em ya know, more than I thought I would. Got an older brother out there somewhere mind, but we fell out; can't even remember what about. Stupid really, life's too short and you don't get a second chance. Probably just me now." He fell silent, then cleared his throat. "Anyway, 'nough of that, talking of burying that's reminded me, I promised to go over this evening to Joe's, his son Sam's finally back from Uni in Adelaide. Sort of welcome home. You remember Joe, he helped me bury Emily's little pony. How long ago is that five, maybe six years? Never forget that. That little girl came over and thanked me for helping put her little pony out of his misery. Me! Me as what caused it. Broke my heart did that." He cleared his throat and sniffed. "What a lovely little girl she is. Did I say little? I saw her lunchtime in the garden with her mum. My word, she's taller than Rose. Wouldn't be a bit surprised if she ain't my height now. I wonder what life has in store for our little Emily? Ya know since I've been forgetting to take my medicine regularly one or two things keep coming back. I'll swear there used to be another girl who lived next door before Emily, I dunno maybe twenty or so years ago, who was a lot like her to look at. I can remember seeing her on the odd times I visited my folks here. I lived just outside Hobart then. Yeah now I think about it she was a tall blond girl too. I remember Ma telling me she had exhibited some of her paintings in Melbourne. Oh yeah and another thing, she used to play the piano real good, just like Emily." Bill looked out over the hill and screwed up his eyes trying to remember. "Yeah strange that, almost like they were twins or something." Bill turned to Max, who avoiding his eyes, got back up from the top step he'd been sitting on.

"I wouldn't know Bill. Anyway I'd better let you get off and I'd best finish up next door or I'll never get home. 'Night Bill. Give my best to Joe and his boy." Deep in thought Max walked down Bill's drive and turned into Windermere's. He was in a bit of a dilemma over Bill's ramblings. He'd have to give it some thought about whether he should recount any of it to Harrington. But decided for now he would sleep on it first. Max spent the next hour clearing up then as twilight stole in he wearily climbed into the Land Rover and set off for home.

As he pulled into the little clearing and climbed out, a row of looped lights were suddenly switched on along his caravan.

"Surprise! Surprise!" Startled, Max looked round to find Rose, Paul, Emily and Bill wearing paper hats and with their arms linked doing a pretty bad impression of a Can-Can and laughing uproariously before giving him a hearty rendition of Happy Birthday and crowding round him.

"Bill you old bugger."

"Happy birthday Max. QT what?" Bill gave a great hoot of laughter. "Got you a prezzy mate." He pressed a small parcel into his left hand while pumping his right hand vigorously. Both Rose and Paul congratulated him with a shared present, which, judging by the packaging, looked suspiciously like a new hat and then Emily wearing a party dress in a wicked shade of blue came forward and gave him a kiss on his cheek and what, Max guessed, might be a little painting wrapped up in gold paper.

"Happy birthday Max." She smiled happily at him. Max beamed back. Bill was right, he too had forgotten how tall she was. As he'd guessed, it was a little painting of himself, well his backside mostly, working on an engine under the bonnet of the Land Rover. Max, smiling his approval, hugged her and quickly kissed her cheek. Then he posed with the straw hat on at different angles and admired Bill's handy gift of new secateurs.

"Thanks everyone. What a lovely surprise, and thank you all so much for your presents." He looked at the caravan. "I'd invite you in but I'm not sure we'd all fit inside." They all laughed and whilst Bill popped a champagne cork and Paul got an open fire going in the clearing, Max took the opportunity to clean up and change out of his gardening attire. Within half an hour they were sitting on chairs and boxes enjoying a barbeque and chatting happily. Emily's parents allowed her a glass of champagne but failed to notice, as she'd obviously intended, that she was topping up her glass when they weren't looking. However Max noticed and occasionally caught her eye with an admonishment to which she poked out her tongue and laughed. Finally Bill got to tell the story he had been trying to tell for the last ten minutes.

"Well I don't know if you tuned into the local radio this morning but the presenter was recounting the story of a retired English teacher whose husband had recently died. They had been living in France with their pet cat who had developed a great liking for tinned duck, to the extent that she would turn her nose up at anything else. Now as the widowed teacher had a sister living just up the coast from Sydney, and no other family, she decided she would up-sticks and asked her sister to find her a small bungalow in or around the same area. So about six months later she arrives in Oz and moves in to her new home with her cat, a very large supply of tinned duck and together they settle down to a life down under. Now it was her habit each morning to give her moggy about a quarter of a tin of her favourite food. But on this occasion whilst dishing out the duck she was on the blower to her sister excitedly discussing the forthcoming state visit of Queen Elizabeth and Prince Phillip and the possibility of visiting Sydney to be part of the welcoming crowd. As a result she inadvertently emptied the entire tin into the cat's bowl and turning away continued chatting to her sister. Well that moggy thought all its Chrissies had come at once, and concerned that its mistress might realise her mistake wolfed the lot down double quick. Well not surprisingly within a few minutes the bloated feline started to feel a bit queer and unsteadily made its way into the garden, where, still feeling crook, carried on down the path. By the time it got to the little hedge that bordered the road it was feeling very disorientated and losing its way wandered through a gap and onto the road, just as a patrol car shot round the corner and ran over it. As the car squealed to a halt the officers looked at each, pursed their lips and climbing out walked back to where they'd felt the bump. They looked down at the mangled remains.

"Jees Bruce, what the hell is that?" His fellow officer squatted down for a closer look.

"That Wayne," he said as he stood up. "Is a Duck-filled flatter-puss!" Bill roared with laughter and they all joined in although Emily, giggling a bit, didn't think that was a very nice thing to joke about.

Well they chatted and joked on into the night, until finally Paul stood up and looking at his watch said they'd better go as it was a busy Parent's Day at the school tomorrow and he would have to be in early.

"Oh, Daddy, it's only ten o'clock, It's Max's birthday can't I stay a bit longer? Please?" Paul looked at Rose, who shrugged her shoulders.

"Well that's up to Max, sweetheart, because he'll have to drive you home." Max shook his head.

"That's no problem, I'll bring her back in an hour after she's helped to clear up." They all laughed as Max dodged a plastic fork thrown by Emily. They waved Bill and her parents off and returned to the clearing where Max started to gather paper plates, some decorations and cooking utensils, while Emily put on another Bee Gee's CD. For ten minutes or so they washed and dried in the little caravan and as Max started to put things away Emily wandered to the other end with another drink in hand and spotted the photographs on the end wall.

"Oh wow Max! All these photos, and look, I'm in everyone. That's one with Fran, and look - do you remember that one of Shandy?" She giggled as the drink started to slur her speech, "I mean Sandy." Max strode across and took the drink from her.

"Well I think that's enough for one night, don't you?" Emily tried to retrieve the glass, but Max, now laughing at her antics, just held it higher. Suddenly, as she reached up again, she put her arms around him and kissed him. It was just a kiss, but to Max it was like no other, to him it felt as though she had kissed him with her entire body. With the curve of her thigh, stomach, breasts, arms and lips she pressed herself against him and for perhaps three fragrant seconds she was like a second skin. Max, completely shocked, held his breath then gently pushed her away just as her legs started to give way.

"Oh Max, I don't feel well."

"I'm not surprised, the amount of drink you've sneaked. Your folks are going to slay me. Come on let's get you outside into some fresh air." They made it into the clearing where Emily, not surprisingly, was sick several times. He sat her down, fetched some kitchen roll and gently cleaned her up. With her head on his shoulder and a supporting arm around her, Max quietly sat with her until her head cleared a little, then he fetched a glass of water and made her, much to her disgust, drink it all.

"It will help with the hangover you're going to have tomorrow, believe you me. Come on I'll get your coat, better get you back and face the music."

Neither Paul or Rose were amused at the state of Emily but accepted that she had brought it on herself and in no way blamed Max, but did think it was a lesson for all of them to assume that an adolescent would be able to act responsibly where alcohol was concerned, bearing in mind that quite a lot of adults struggled with the same problem. He waited until Rose had taken an unsteady Emily up to her room then, with an apologetic glance at Paul, went out to his Land Rover.

The drive back was full of emotion for Max. What had happened in the caravan troubled him greatly not least because he realised that he had been on the brink of responding to her amorous embrace. He broke out in a cold sweat as he relived the moment, and how close he had been to doing just that; for him that would have been a terrible breach of trust. On another level the few seconds of the kiss, her perfume, the clinging nature of the embrace and the softness of her through the cotton dress had awakened feelings for her that he had not really been aware of but obviously were just below the surface. What frightened him most was the seismic charge that involuntarily thrilled his body and whether Emily had been aware of it. He hoped the effects of the alcohol had masked that but he knew it would be an anxious wait until tomorrow when he visited the house. For the first time in fifteen years he was not looking forward to being in her company.

But, apart from the uncharted waters surrounding Emily moving from adolescence to womanhood, Max had other more pressing matters on his mind. The growing awareness of Bill to the previous occupants of Windermere and his startling reference to twins. He remembered telling Harrington that Bill was no threat to him because he was on anti-depressants and hardly knew what time of the day it was. Clearly that was no longer the case, not only for what Bill had admitted, with respect to not always taking his medicine, but for his improving memory and observations of next door. Max wondered what effect it would have on Bill's memory if he stopped his medication altogether. The last thing Harrington would want was an observant ex-policeman on his case with time on his hands and particularly one with such a close association with the main participants. In fact, with the exception of some bit players like Theresa and McGregor, Bill was familiar with five of the six main players; himself, Paul, Rose, Emily and to a much lesser extent Felicity. Still Max was reluctant to draw attention to Bill, feeling that since he was here and a personal friend, he would be better able to influence and keep a lid on events without being pressured externally by Harrington.

At eleven o'clock the next morning a hesitant Max parked the Land Rover in the shade and walked down Windermere's drive. He wasn't sure what he would do or say if Emily remembered what had happened and expected him to continue with what she might think was an actual liaison. He tentatively knocked and stood back, waiting several minutes before a subdued, fragile looking Emily with tousled hair, no make-up, wearing pyjamas under an open dressing gown, opened the door and silently beckoned him in. He followed her into the kitchen where he noticed a mug of steaming coffee on the counter and, with some alarm, that they were on their own.

"How you feeling? You look awful." She pulled a face.

"Thanks for that Max. Yes I guess this is what a hangover feels like. Phew." She heaved a sigh, drew in her dressing gown a little more securely and took a sip. "Never again."

"I know, been there, done that a few times when I was younger. You'll be alright. Drink plenty of water. The hangover is the result of dehydration brought on by excessive alcohol. The water will help flush it out of your system and re-hydrate you. If it happens again, as well it might, just remember to drink as much water afterwards as you can. If you're lucky the drink will just make you sleep well and you'll wake without a bad head. As you found out getting drunk sneaks up on you, one moment you're fine the next you're sick and on the verge of passing out. Anyway enough of that, apart from coming to see how you are this morning, I just wanted to thank everybody and especially you for my surprise birthday party. I loved it." Her frown disappeared and she smiled up at him.

"Yes it was great fun wasn't?" Then she looked nervously at him. "I didn't do anything silly, did I?" A relieved Max leaned forward and patted her hand.

"Of course not. Whatever gave you that idea? Anyway I wasn't drunk, so I would have remembered if you had, right?"

Chapter 9

2009

Emily, now sixteen, spent most of that summer with Sally and her twin sister Fran. She had discovered, as Harrington intended, a most wonderfully secluded stretch of river with a waterfall at its head, that tumbled some fifty feet in a cool torrent into a shallow basin. Although more than an hour by bicycle along a dusty track, once and sometimes twice a week during those long hot summer months the three friends would endure the ride for the utter luxury of their destination. They would take packed lunches and colourful beach towels and by late morning they would take up their usual favourite spot on a flat rock overlooking the little lagoon, where they would either lie in the sun or swim in the cool shade of the willows that edged the lake.

Fran was the first to swim naked but it was not long before the others did as well. They would laugh and splash each other and cavort about safe in the secrecy of their location. As the summer wore on each had a seamless golden tan from lying out on their towels on the warm flat rock.

Then, late one evening as the sun dipped towards the horizon, the three young women climbed naked out of the lagoon and up onto their rock. It was time to go home, but their towels were nowhere to be seen. More importantly neither were their clothes, until they spotted them about twenty feet away neatly draped in a line over the bushes. With a gasp they dropped to their haunches and held their arms across their breasts. For perhaps ten seconds, like cornered animals they huddled there, their eyes everywhere at once, acutely aware of their vulnerability. Neither could they look each other in the eye, for what had seemed perfectly natural just five minutes before now appeared to be inexplicably unnatural and embarrassing. Mortified, together they half crawled, half crouched towards the bushes, snatched their clothes back and hurriedly dressed. They never went back, for on that day in a little corner of paradise, they lost for ever their childhood innocence.

Unseen Max drove back to Windermere before them and from an unseen vantage point watched the subdued girls cycle up the drive. He flipped up his mobile phone and reluctantly dialled Harrington.

Chapter 10

Alfonso Maldini tucked his half moon spectacles into the top pocket of his calico jacket and with his hands on the waistband of his corduroy trousers, stretched his back. He was feeling all of his sixty-two years. Slowly he relaxed, thrust his hands into his pockets, and sighing looked out across the playing fields to where the last few students were strolling out of the school gates. Then he turned and wandered around the art room collecting the still life paintings that had been the subject that afternoon for the twelve girls that made up his class. He took them to his desk and then entered the stock room.

Every shelf told a story that stretched back for the twenty five years he had worked there. Occasionally, amongst the young women he taught, he would discover a natural talent for whom composition was not contrived and who needed no lessons from him concerning the use of colour. For such as these he would largely leave them to their own devices, allowing them to develop their talent with the minimum of interference but with the maximum of encouragement. For the others he would painstakingly teach them the mechanics of perspective and try to impress upon them that a painting could work for as much as you left out as that which you put in - that it was a question of balance. He spent fruitless hours pointing out that nothing had a line round it, but was merely one texture against another, in a closer or more distant plane, in more or less light. He even tried to get one class to draw in only the background around the fleshy young life model in the hope that at least one would breath life into the space that was left. But to no avail. There was little that Mr Maldini hadn't seen during his forty years teaching. If he had to put a figure on it he would probably say that a real talent only surfaced in about one in ten thousand and if he was really honest with himself it was probably even rarer than that. Once, it must have been twenty years ago now, there had been a girl that talented, but he had already accepted deep down that it was highly improbable that he would ever come across another, until the day Emily enrolled into the art class and in her he found that elusive improbability.

What actually impressed him most was her serene confidence with whatever medium he placed before her. She seemed to know quite instinctively when working with watercolours that the light source was the paper itself. She puddled and layered like she had been doing it all her life. She never overworked the paint and in fact her great forte was in her understatement. Her flowers dripped nectar and freshness. So it was of no surprise to him, but of great delight to her, that on returning after lunch to her easel one day she actually found that a peacock butterfly had settled on one of her delicately painted flowers. They even managed to photograph that. Then of course there was the girl herself. Striking in every way. Tall, willowy, graceful and very feminine. But of all her enchanting attributes, it was her eyes. They were quite simply unforgettable. To Maldini they were the most beautiful he had ever seen. They were an indescribable blue tinged with a smoky grey. Like the sea they seemed to constantly change. One moment he thought he had the colour and in his mind he reached for the cobalt blue, then another wave would ripple over them and stayed his hand. Then some days they would glitter, as though lit up from within and lights danced in them. Whenever he spoke with her, he would be so captivated by them that he would frequently lose the thread of what he was saying, breaking the spell only by looking away.

As he stood gazing round his stockroom at the years of work from countless classes, he stroked his chin and tried to rationalise where he was to make space for the work of the coming term. Eventually he moved to his right and started to move piles of work from classes years back.

Now Mr. Maldini was a creature of habit. Every year he took the same holiday in Melbourne where he visited his widowed sister, and every Saturday he went to the same restaurant in Tumbleweed Road where they served him up an excellent homemade ravioli, with a comparable sauce. Every Sunday he rang the retirement home in Geelong, south west of Melbourne and spoke for half an hour with his father, now in his late eighties. Living close by, he cycled the same route into school each morning, collecting his paper and probably receiving and giving the same salutation to the same lady behind the counter who expanded imperceptibly in deference to the passing years as Mr Maldini grew thinner. So, when it came to his art classes he set the same subjects year in year out. The same still life, the same landscapes and so on.

For the class that afternoon he had set up a still life of classical plinths with plaster busts that he had been using for almost twenty-five years. As he looked down at the art work before him, he realised that he must have carried Emily's still life in with him and inadvertently placed it on another year's work. Clucking to himself he picked it up and went back out to his desk.

He placed it on top of the pile and turned to go back into the stock room when he stopped. He turned and walking slowly back to the painting lifted it to expose the one beneath. For just a moment his vision clouded and his heart sounded hollowly in his ear, then the noise abated and he could see clearly again. He was witnessing the impossible. They were absolutely identical.

In a cold sweat and unable to support himself he sat down heavily in his chair. Disbelievingly he looked again, but this time he fished out his glasses and perching them on the end of his nose set the two paintings side by side and studied them minutely. For almost half an hour he examined them, until finally he rose unsteadily to his feet and taking out a handkerchief mopped his damp brow. He turned them over. Each painting was detailed on the reverse with the name and the year of the student. One read Felicity Harris Class V, and the other Emily Beresford Class V. He went back into the stockroom to find his old class assessment records. Half an hour later, with the light starting to fade, an ashen Mr Maldini found what he was looking for and went home.

That weekend Mr Maldini did not visit the little Italian restaurant and take up his usual Saturday table by the window and on Sunday his ageing father stared at nothing in particular as he waited patiently by the phone for the call that never came. For the art master was, for the first time in his simple yet hitherto organised life, both troubled and disturbed. Everything he had taken for granted all his life, the building blocks of reason and logic, had shifted slightly beneath his feet and unbalanced him. The uniqueness of an individual, the randomness of nature, the incomprehensible vastness of the universe, the invisibility of an atom; all this and much more rumbled and echoed in his mind as he searched for equilibrium. In his quest for comprehension, he took reason with him and let it off the leash. It was gone for a while but then from time to time, through the swirling mist that beguiled the path, returned to lay ideas, theories and suggestions at his feet. It brought twins and telepathy and grinned and wagged its tail as it dragged intuition into view. It sniffed at the door of spirituality but finally sprawled before the infinite corridor that led to the labyrinth of man's ingenuity and invention. Unconvinced Maldini let his soul free with nothing but a spider's cobweb of faith with which to reel it in and when he did so it brought back with it the unmistakeable smell of corruption. But nothing that he saw, touched or sensed really answered the two questions that permeated that strange elusive journey. How and why?

There is behind the school a wild flower field, where the butterflies rise and settle constantly, sometimes to be reflected in a little stream that tumbles and turns as it threads its way through to the acacia wood beyond. Eventually in a myriad of bubbles and little eddies it swirls into a glittering silver river that meanders under a fine stone bridge where Mr Maldini and his class of twelve pause to catch their breath and admire the view of the little church with its white weatherboard spire. Each of the students, of which Emily was one, had a folding stool, an easel, sketchbook and watercolours in little pine boxes. He told them to find their own preferred view of the church and that he would return at the end of the afternoon to see how they had progressed. He watched them as they fanned out, then with his hands in his pockets strolled thoughtfully back towards the school.

He pulled from the drawer of his desk the view of the church painted by Felicity from beneath a willow all those years ago, and studied it. He rocked back on his chair, steepled his fingers and with his eyes shut tried to conjure her up. He used his training and his eye for detail and gradually she coalesced behind the semi darkness of his eyelids. He saw once again the slimness of her, the long blond hair, the oval face and the beautiful sparkling eyes. But there was something else that he half remembered about her, but that would not come. It was something silly, but it had been peculiar to her. He screwed up his eyes, but still couldn't recall what it was.

Later that afternoon with his unlit briar pipe clenched between his teeth, Mr Maldini crossed the bridge, and avoiding the willow to his right, turned left on a circuit of the Church in search of his students. For the first time in his life, as he found the first few students, an apprehension started to build. As he continued to discover them the feeling grew until he had found the eleventh. But Emily was not amongst them. Perhaps he had missed her, in his haste walked by her without seeing her, but he knew he hadn't. He had now almost completed the circuit of the church and fifty yards in front of him was the willow tree with its branches sweeping the ground and the little bridge just beyond. With his heart thumping he quietly approached the willow, its branches screening everything within.

With trembling fingers he reached out and parted the thin suspended leaves. Emily was sitting with her back to the bole of the tree totally engrossed in her painting. From where he was standing, unseen behind her, Mr Maldini was not really surprised to see the identical picture forming to that in the desk drawer, but what really caused the hairs to rise on the back of his neck, was that suddenly he remembered what it was he'd forgotten about Felicity all those years ago. She used to whistle softly under her breath while she painted.

And Emily was doing the same.

Chapter 11

At seventeen, Emily was like any other teenage girl, she loved to party. She didn't smoke, but she loved to dance and was not adverse to a shandy or even a beer on a hot day or a vodka and orange in the evening. In the early summer, following her first year studying for her Higher School Certificates, she could often be found with a crowd of friends enjoying the atmosphere of a beach party. They would light small bonfires and roast snags over them and party until late into the night, and often into the small hours. They wore swimsuits or bikinis and, as the night cooled, floppy T shirts. They swam and sunbathed and of course they talked.

It was during that summer that she met Wayne. He was on holiday from the mainland and literally tripped over Emily, who was lying topless face down sunbathing, as he walked along the beach admiring the wind-surfers.

"Hey!" Emily crossly spun over and clasped her foot. Wayne picked himself and turned back.

"Gee, I'm sorry." He trailed off because in turning over to massage her foot, Emily had completely forgotten she was topless. Her lovely breasts bobbed as she rubbed, then she realised and with a little yelp, covered herself with her arms and blushed. He squatted down. "That was all my fault, I'm really sorry, I guess I wasn't looking where I was going. You alright?" He looked down at the red mark on her ankle and suddenly sprang to his feet and strode quickly into the sea. He took off the towel draped round his neck, immersed it and hurrying back quickly wrapped it round her foot. The relief was almost instant.

"Ooh, that's better." She looked up at the sandy haired lad as he held the wet towel to her foot. She smiled and shrugged her shoulders. "Not your fault, I suppose I should have been sunbathing further up the beach." He grinned back at her.

"Well lucky for me you weren't or I would have tripped over someone else. Knowing my luck a bloke." They both laughed and he wandered off and came back with a couple of cokes. They chatted through the day, shyly exchanged names, shared each other's sandwiches and took a swim, although he had to help her in and out of the sea as she was still hobbling slightly.

Sitting on the beach that evening, Wayne told her that his holiday would soon be over and he was leaving on the 24th, the Sunday, for the mainland. They were silent for a moment, but then each knew they had the rest of that week to look forward to. The time seemed to flash by as they spent many carefree hours in each other's company, so by the time the Saturday night beach party arrived, he was part of the group and automatically included.

They partied long into the evening and Emily had a few more beers than normal. At around eleven that night as she came out of the moonlit surf, she felt Wayne's arms around her waist. Turning she put hers around his neck and they kissed. She could taste the sea on his lips and feel the coolness of his skin. When he touched her breast she didn't flinch but when he gently squeezed her nipple she felt a moment pass through her body that she wanted to experience again. Eventually they lay on the beach just above the surf. In the pale light of that starlit sky Wayne very gently caressed her, softly following her contours until his hand slipped beneath her bikini. Slowly his fingers explored and softly massaged as he kissed her breasts and took her nipples in his mouth. When her first orgasm rippled through her she moaned softly, clasped him tightly, and smothered him with kisses. She felt no pain as he entered her and she felt no regret, for she knew this day would come, and preferred that it should happen unplanned and with total spontaneity. Although she knew deep down she didn't love him, she gave herself completely to him, for somehow, and for reasons she couldn't explain, she knew this was her time.

Harrington looked for the last time at the entry in Felicity's diary, then with a stony expression quietly left the room, switching off the light as he did so. In the vacant silent room with its dark reflections and darker shadows the moon cast a rectangle of light through the window upon a hand written line on a page of a book headed Saturday, 23rd January. It was the second shortest entry in the diary.

'Made love to Mike on the beach.'

On Sunday Max was waiting by the bus as Wayne wandered up. Max drew him to one side and handed over an envelope.

"Everything go OK?" Wayne glanced up at him sullenly.

"Yeah, yeah." Max regarded him with undisguised distaste. He was absolutely furious when Harrington first muted the idea of arranging for Emily to lose her virginity, just as the diaries had described, during her first summer beach holiday without her parents. Harrington had listened to Max's objections, including the risk of sexually transmitted diseases, but he was adamant that it was going to be arranged feeling that it was essential that they followed exactly the events in the diaries. The only difference was, that this time, Harrington would make the arrangements to find someone suitable from the mainland. Max still hated the idea and lamely suggested that perhaps Emily was already sexually experienced. But Harrington was having none of it, sighting the fact that there was no such entry in her diaries, of which he had a perfect view from the tiny zoom camera in the light fitting of her bedroom. Max remained silent on that. He really hated the idea of the camera in her room, since it meant she had no privacy at all. It would be quite normal, for Emily to feel that her bedroom was a safe haven from the world and to walk around it naked or otherwise as she chose. He couldn't help wondering how often Harrington spied on her. Max eyed Wayne up and down.

"You did use something, didn't you?" Again the same look.

"Yeah, Yeah." Max wasn't sure he believed him, but motioned towards the bus.

"Well you'd better get going." Wayne made a move towards the door. "Oh and," he turned and regarded Max, waiting for him to finish. Max fixed him with a hard look. "Don't come back." Wayne opened his mouth to say something, but Max held his hand up and stopped him. "Yes I know. Yeah, yeah," and turning walked quickly and angrily away.

Chapter 12

2010

Bill hadn't felt so good in years. He whistled as he limped down his drive towards the post box, noting that even his walking had improved and he couldn't for the life of him remember when he'd last used his cane. It was 10.15am when he heard the unmistakable sound of a branch cracking and plunging from a tree followed by a hoarse shout for help from someone in a great deal of pain. Bill hobbled over to the picket fence and peered over. He squinted into the shadows to his left and could just make out someone lying awkwardly about forty feet away. He shaded his eyes.

"Is that you Pom, you alright boy?"

"Jesus!" Bill recognized the voice. It was Max.

"You need some help?" Max groaned and tried to sit.

"Yeah, fuck it, I think I've bust my arm. Jesus."

"Right you stay put Pom, I'll get the car and take you to Launceston General." Bill ran and hobbled, not unlike Chester in the old Mat Dillon series, and got the garage door up. Within less than three minutes, he had the car reversed into next door's drive and parked as close as he could to where Max had now propped himself up against the tree he had been climbing.

Max looked a sorry sight as Bill puffed over to him with a length of sacking and a bottle of water. He knelt down beside him and from his shirt pocket took out a couple of aspirins and showed them to Max. Max closed his eyes in acquiescence and Bill pushed them into his mouth and uncorked the water. He then quite skilfully and very gently, since any movement caused Max to groan and break out in a sweat, managed to get the sacking under the cradled arm and knotted diagonally round his neck.

"Right Pom, let the sling take the weight nice 'n' easy. That's it." Bill stood up and looked the fifty feet across to his car, trying to judge the best route through the trees and shrubs. He looked down at the drawn features and the paleness beneath Max's tan. "Reckon you can stand if I help?" Max screwed up his face, took a deep breath and to Bill's surprise rocked backwards till his legs were in the air, then crossing them sat on them as he rocked forward and with sweat pouring down his face and grunting with pain he stood up in one smooth gymnastic movement. Bill's face cracked into his version of a smile. "Gettaway. Better stop calling you Pom eh, Max." Max managed a weak smile and slowly, with Bill steering him, skirted the trees until they reached the car.

Bill looked at his old Timex watch and stuck it to his ear. He looked suspiciously at it again. He glanced at Max who with his head bowed had his eyes shut.

"Christ it's 1.45, where is everybody?" He looked round the casualty waiting room. They were the only ones there. He got up and went to reception in the adjoining corridor where a nurse was talking on the phone. She looked up at him and nodded and crooking the phone with her shoulder pointed to her watch and held up five fingers. Bill was pleased that she was occupied for the extra three minutes. He chuckled at his own joke and shuffled back to Max and whispered in his ear.

"Just spoke to the nurse, mate, and they're gonna fix you up in five minutes. You take it easy, I'm gonna shoot off. They'll probably sort you out a ride home. I'll be in touch later." Then he patted him twice on his good shoulder and headed off toward the car park.

Bill wound down the window of his car and let the slip-wind ruffle his hair. He thoroughly enjoyed his thirty minute drive as the road followed the estuary. The mudflats were dotted with waders and the scattering of white clouds drifting leisurely over the green hills were mirrored in the silver band of the Tamar. He pulled up outside his garage and walked back down the drive, along the road and through the Beresford's gateway. He had remembered seeing Max's coat by the tree and as it might rain later, thought he had better bring it in. He crunched over the brown leaves until he reached the tree where the coat lay and was about to leave when he spotted a mobile phone lying close by.

"Musta fallen out of his pocket when he fell," he mumbled to himself as he picked it up. He talked a lot to himself these days he noticed. He was halfway up his own drive when the little phone he was carrying rang. He stopped looked down at it and cautiously flipped open the top. A voice he had never heard spoke.

"Have you fixed the Bentley yet Max? Hello? hello? I said, have you fixed —- useless bloody phone!" Suddenly, before Bill could say anything, it went dead. He stared down at it, closed it, then shrugged and with

Max's coat slung over his arm and the phone tight in his hand headed for the veranda and a well earned tinny.

A relieved Max came out of the cubicle with his arm in plaster from the wrist to the shoulder. Two fractures, each above and below the elbow necessitated that. Still they had given him a shot of pain-killer and he felt better than he did an hour ago although still a bit unsteady. He reached for the phone that he habitually kept clipped to his belt. He swore under his breath when he realized it was missing and with a resigned sigh went off in search of a public telephone. At the fourth ring he connected with Harrington.

"Yeah it's me, I've had an accident and bust my arm. I've got it in plaster."

"Bad luck Max. How did you manage to do that?"

"Climbed a tree this morning to do some pruning and the branch I was standing on gave way -" Harrington interrupted him.

"- Did you say this morning? So where are you now?"

"I'm still at the hospital, the old guy Bill next door brought me in, but they didn't start working on me until 2.30, I've been more than an hour having the plaster put on. I've just come out, found a phone in the corridor -" Harrington cut sharply across him.

"- What's wrong with your mobile Max?"

"I dunno, I must have dropped it when I fell out of the tree."

"What!" There was an angry pause, then Harrington said evenly, "I made a call on your mobile at three Max, and someone took the call." Harrington tried to think calmly, but in reality he was panicking. Somebody had picked up that phone and heard him talk about the car and that was bad news. He wondered who that might have been. Bill? "Right Max. Bill. Tell me about him." Max screwed up his face and tried to get more comfortable, but his arm refused to cooperate.

"Well he lives next door, has done since he was a boy, apart from a few years when he was married and lived in Hobart, knew the first family a bit. He's a retired cop -" Max stopped as he heard a sharp intake of breath from Harrington. "You still there?"

"Yes, go on." But there was grim edge to the invitation.

"Well as I said he's a retired cop. Invalided out I think. Some accident made him flip. Lives on his own. Anyway," sensing why Harrington wanted to know, added, "he's been on anti-depressants for maybe twenty-five years, he hardly knows which day of the week it is. He just bumbles around in the garden." Harrington listened attentively. While Max talked he was weighing up on a scale of ten the threat factor to his plan that Bill posed. Emily was now eighteen and to date there was no sign that Bill had in any way influenced any of the many events Harrington had manipulated in her young life. In fact he doubted that he even appeared in her diaries. He hadn't appeared in Felicity's. He reckoned the factor was four and relaxed slightly. But it was still high enough for Harrington to make a mental note to add him to the growing list on the back of the door. Harrington made some quick decisions.

"Right Max, this is what I want you to do. You are certainly in no shape to do anything so I want you to go back to your caravan and rest. I'll come over straight away and sort everything out. But stay put and on no account go to work. You got that? Good, I'll see you in a couple of days."

As the line went dead, Max hung up and although his arm hurt like hell, he stood there for a moment trying to take in what Harrington had just said. He was coming over. He could hardly believe it. Harrington always told him that he would never visit Tasmania while Emily was there. It was too risky, if she accidentally saw him now it might raise awkward questions later. Max shook his head and raised his eyebrows at the turnaround, then noticing the number of a local taxi rank above the phone, picked up the receiver again and dialled. He just wanted to get the hell out of there. Jesus, his arm hurt.

Even before Max had replaced the phone, having called for a taxi, twelve thousand miles away Harrington was on the move. He unlocked a drawer to his left, and rifling through its contents retrieved an envelope with a new identity in the form of a passport and driving licence which he had hidden away for just such an emergency. Finally he shuffled through a dozen credit cards before pulling one out. Then he paused and, deciding that the card was an extra risk of being traced, threw it back in the desk and instead opened a battered tin box and counted out two thousand pounds in twenty-pound notes. Placing the money with the passport and driving licence he locked the drawer, rang for a taxi and went into his bedroom to change. From a carved wooden box inlaid with ivory he selected a heavy antique silver signet ring. He slipped it on but not before he had flipped it open, checked that the tiny concealed cavity below was still filled with a fine white powder and snapped it shut.

Dressed in an old khaki jacket, slacks, wearing desert boots and carrying a canvas rucksack from his student back-packing days, he descended the main staircase, told the maid that he was away for a long weekend, that he could not be contacted and would she tell his valet. Then he went out to the waiting taxi.

At Heathrow, having exchanged his pounds for Australian dollars and after a wait of some three hours, Frank Carter stretched his long legs beneath the narrow seat in front as, at six hundred feet and climbing rapidly, a British Airways 747 flight number BA15 bound for Sydney, drew up its undercarriage and banked towards the sun.

Chapter 13

January 5th

At 10.27, local time, Harrington walked with the other passengers across the apron to the Hobart terminal. As he did so he pulled from a patch pocket a canvas, floppy brimmed hat and from another a pair of Polaroid sunglasses and put them on. Witness to his long tiring journey, he had more than a day's stubble on his chin and his clothes hung limply from his tall frame. He stood behind another traveller at the Hertz desk and eventually hired a white Toyota. They photocopied his driving licence and counted out the dollars he placed on the counter. Relieved to find that the little car had air-conditioning, he threw his bag and hat on the back seat and took the main road that headed north towards Launceston. At any other time he would have probably taken the coast road and toured through the unique scenery that was, to many, the allure of the island. But he was on a mission and time was running out. He cleared the suburbs and increased his speed. The time was 11.15am.

Three miles south of the road that turned off for Windermere, Harrington drew up to a convenience store and climbed the steps to the shady veranda. He took off his sunglasses, ran his fingers through his hair and entered. A pressure bell rang as he stepped on the mat just inside the door. A few strides further took him beneath a large ceiling fan that lazily turned but noticeably disturbed the air. He stood below it and looking round at the aisles of general groceries on display, spotted what he was looking for. From a top shelf he took down two bottles of whisky and from a glass-doored refrigerator further along a bottle of spring water, before slowly making his way round to the checkout. A slightly overweight woman wearing a shapeless dress, her greying hair tied back, was chatting earnestly to the owner who was scanning in her purchases and packing them as he went. Harrington waited patiently in line. He had made good time. It was Wednesday, January 5th and it was 1.30 in the afternoon.

The bell rang at the entrance to the shop, as someone entered. Harrington looked across and momentarily froze. Then he quickly turned away and head down hurriedly put on his sunglasses. Emily had just walked in. She was at the far end of the shop and starting to walk slowly down the furthest aisle. Harrington could feel his heart racing and his mouth felt very dry. He put his bottles down on the counter and tried to catch the attention of the man at the till. He glanced up disinterestedly at Harrington, and continued at the same pace. Without looking round Harrington tried to block out their conversation as he desperately tried to work out where Emily was in the shop. Then he heard her starting up the next aisle. He coughed and theatrically looked at his watch, but the lean man with the unbuttoned white coat was not to be hurried. Harrington thought about just leaving, but that was sure to evoke a response from the owner and the last thing he wanted to do in the present circumstances was draw attention to himself. So with rising panic he stood there willing the items into the carrier bags. While he waited he fished out three ten dollar bills and moved his bottles a little closer. The man glanced at him and unmoved returned to his task. If anything to Harrington it looked like he'd appreciably slowed down. A rivulet of sweat ran down Harrington's back until it touched his shirt. Her footsteps were louder now, they seemed to be echoing they were that close. Any moment she would turn the last corner and stand behind him. Inwardly Harrington was cursing that his hat was on the back seat of the car. His nerve endings were stretched out like antennae as he tried to pinpoint her exact whereabouts. He could hear his heart thumping and his pulse seemed to be racing uncontrollably. Her footsteps filled his head. He was trapped and he knew it. He just wanted the ground to open up.

"Two bottles of famous Grouse? You alright mate?" Harrington snapped back, the sweat was pouring down his face. For a moment he looked blankly into the enquiring eyes behind the counter, then suddenly he tossed the bills on the counter, snatched up the bottles and fled. "Here mate what about ya water?" Harrington, didn't stop. "And ya change." He was out the door, down the steps in a stride and behind the wheel in seconds. As he slammed it into gear and floored the accelerator he peered frantically in the mirror, illogically expecting to see Emily running after him. But there was nothing, only the dust cloud of his tyres as he snaked away. For several minutes he crouched behind the wheel shaking as he relived every moment of the unnerving encounter. Finally he glanced just once more in the rear view mirror to reassure himself and then at the speedometer. He was doing just over eighty miles an hour.

Twenty minutes later at 2.05pm, Harrington parked the Toyota just off the road in the shade of a tall Eucalyptus and carrying the bottles of whisky walked up the grassy track that led to Max's caravan. He came to a neat, circular, clearing where opposite him sat a little ramshackle weather-boarded shack with a corrugated metal roof and at right angles to it and forming an L, a partially shaded cream coloured caravan with the door pinned open. He stuck his head in the door and looking left, immediately saw Max lying on a bed across the far end. Max heard rather than saw Harrington and turning his head managed a painful grin. Harrington grinned back and climbed in.

"Max, how are you? No don't move, let's get you comfortable." He put the whisky on the draining board of the sink to his left and stooping slightly, took the two strides that brought him to Max's bed.

"Sorry about this, but as you can see I'm out of action for a while. Bloody stupid thing to do. Never fallen out of a tree before in my life." Harrington plumped up his pillows and eased him back.

"Well you've never been forty-five before either, old chap. We've both put on some weight you know." They grinned at each other and Harrington looking round, pulled up a small wooden chair and eyed the plaster cast.

"Painful?" Max pulled a face.

"Guess I'll live." Harrington, picked up one of the bottles of whisky, spun the cap off and put two good measures into a pair of chipped mugs he found above the sink. He passed one across to Max.

"This should do you good. Cheers." Max took a mouthful and closed his eyes as the fire descended and the warmth of it gently spread. "Have you eaten today?" Max shook his head.

"Couldn't face it, but..." and he unashamedly held out his mug. Harrington laughed as he filled it up.

"Do you good, help the pain." They drank in silence for a while. Max taking in great swallows and Harrington quietly sipping. Finally Harrington broke the silence. "Well Max it's been a long time and you've done a fantastic job here and I just wanted to let you know that." He took out a packet of cigarettes and lit one from the box of matches beside the sink.

For well over an hour the two old friends reminisced about their time at Langbourne. They laughed and joked at each other's expense, and as they did so the years slipped away and for a while they were young again. Then Harrington drew his seat a little closer to Max's bed and laid his hand on his arm.

"Guess it's time to think about getting you back to England, Max. We're almost done here and as I said you've done an amazing job and I can't thank you enough. Just one other thing to sort out, have you got the keys to the Bentley?" Max raised his eyes to a hook just inside the door, and took another gulp. Harrington noted the keys and turned back to Max. But Max had gone quiet. When next he spoke there was a definite slur as the whisky he had taken so quickly started to take effect.

"I don't like it Harrington." Harrington paused in mid sip. Max had called him Harrington. In all the years they had been together growing up at Langbourne, Max had never referred to him by name. Up until that moment he had never given it a thought. Now he did, and it suddenly dawned on him that there had always been that imperceptible difference between them, unrecognized until now. The heir to Langbourne and the son of the chauffeur. Equal in every respect except by birth. Unquestionably loyal, only now, with Max calling him by his Christian name, did Harrington detect a slight shift in their relationship. At first he put that down to the time they had spent apart, but as he reflected on that he realised that was too simplistic. There was something more fundamental. Max had come of age, he had found himself. He was more independent, more self sufficient, more inclined to express his own opinions, without deference to status or tradition. Thinking back on that he realized now the difference in the telephone conversations as the years had passed. He had called him Harrington and it was a direct challenge. He no longer followed a pace behind but stood shoulder to shoulder with him as an equal. Master of his own destiny and in that moment Harrington realised that the old order had been left behind and they had grown apart. Amongst the many things Max took with him and it became rapidly evident as the whisky loosened his tongue was, for Harrington, his most precious asset - his unquestionable loyalty.

"I went along with everything else, because I knew how much you loved Felicity. I guess I got sucked in little by little. Causing the death of that dog all those years ago; arranging it so she missed dates; getting hold of those exam results and altering them. Getting that arsehole Wayne to sleep with her last year and paying him. Jesus, I don't know why I agreed to that. There was no need for that Harrington." He took another swill from the mug and as his head started to swing round any reticence to express his opinion disappeared. "And now the parents. Bollocks! I can't go along with that." He propped himself up on his good arm and looked blearily at Harrington, his eyes red from the three quarters of a bottle he had consumed. "No bleedin' way. You know what you are, don't you?" Max pointed an unsteady finger over Harrington's shoulder and with his head weaving and bobbing as he tried to stay awake, muttered to no one in particular, "a murderous bleedin' bastard ...." and slumped into a drink induced sleep.

Throughout all this diatribe Harrington said nothing. He listened as Max moved from being the loyal servant to the bitter man that could put the finger on him. He leaned forward and took the empty mug from where it rested on Max's chest and getting up stretched his back and looked round the caravan. Then he saw them. Photographs, probably a hundred of them taped to the far wall. He leaned over and peered at them. They were all of Emily. As a baby; with her dog; playing in the school orchestra; going to her first party as a teenager; shots of her on the beach; a big one of her nude out by the waterfall with its flat rock. Dozens of others all saying one thing, and one thing only, loud and clear to Harrington - Max was in love with her.

He glanced at his watch it was 4.45pm. Surprisingly he had been there more than two hours. He walked slowly back to the stupefied snoring form on the bed and gazed down at the man he had known most of his life. The Harrington of twenty years ago would have smiled down at him and left him to sleep it off, but twenty years later this was a different animal that looked down. There was lunacy in the eye, and a tenseness to the body and this Harrington came to another decision. He quickly unscrewed the other bottle of whisky and poured it over the sleeping Max. He doused the bed linen, shook some on the curtains and tipped the rest on the carpet before placing the bottle alongside the bed. He worked methodically and without feeling. But just before he picked up the box of matches, the door that belonged to the old Harrington inched open and he looked down at his old friend.

"Sorry Max," he whispered. Then the new Harrington stepped forward and savagely slammed the door shut. Steely-eyed he stepped out of the caravan, struck one match to light the rest, threw the spluttering box inside and without a backward glance walked unhurriedly back along the grassy track to his car.

He was in third gear and some two hundred yards down the road when the gas cylinder exploded and sky-rocketed. He was four hundred yards down the road when, with a vehement oath, he realised he'd left the Bentley keys in that inferno.

It was 4.52pm.

Chapter 14

The obsessed are the last to know that they are so. And so it was with Harrington. As he constantly looked at his watch in the fading light of the little knoll that overlooked Windermere House he was unaware of that obsession. For Harrington as twilight ghosted in and brought its dark companion it ruled him like a rod of iron. Time had become both his closest friend and most implacable lover. Everything he did he subconsciously played to that unquenchable and unforgiving mistress. He had become a control freak. However the most freakish part of it was that he himself was being controlled. Initially it manifested itself in his obsession with the actual time pieces. Langbourne itself imperceptibly seemed to settle on its footings under the sheer weight and number of them. It seemed that Harrington would become agitated if he was unable to see a clock wherever he turned. So wherever he turned there was a clock. On the hour they boomed, chimed, tinkled and jangled down long corridors and in every room. To the despair of the servants, who were constantly winding them up, the blind faces of the plain, the ornate and the painted ticked and tocked everywhere, until they seemed part of the very fabric of the building. There was no escape, but Harrington himself heard them not at all for they were in his blood, the incessant pulse that primed his obsession.

For Harrington it had all begun with the diaries. For what they did was to bring to him in the midst of his inconsolability and aimlessness, a focal point. Something against which he could brace and steady himself. But instead of it being just that, he found that like a walking stick used while recovering from a broken leg, the habit of walking with it remained. Inevitably his dependence on the diaries grew, until over the years they governed his every waking thought. And imperceptibly, as he submerged himself in the detail, he entered a time warp that he rationalized into parallel time. It was no longer enough that events in Felicity's life should just happen to Emily, it was imperative that they happened at exactly the same time. The day he always knew, for that is the nature of a diary, but what made it an obsession was his continual reading and exploration of them in the hope that he could pin the writings to the hour or even the minute. But to no avail, he could never define those entries closer than a morning or afternoon and sometimes the evening or night. However that was all to change, for on the very last page of the last diary it was recorded that her parents died, according to the broken watch, at exactly 11.47am on January 6th 1987.

Alone in a strange land, half a world from his own, in the utter stillness of the night Harrington's eyes gleamed as yet again he looked at his wristwatch. By the light of the full moon his eyes greedily watched as the sweeping second hand brought the day to a close, then his lips curled back in a mirthless grin as another swung into view.

At last it was the 6th of January and Harrington closed his eyes and fell into a deep, deep sleep.

Chapter 15

He awoke to the sound of a car door slamming. It was 9.35am and in the light breeze the sun spangled through the dancing leaves above his car. He fisted his eyes and wiped the condensation from the driver's window. From his canvas bag he retrieved a pair of binoculars and trained them on the house. The Beresfords were preparing to leave. Their suitcases were loaded and while Rose lifted over a cool box to the foot well behind the front seats, Paul closed the boot and walking round the car made one last inspection of the Bentley. Then Emily appeared at the door. They quickly embraced her and with several asides and some laughter they climbed in, slammed the car doors and drove smoothly down the drive.

Harrington watched and waited until the last waves had been exchanged and the great red Bentley turned out of the gate and accelerated away. Unhurriedly he sat there until Emily had turned back and closed the front door behind her. Then with a map open on the passenger seat, he fired up the engine and slipped quietly away in the opposite direction. It was 9.53am.

Without the garage key Harrington had been unable to get at the Beresford's Bentley. He was more than a little annoyed at himself as he slipped along the lanes south towards the Wild Way and as he drove he still had no idea what exactly he was going to do. His eyes flickered to the dashboard and noted two things. He was doing fifty-five miles an hour and the time was 10.32am. With one eye on the road he glanced at the map and calculated that he needed an hour to get to Devil's Pass before the Beresfords. With the sun behind him he pressed on, the only witnesses the haze of dust and spiralling leaves that he left in his wake. But they too settled and it was as though he had never passed.

The Beresfords had been looking forward to this holiday for several months. This was a part of the island they had never visited and by all accounts it was very spectacular. Deep gorges and cliff edged mountains with narrow roads that snaked along their flanks. At the junction that would take them along the Wild Way and towards Devil's Pass, they stopped at a roadside store, to fill up with gas for their onward journey. They got out and stretched their legs as a gangly man in his fifties, wearing a pair of green overalls and sporting a battered straw hat, descended the steps below the Bentwood Creek General Store sign. He gave them a friendly smile and looked admiringly at the gleaming red Bentley as he unhooked the pump and started to fill her up. Rose went into the store.

"That's one helluva car you got there. Used to be one just like it. Called in dead regular every summer. Must be over twenty years ago. Same colour too. If I didn't know better I'd swear it was the same one. You folks on holiday?" Paul nodded as he cleaned his sunglasses. "Yup these people lived near Launceston." He re-cradled the pump, and taking off his hat scratched his head. "Yeah now I remember. The Harrises. Lived at a place called

Windermere somethin' or other. You know it? That will be twenty-three dollars ta." Paul opened his mouth to say something, then, stooping to pick up the glasses he had dropped, handed over the money.

"Did you say Windermere?"

"Yeah. Windermere. Sure of it. I remembered the name 'cos my folks emigrated here from the Lake District in England. Anything else I can get ya?" Paul didn't say anything, so taking that as a no the attendant turned and climbed the stairs just as Rose came out with a carrier bag. He tipped his hat to her and went inside. As they drove down the road, Paul was silent for several miles, then he said.

"Do you know what that guy told me at that garage back there? He said he knew this car. Swore on it in fact. Said it belonged to a couple called the Harrises." Rose looked across enquiringly at him.

"So?"

"They lived at Windermere House."

"You're joking." Paul glanced at her and then stared ahead.

"Now how come we've been given the same car by the Trust as that owned by the Harrises who lived in the same house. That's a bit weird isn't it since I'm positive Max told me the car had been shipped over for us from England." They drove on in silence for few miles. "And that's another thing, thinking about Max, have you noticed that he does everything in the house. I don't even get to change the light bulbs. We can't change anything in the house. It has to be left exactly as it is. When Max decorates it is always with exactly the same colours on the walls and exactly the same fabrics to replace the worn ones on the sofas and chairs. It's like a time capsule.

A sort of mausoleum, almost as though someone had died there and for some reason it had to be left exactly the same, in case they came back. Now why would that be I wonder? I mean what exactly are we doing there? It's almost as though we are understudies. What's the real reason the Trust employed us? What's its real purpose?" He worked his mouth and squinted as he grappled for answers just out of reach. They drove on, each deep in thought and as they did so the road narrowed as it started to skirt the side of a gorge. Finally Paul looked across at his wife, smiling he searched for and squeezed her hand.

"Well enough of all that. We're on holiday. We can worry about it when we get back. Right now we've got this road to get up and then down to the bridge over Devil's Pass and according to the map, there's a picnic area after it. We'll be there in ten minutes, we can stop there for lunch. Now, just look at that view Rose. Isn't that something?" She looked out at the tree covered slopes that fell steeply away to their right, and the ribbon of river far below. Rose snuggled up to his arm.

"Yes, it's absolutely beautiful."

At 11.31 Harrington searched nervously with his field glasses for any sign of the Beresfords. He had been doing so for the last ten minutes. At 11.35 there was still no sign of them and Harrington was starting to panic.

"Come on, come on," he implored beneath his breath. Then he saw them. A small red dot low down on the far side of the rocky valley, leisurely climbing the cliff road. He ran back to his car parked in a small lay-by hacked out of the overhanging cliff. He sat behind the wheel, put on his canvas hat and sunglasses. At 11.41 he switched on the ignition, took off his watch and taped it to the steering wheel boss and waited. At 11.45 the Bentley swept past, crested the hill fifty yards beyond and started the long descent to the hairpin on the sheer cliff edge before the Devil's Bridge.

Harrington put the Toyota in gear and accelerated after them until he was about forty yards behind and kept pace. He glanced at the watch. It showed 11.46. He looked again, less than a minute. His knuckles whitened as he gripped the wheel and his jaw muscles started to work. Behind the sunglasses his eyes narrowed.

45 seconds. His heart started to pound at the same moment his mouth dried up. They were half way down the descent.

35 seconds. He could feel his shoulders hunch and his breath starting to labour. Glanced again.

28 - no 27 seconds. The sweat sprang from his face.

25 seconds. He took a very deep breath and floored the accelerator. The car shot forward and rammed the Bentley. He felt rather than saw his headlights implode and the bonnet buckle.

20 seconds. Two startled faces jerked round to look back, then he saw Paul turn back hurriedly to straighten up the wheel.

14 seconds. Harrington surged forward and rammed them again. This time as he shot forward with the impact his hat flew off and his glasses fell between his feet.

8 seconds. He looked up. Paul, his left arm hooked over the back of the seat, was looking incredulously straight at him. Recognition flooding across his face.

6 seconds, the lighter Toyota reeling from the collision slithered across the road, broadsided into the barrier, spun through 180 degrees and stalled. Harrington's head

slammed into the steering wheel. Horrified Paul stared back.

"Blaine!"

Rose screamed at exactly the same moment as ear-splitting air horns dragged Paul back. A huge chromium radiator, dazzling in the sunlight, filled his vision. He instinctively heaved the wheel to his right, and the great heavy car ploughed into the road barrier. With a shriek of tearing metal and the pungent smell of smoking rubber it buckled and parted beneath the impetus and weight of the Bentley. As their momentum propelled them off the high canyon road and to their certain death the image of Harrington Blaine was indelibly burned into Paul's retina. With only seconds to live a screaming Rose found and gripped his hand and together their very last terrified thoughts were not for themselves, but for their darling Emily.

As Harrington lifted his aching head the first thing he saw was the blood stained watch. Groggily he wiped it with his sleeve. The glass was cracked. It had stopped.

The time was 11.47.

Chapter 16

Bill was in his garden spading an edge to his lawn when Emily came running up his drive.

"Uncle Bill can you drive me to Hobart General? Mum and Dad have had an accident, the police rang and asked me to get there as soon as possible. They didn't have any other details. I've tried phoning Max but he's not answering." Bill took one look at the flushed anxious face and threw aside his spade.

"Too right. I'll get my coat, you get in the car. Won't be a sec. I'm sure they're OK," he squeezed her hand and making the best speed he could with his bad knee ran to get the keys.

They drove practically in silence for a little over two hours. Most of the time Emily stared out of the window pulling nervously at her lower lip. As he drew up to the hospital emergency entrance, Emily was out of the car and had run inside almost before Bill had pulled up the handbrake. He parked up and hobbled in after her. The smell of antiseptic hit him as he turned down the polished corridor to his left to where he could see reception. There was no sign of Emily. The receptionist looked up as Bill leaned on the counter.

"Er, Beresfords. Which room?"

"Are you family?"

"Nope, just drove the daughter in. Emily Beresford."

"Ah yes, would you like to take a seat, she's with the Doctor-" she broke off as startled they both heard the scream. Bill shot off down the corridor in its direction. He spotted Emily through the wired glass window of the second door, and barged in. A Doctor in a white coat was trying to pick her up off the floor. Bill pushed him aside and in one movement bent down and picked her up. The Doctor moved quickly round him and pulled back a curtain to expose a steel framed bed against the far wall. Bill staggered across and gently laid her on it. She was deathly pale. He glanced round as the Doctor reached past him and felt for her pulse. He stood there looking at his watch for a while before placing her hand back across her stomach. Then he unfolded a blanket over her.

"She's in shock. I'm afraid there was no easy way to break the news. In fact I didn't say anything. She just looked at me, as though she knew already. Then she screamed and fainted. She'll be alright but we will need to keep her here for a few hours. You a relative?" Bill ignored that.

"What happened to her parents?"

"Car accident, they went off the cliff at Devil's Pass." Bill felt suddenly cold and shivered.

"Jesus. Anybody else involved?"

"Yes, but no one else hurt. They apparently went through the barrier to avoid a transporter. The lorry driver radioed in. He said that there was another white car much further back, but it drove off." Bill's face sparked with anger.

"Bastard! They know who it was?"

"Well you'd have to speak to the local police about that, I've no idea. As for the accident, there is a garage about eight miles beyond Devil's Pass at Swallow Falls, I think they took the Beresford's car there. By all accounts it's a complete mess. They had no chance. They were dead on arrival." Bill rubbed his chin and turned away. Then he looked back.

"If Emily wakes up -" the doctor raised his hand and smiled kindly at Bill.

"No she won't for a while, I'm going to give her a sedative now. She'll be alright, but she'll sleep and that's what she needs. Terrible shock for her. I'm really sorry."

As Bill made his way towards the Wild Way, on the horizon of his consciousness thunderheads were forming. The Devil's Pass. At the back of his mind, where the medication that he no longer took had clouded his memory, the great rusty bolts that locked the door to his past, were starting to slide back. There was something about the Devil's Pass that rang a bell, but for the life of him he couldn't put his finger on it. He mulled over it as he drove. What was it? In his frustration he worried it like a bone. He gnawed it for a while, then several times he turned his back on it while his brain made a fruitless circuit and tried to sneak up on it from another direction. But each time it lay just as he left it and he was still none the wiser.

It was not until he started the switchback climb towards the pass with its accident warning panel that a spark jumped from one thunderhead to another and Bill had the oddest suspicion he'd been there before. As the old Holden laboured upwards that feeling grew and so did the unpleasant one in the pit of his stomach. That which had lain there for more than a dozen years insidiously dividing and multiplying started to ferment. Still unrecognized, Bill belched to release the pressure. But there was nothing, just the momentary evil taste of bile.

At 5.18pm Bill reached the summit and coasted down towards the Devil's Pass. A hundred yards from the corner, he pulled over, ratcheted up the hand-brake and got out. Opposite where he'd parked, tyre marks careered and abruptly stopped where the barrier bent noticeably outwards. Walking past he glanced down at the splinters of glass and noted the flakes of white paint amongst them and on the barrier. But he didn't stop.

As Bill limped towards the sharp bend at the bottom of the descent, those rusty bolts fell away and the door that his illness had kept closed for all those years swung slowly open. All the fragments and shards of his past both half remembered and long forgotten started to emerge and blink in the light of his new awareness. He'd seen this before.

By the time he had reached the smashed and flattened barrier overlooking the sheer drop, it was more than just deja vu. The last time he'd looked over that barrier he'd been a young ambitious patrol man, and for the first time in many years he remembered everything. The memories of that former life and his time with Sandra flooded in, but this time it did not hit him like a tidal wave and sweep him into oblivion. This time it was different and so were the emotions. Twenty-five years ago he had surrendered to the wall of agony and anguish and paid the price. But he was stronger now, the intervening years and even perhaps his medicines had buttressed him against this moment. But he was unprepared for the new emotions of anger and fear that overwhelmed him as he looked down from those dizzy heights to the tree canopied floor of the canyon more than eight hundred feet below. Anger that the accident had happened at all and fear because he realized that it could not have been a coincidence.

When he got back to the hospital, a woman police officer was waiting at reception. Bill introduced himself and after a brief discussion it was agreed that if Bill was prepared to identify the victims it would spare Emily that ordeal when she woke up. In the presence of the hospital registrar and the police woman, Bill formally identified Paul and Rose despite their horrific injuries.

That same afternoon a hundred and ten miles north, Harrington parked the battered Toyota on the outskirts of Devonport. He carefully wiped the car clean of his prints and with a bottle of water washed any traces of his blood from the steering wheel. He then collected his canvas bag and within half an hour had walked the two miles to the ferry port, where he booked a cruise seat ticket for the night sailing on the Spirit of Tasmania. Later that evening, three miles out in the Bass Straights, Harrington walked out to the stern railing and nonchalantly dropped the Toyota keys over the side.

Chapter 17

After the funeral Bill drove Emily back to Windermere. They sat outside in his car, in silence, each alone with their thoughts. Emily had tried several times to contact Max but of the numbers he'd given her only his mobile rang and that was on Bill's kitchen table. When Bill had read of the fire in the little wood and the report about a man's charred remains found there, he was pretty convinced it was Max, so the day before the funeral he went to the police station at Launceston. After a short wait, he was shown into a small office where a balding man in a blue short-sleeved shirt was studying a file spread out across his desk. He looked up, took of his glasses and indicated a seat to Bill's right.

"Mr. Rodgers? Take a seat I'll be with you in a moment." Bill waited while the officer glanced briefly at another page, folded it and pushed it into a tray laden with others just like it. Then, half rising, he reached across the desk and shook Bill's hand. "I'm Inspector Wainwright. Right, reception tells me it's about the accident at Devil's Pass, Mr. Rodgers. Have you got some information?" Bill edged forward to the front of his seat.

"Well I guess you'll have to decide that. It's a bit of a long story, but before I tell you that, have you been able to identify the body in the fire out at Jacob's Copse? The reason I ask is that next door's gardener, Max, he worked for the Beresfords, hasn't shown up for over a week since I took him to the hospital last Monday, and though it's a couple of years since I visited him, I'm pretty certain he lived at Jacob's Copse."

"To the hospital you say. What was wrong with him?"

"He reckoned he'd bust his arm. I reckon he did too. Fell out of a tree in the Beresford's garden. Wouldn't surprise me if he hadn't bust it in a couple of places." The officer looked keenly at Bill for a moment and rang out to reception.

"Pete, have we got the Pathology report in yet about the victim of that fire earlier this week? You have? Could you bring it in straight away." The duty desk officer brought it in, nodded at Bill and closed the door behind him. Wainwright thumbed through it. Then he paused and adjusting his glasses read one of the pages more slowly.

"Seems you are right Mr Rodgers. Pathology reports a fracture in the left humerus and a clean break in the radius. They estimate the man to be Caucasian and aged between forty and fifty. That about right?" Bill nodded and his shoulders slumped.

"Jesus! Poor bugger." He swept his hands through his hair. Wainwright got up and opened a window. He looked down at Bill and rested a hand on his shoulder.

"I'm sorry mate. I'll get you some water." As he opened the door he turned back. "You know, Mr Rodgers, it's a long time ago but your name seems vaguely familiar. What did you used to do?" Bill sighed.

"I was a cop. Highway Patrol. Hobart, North West Precinct. I'm retired now, getting on for twenty five years I suppose." Puzzled, Wainwright paused.

"You must have been pretty young ."

"Well when I say retired I was invalided out." Five minutes later the inspector returned with a plastic bottle of spring water and a beaker. Bill drank gratefully.

"Right Bill. Alright if I call you that? Why don't you start at the beginning and tell me what you know. You don't mind if I take notes, do you?"

For the next ten minutes Bill told him everything he knew and had seen. Starting with the first accident at Devil's Pass in which Sandra had been killed, his observations about the Beresfords themselves, the phone call on Max's mobile and finally the second accident in the identical car involving the Beresfords, who coincidentally lived in the same house. Wainwright said nothing while Bill recounted his story. Even when the duty sergeant stood outside the door with its small glass window, not a flicker of emotion shadowed his features as he looked at Bill, but took in the mime taking place outside. For the sergeant was pointing first at a dossier then at Bill's back, then into his mouth before pedalling a finger to his own head indicating that Bill was loco.

But unbeknown to both of them, this was not the Bill in the dossier. This Bill was no longer on medication so he no longer looked through the wrong end of a telescope. Everything he now saw he did so with not only clarity, but with the trained eye of his old profession. So he did notice the infinitesimal muscle adjustment of Wainwright's eyes as he pretended not to look behind Bill. But what really gave the game away was the minute change in focal length as the eyes imperceptibly glazed. The attention span had gone into auto-pilot. Bill recognized that as someone who was not really listening and tailed off. There was an awkward silence broken only by the sound of the inspector writing. Finally it was over and they both stood up. Wainwright walked round from behind his desk and stuck out his hand.

"Well thanks Bill for coming in. That's been really helpful. We'll take it from here." Inspector Wainwright waited until Bill had hobbled from the building before screwing up the notes he had taken and lobbing them into a waste paper bin by the door.

Chapter 18

Eventually, when Bill walked Emily to her front door she didn't immediately enter. It was as though she was steeling herself to enter a house in which up until the last few awful days she had only known happiness. Now there was for the first time a terrible stillness and a wall of silence seem to surround them. But there was also something else. The house seemed to be waiting. They could both feel it. There was a sort of restlessness about the lovely old weatherboard house. Nothing tangible, just a feeling, that somewhere just out of reach on the edge of intuition something wasn't right. Emily sighed, then opening the door she turned round and faced Bill. She looked so tired, her pale face accentuating the deep shadows of sleeplessness around her eyes. Bill could see that she was making a monumental effort not to break down in front of him. He felt completely useless at that moment and could think of nothing to say that might comfort her. So he didn't; he quite simply stepped forward and put his arms around her. And she wept.

As her tears soaked into his shirt Bill pulled her closer and then he too cried. He wept for the injustice of it all and the lives wasted and all the love that Emily had to give and would not now receive. But most of all Bill wept for Sandra and with that simple act, after a wait of more than twenty years, gently started to turn the last few pages of their life together. Yes he would weep again, but at last the healing had begun.

Eventually Emily pulled away and looked up at Bill with brimming eyes. They exchanged the saddest smiles and shared his handkerchief. Then she quietly surveyed the garden remembering all the good times and happy memories that it evoked. Gradually she composed herself.

"I'm going to England Bill. Tina, my pen pal rang, having heard about the accident and suggested that I should get away; go and stay with her and her mother in London for a few weeks. She'd even reserved a seat for me on a Qantas flight leaving this evening from Melbourne. That was so sweet of her." She looked across to the empty garage "I can't stay here right now Bill, I need to get away for a bit. Will you drive me to the airport? There is a connecting flight from Hobart at 5.20 that will get me to Melbourne in time. My bags are all packed they are in the hallway." She looked apprehensively at Bill "I think Mummy and Daddy would understand, don't you Bill?" He squeezed her hand reassuringly. He knew he was going to be very sorry to see her go, but he also realized that to cope with the nightmare she would be much better off out of there and with someone her own age and better able to handle the news about Max when she returned.

"Of course they would. I reckon you're doing the right thing girl." He gave her a quick hug. "Come on let's get your clobber in the car." Then he swung up the boot lid and between them they fetched and loaded her suitcases.

When flight 1662 to Melbourne was announced over the Tannoy, Bill walked Emily through the small waiting area to the departure gate. There was only one. He put his arms round her and she hugged him back.

"Now be sure to write lass and let me know you're OK 'cos it's going to be kinda lonely here without you."

"Oh I will Bill. You've been so good to me I'm going to miss you so much. Will you say goodbye to Max for me and that I hope his arm is on the mend and I'll see him when I get back."

"You bet, I know he was so sorry that he couldn't come to the funeral, but he was in too much pain, and he's promised to get his mobile fixed. Oh yeah, and don't worry about the house, I'll keep an eye on it. I've got the key. You just find yaself. Now don't start crying or ya gonna set me off as well." Bill held her close again then he reached up and cupped her face in his leathery hands. Very gently he thumbed away the tears and noticed as he did so a tiny scar just below her left eye, the only flaw in an otherwise perfect face. Then with a final hug he quickly kissed her forehead and let her go. With a last anxious look back and a tremulous smile Emily walked through the gate.

Bill cried for much of the long, lonely journey back to Launceston. He recognized that a part of it was self pity but then why not. Who else was going to feel sorry for him. But deep down he felt desperately sorry for Emily. As he had watched her walk out to the little Lysander for her flight to Melbourne he was suddenly struck by how young she was, how vulnerable but yet somehow how brave. He watched as the little plane climbed, banked and headed north. He watched until it was a mere dot low in the sky and, as much for himself as for Emily, he gave one last wave. His arm slowly dropped to his side and as he turned back to his own life, he suddenly felt very old.

As the last rays of the sun gave way to twilight, Bill heaved himself out of the rocking chair on his veranda and went into his sitting room. He stood at the window gazing out across the side lawn, to where beyond the tall picket fence he could just see the gable end of Windermere House nestling amongst the acacia and eucalyptus. He was thinking of Emily. For a moment he was there again at the airport holding her face in his hands. The more he thought of her the more convinced he became that he'd seen all this before. As his recollections of his youth sharpened he began to think about the family that lived there before but found himself confusing them with the Beresfords. In fact the more he pursued that train of thought, the more the images overlapped. Then he had an idea. He went to the old bureau in the alcove to the right of the mantelpiece and pulling out the top drawer tipped out its contents.

For more than half an hour in the diminishing evening light he sifted through the hundreds of family photographs and several albums. Occasionally he would pause and half smile at the memories evoked, but pressed on in his search for any photos of the previous owners of Windermere House. He found many of the Harris family, but few with their daughter except when she was very young. There were two of her in her early teens, but perversely she was fooling around in one and had her hand over her mouth clearly to conceal amusement at something in the other. Bill rocked back and puffed out his cheeks, it was obvious she was blond and slim but -. He went back to the bureau to look in the second drawer. Suddenly Bill stopped he had seen something. He reached into the space where the first drawer had been, and drew out a photograph that had partially slipped down behind the second. It was a full face studio portrait of Emily. But it couldn't be. Holding his breath, Bill turned it over and there, pencilled on the back, was the name of the studio in Hobart, the date, more than twenty years before, and the name Felicity Harris. Yes that was her name and as that piece of the puzzle neatly dropped into place each recollection of her triggered another. As the colour separations of those memories aligned she came sharply and almost tangibly in to focus. He remembered her and rubbed his forehead. It felt clammy. For a moment Bill hesitated as he turned it once more to reveal the now familiar lovely face. Then hesitantly he reached for a magnifying glass. The clamminess had spread to his hands and they trembled slightly as he moved it slowly across Felicity's photograph.

Bill got shakily to his feet and pouring himself a large whisky from a dusty decanter, that had remained untouched for many years, took it to the window. Staring out with unseeing eyes he took a steadying sip from the tumbler then slowly walked back and looked down at the magnified image. Even from that height he could clearly see below the left eye the unmistakeable evidence of a tiny scar.

Carrying the photograph and the remnants of his drink, Bill wandered out onto the veranda, switched on the outside lamp and made for his rocking chair. Bill shivered in the mild night air and the clamminess spread extinguishing the warmth of that last sip of his whisky.

Then a phrase that had been wandering around in circles finally stumbled and Bill heard himself say, 'My pen pal rang, having heard about the accident.' Bill sat up and the rocking chair followed, thumping him in the back.

"No way," he breathed. Everyone in and around Launceston, teachers, parents, school friends and many others when they heard about the accident had been very supportive, offering whatever help they could, but Bill knew Emily had found it impossible so soon after the accident to talk to even her closest friends let alone someone she had never met. And this girl had called Emily - how had she heard? Well a car accident in Tasmania, unless it involved celebrities or VIPs, wouldn't make the English tabloids or TV. It couldn't have been Max because he was dead in the fire of his caravan before the accident that killed Emily's parents. That all looked a bit too close for comfort too. Two separate fatal accidents within a day of each other involving people so closely associated? Almost looked like contract killings. So who else could it have been? Bill frowned and tried in his mind to eliminate anybody who knew the Beresfords who might also have had some connection with the UK. Wherever his mind wandered it returned empty handed, until he started to think about the accident itself and the elusive white car reported by the lorry driver. If the driver of that car had nothing to hide why had he driven off? Then Bill remembered the broken headlight glass on the road and flashes of white paint on the barrier. Yeah he might well have driven off if he'd caused the accident. Bill, using his old police training, assimilated the evidence as he recalled it, especially the distance between the damaged barrier with the white paint and the twisted and broken part much further down the hill with its tell-tale red paint from the damaged Bentley. Did the white car deliberately ram the Bentley from behind? He weighed it up for a few minutes and decided that it probably had. That driver and car had disappeared, so could the driver be the conduit behind the phone call from Tina? But putting all that on one side, why would anybody want to deliberately cause an accident to a couple of ordinary teachers that would, bearing in mind the location, almost certainly result in death? Then there was the darker issue of the same car, the same place and the same result but twenty-five years earlier. Now that was interesting. A copycat accident. Only accidents can't be copycat, because they can't be planned. That would be a contradiction. So that means it was intended. It was cold blooded murder. But who and why?

Bill shivered. Suddenly, without being able to explain it, he felt very scared for Emily. Several times during the last few weeks Bill had found himself glancing nervously over his shoulder sensing there was something darker in the twilight shadows. Of one thing he was sure something sinister was going down. Evil forces were starting to break cover and he knew he could not let Emily face those alone.

Chapter 19

From the ferry port at Melbourne, Harrington took a long haul bus to Sydney and a taxi to the airport. At the check-in he presented his ticket and the operator scanned in his name.

"I'm sorry Mr Carter, your flight is for tomorrow -"

"Yeah, I know, but my daughter is gravely ill in hospital following an accident and it's imperative that I catch this flight back. Are you full?"

"Yes we are, although we are still waiting for some passengers to check in. The best I can do, I'm afraid, is put you on the waiting list. You'll have to wait and if there is a spare seat I will Tannoy you." She smiled brightly at Harrington. "There's a coffee bar and restaurant on the next floor up." A disgruntled Harrington turned to go, then looked back.

"Anybody else waiting for a seat?" She conferred once again with her screen.

"Er no. You're the first. We don't close the check-in for another hour. Don't worry I will call you if there is a cancellation or a no show." Again the smile.

Harrington heaved himself up onto a bar stool and looked around. The restaurant was about half full. He glanced down at some of the luggage tucked in and around tables occupied by travellers enjoying a last drink before checking in. Even from where he was sitting he could recognize the London Heathrow stickers. Then he spotted a middle-aged man, dressed in a grey suit, sitting alone at one of the tables. He walked across, signalling to a waiter as he did so and sat down at the next table.

"I'll have the same as that gentleman, thank you."

"I wouldn't," said the man in the grey suit. "Unless of course you are particularly partial to Kangaroo's feet." Harrington glanced quizzically across to him, only to find a pair of very blue eyes dryly contemplating the plate before him. Harrington laughed.

"In that case, I'll have a BLT and a beer. Thank you." Harrington settled himself in his seat. "You on the BA flight to London?"

"Indeed I am. You?"

"Yes. Holiday cut short, illness at home I'm afraid." Harrington stuck out his hand. "Frank Carter."

"Andrew Bannister. Nice to meet you." They shook hands. The two men chatted for about twenty minutes before Harrington suggested a coffee and went to the counter to fetch them. Twenty-five minutes later, in response to the Tannoy he presented himself at the check-in.

"Well it seems you are in luck, Mr Carter. It appears one of the passengers has been taken ill in the restaurant." She broke off as a hospital stretcher bearing a man in a grey suit was hurriedly wheeled past by several paramedics, one of whom was holding up a saline drip whilst the other adjusted the patient's oxygen mask. "Do you have any luggage?" Harrington smiled, shook his head and passed her his ticket and passport.

As he waited at the counter, Harrington absently turned the empty signet ring round and round his finger.

Chapter 20

Bill picked up the key that Emily had left with him and with the aid of a torch made his way across the garden to the deserted Windermere House. As he entered the hall and switched on the light it suddenly occurred to him that despite having lived next door for so many years this was the first time he had actually been inside. The silence disturbed him and not least the reason why it was so, but undeterred he limped from one room to the next until eventually he stood at the foot of the stairs.

In Emily's bedroom he found what he was looking for. Pinned to a board over her desk was a letter with a photo attached. Bill leaned forward and peered at it. It was a letter from her pen pal Tina and the London address was at the top. The photo was of a pretty young girl and he guessed her mother, a handsome woman with long straight brown hair and large dark eyes. Bill reached forward to unpin it but in so doing the photo slipped down behind the desk.

"Course it would," muttered Bill, and with a pursing of his lips pulled the desk out to look for it. He groped around for perhaps a minute getting more and more irritable, until by pulling the desk out even further he saw that it had actually fallen behind the skirting board itself where it had slightly pulled away from the wall. As he tried to pull it out it slipped even further behind. With a dark oath he went downstairs and returned with a very solid looking chopping knife which he inserted behind the board. As he levered outwards the board suddenly gave way along its length and fell flat on the carpet. Bill stared in amazement, he had never seen so many wires and co-axils in his life. He retrieved the photo and by pulling off more and more skirting board, followed the wires to where, bunched together, they passed through the wall. He went out of the bedroom to see where they exited and found a hall cupboard. Opening it he could see nothing of the wires until he realized it had a false back. He levered that off to expose even more wires. He reached up and opened the loft hatch and pulled down an access ladder. He traced one of the many coloured wires back to the ceiling rose of Emily's bedroom and climbed back down. Standing on her chair he looked into the multi globed lamp, and eventually pulled out a small black tube, no more than half an inch in diameter and perhaps three inches long. He'd seen something like that before. Bill was ninety percent sure it was a miniature camera. He looked over his shoulder to see where the camera had been pointing. It was her dressing table. He climbed back into the loft and when, on descending, that led him to find another concealed camera and miniscule microphone further down the hall, Bill picked up the letter and hurried from the house.

Bill had just brought out his suitcase and dumped it on the veranda, when a car travelled slowly up his drive and caught him in its headlights. Bill shaded his eyes against the glare until it came to a halt. A smallish man with a goatee beard got out and approached.

"I'm sorry to call so late, but I'm looking for Emily Beresford. There is no one at the house and I saw your light on. Would you happen to know where she is?" Bill looked down suspiciously.

"I might. Who are you?"

"Oh I'm sorry, I should have introduced myself. My name is Maldini, Alphonso Maldini and I'm the art master at her school."

"Well, you've missed her I'm afraid. She'll be on her way to London by now. I took her to Hobart for her connecting flight this afternoon." Suddenly the clouds that had been building all day in the prickly heat unleashed their static and a great sheet of lightening splintered across the low hills behind the house. Within seconds it started to rain heavily.

"You'd better get up here on the veranda, before you drown mate." Mr Maldini mounted the three steps and sank gratefully into the chair Bill waved him to. Bill went inside returning with a clip of four cans and set one by Maldini's chair while the art master dried his face with a handkerchief. They sat quietly with their beers behind the shimmering curtain of water that cascaded from the veranda overhang.

"I'm going to England myself tomorrow, if it was something you wanted her to have, or a message perhaps." Maldini nursed his can and looked across at Bill.

"Well, no it wasn't that, it's a bit difficult to explain." He paused obviously unsure how to continue. "Have you lived here long? Sorry I don't know your name."

"Just call me Bill. All my life except for a few years in the south when I was married, but that was more than twenty years ago."

"Ah, so you know Emily quite well then?"

"Well mostly as a neighbour, but yup I suppose I do mate."

"It's just that there have been certain things happening at the school that just don't make sense, and so I thought I would just like to talk to her to see if she could throw any light on them."

"Like what?"

"Well, she paints exactly the same pictures as another girl that used to be at the school over twenty years ago -" Bill tensed and leaning forward uttered one word.

"Felicity." Maldini's jaw dropped and he stared at Bill in astonishment.

"How on earth did you know that?" Bill rubbed his arm, it was clammy again, then he settled himself more comfortably in his rocking chair.

"I'll tell you later. Here have another tinny and tell me what you know." So for the next quarter of an hour, Maldini told his story. When he had finished Bill said nothing for several minutes, then spoke.

"That girl Felicity used to live next door in the same house as Emily about twenty five years ago. Felicity left for England when her parents died in a road crash. Emily's parents died the same way last week. That in itself is bad enough, but it don't stop there mate. Not only did they live in the same house, but the parents died in exactly the same place and in the identical car. A big red Bentley. Yeah, thought you'd find that spooky. But now listen to this - no better, look at this and tell me what you think." Bill went inside and came out with the photograph and his magnifying glass, He passed the photo across. "Who's that?" Maldini, looked at Bill in puzzlement, and shrugged his shoulders.

"Well Emily of course."

"Well turn it over mate." Maldini looked on the back and then again at the photo.

"But I don't understand," nonplussed he looked at Bill for help.

"No mate, hard as it is to believe that is Felicity Harris. So what do you make of that?" He passed over the magnifying glass, "and something else, when I saw Emily off at the airport she was crying so I wiped her tears away and noticed a tiny boomerang scar below her left eye." Bill sat back as Maldini stared at him. "Go on then mate, have a look." With mounting trepidation Maldini nervously passed the glass over the photo.

"Mamma Mia," he whispered

"Yeah, Mamma Mia," Bill repeated grimly.

Chapter 21

Inspector Wainwright turned on the fan and opening another button of his shirt settled down to read the preliminary report of the Devil's Pass accident. What made him take interest and narrow his eyes was the mention of traces of white paint found on the rear bumper, valance and boot lid of the Beresford's mangled Bentley. He remembered the lorry driver saying that there had been another white car further back, that had driven off the other way up the hill. He pressed the intercom and leaned towards it.

"Nick can you check with Hobart North and see if they have any report of a damaged white car. Haven't got a make, but driveable, possibly front and side damage. Get them to check the local garages."

"Right Guv. You say you don't have a make?"

"No, why?"

"Well routine report just in from patrol saying there is an abandoned damaged white Toyota been reported just outside Devonport on the slip road to the Bantree estate. According to a resident reckons it's been parked there for a couple of days."

"Has it now. We got the registration number by any chance?"

"I'll have a look." Wainwright drummed his fingers on the table. "Yeah B17845 T. Belongs to Freedom Hire in Hobart, just ran it through the computer. Want me to check who they hired it to?"

"Too right, and make it snappy." Within three minutes the duty desk sergeant rang through with the name Frank Carter. An Englishman.

"Did they say how he paid by any chance?"

"Yeah thought you'd want to know that. Cash."

"Thanks Nick. We'll make a detective of you yet."

Wainwright got up and looked at the Island Map on the wall, then he muttered to himself. "Bugger, he caught the ferry."

"Nick check with Devonport to see if a Frank Carter caught the ferry to Melbourne in the last few days, and at the same time, check that out with all the airlines, Adelaide and Sydney. Oh yeah and one more thing Nick see if we have a paint match with the Beresford's Bentley, and you'd better bring me that dossier Hobart sent up on Bill Rodgers. I've an horrible feeling that we might have been a bit hasty there."

"Right Sir."

Around midnight Mr Maldini drove away, but not before leaving his address and a promise from Bill that he would, from time to time, write with his progress once in England. They had talked for almost two hours and by the time he had left, each had made a new friend. Maldini had hooked Bill's spare door key onto his own key ring, and had agreed to drop into the farm while Bill was away. He would collect his mail and leave it on the kitchen table and told Bill he was not to worry as he would be more than happy to keep an eye on everything for him. They had shaken hands on that.

Bill lay on his bed, wondering what the next few days had in store. He was not without courage, but there were things afoot and some things yet to show themselves and as he lay there the clamminess, that now covered his entire body, gave off an odour that he finally recognized for what it was. Fear.

At 11.20am Inspector Robert Wainwright was cursing all and sundry as with siren blaring he tried to thread his way out of Launceston. Eventually he made the south highway and with startled birds vacating the trees before him accelerated. On the seat beside him there were several sheets of crumpled notes that he had retrieved from his wastepaper bin. When Forensics confirmed the paint match, and both the ferry company and British Airways out of Sydney confirmed the existence of Frank Carter, Wainwright realized he'd been a bloody fool. He could have been on this at least a day earlier. But whatever role Carter had played, and it looked sinister from any angle, he was undoubtedly in England by now and the trail was not just cold, it had a rime of frost on it. But good policeman that he was he informed Interpol with what they had anyway. Nevertheless Wainwright felt he should at least talk to Bill Rodgers who clearly knew more than anyone, and with some prompting might come up with a bit more. As Wainwright turned into the road leading to Bill's bungalow he had no way of knowing that Bill was already travelling south towards Hobart having left not five minutes before.

Harrington was less than pleased to find himself in the lounge at Singapore Airport, more than three hours after they should have left. Not unnaturally any delay that kept him from being Harrington and left him as Carter gave him a great sense of insecurity. He wondered how long it would be before they found the car. His calculations showed that a two day margin would be ample to get him back into the UK, but that was without the one thing he had not anticipated, a engine light showing in the cockpit as they came into refuel. He could see from the lounge the army of technicians crowded round the inboard number three engine. When the announcement came that passengers would have to stay in a hotel that night while a new part was flown out and fitted he could see the margin for error increasing dramatically. He looked at the inbound and outward flight board, but could see no solution there. He could get a seat back to Sydney, but most certainly didn't fancy that. The problem was that if he left the aircraft as Carter and climbed aboard another as Harrington there was just a percentage risk that he might be discovered and if that happened he was done for. No, he would have to take the risk and sit it out and hope that the Aussie police were adding up tinnies not numbers.

At Interpol headquarters the fax ran practically all day, but today it had a printing fault and a harassed engineer was doing his best to put it right. Neither did it help that the spare he'd brought had been dropped when he barged into a swing door at exactly the same time as someone from the opposite direction. So by the time he had fixed it and reloaded the paper almost two hours had passed and Flight BA9001, delayed at Singapore, had landed at Heathrow almost twenty minutes earlier.

Harrington passed through passport control and made his way to the gentlemen's toilet. He went to a cubicle, washed his hands, then walked from the terminal, hailed a taxi and climbed in at exactly the same moment plain-clothed police took up position at every door. The taxi filtered smoothly into the traffic and headed for the Heathrow underpass, where quite suddenly they found themselves in a queue. Harrington waited patiently in the back whilst the driver cursed fluently in several languages. Eventually they got to the head of the queue and a neatly dressed man with greying dark hair and clipped moustache tapped on the nearside back door window. Harrington wound it down, his hands were sweating and his mouth went very dry.

"Passport please Sir."

"What's the problem?"

"Just the passport please Sir." Harrington reached into his inside pocket and handed it over. The man studied it for a moment then referring to a list looked at him.

"Date of Birth?"

"September 29th, 1967." The man looked once again at Harrington and the passport, then politely asked him to get out. Harrington's mind was racing. How had they got to him so soon? Surely they wouldn't have made a connection with the car that quickly. He watched in panic as the plain-clothed officer looked inside the back of the car. Then he turned to a uniformed official standing close by and nodded. The official approached.

"Would you mind turning out your pockets please Sir." Harrington decided he had no choice, and with his heart racing, emptied his jacket and trouser pockets under their watchful eyes into a small plastic basket. They looked briefly into it.

"Now look."

"Thank you." The man held out the passport. "OK drive on." Trying to remain outwardly calm, Harrington re-pocketed his possessions, got in, wound up the window and sank back into the seat. Harrington waited until they were heading for the motorway before he heaved a sigh of relief. It was only on a whim that bits of Frank Carter's passport and driving licence were floating in the airport toilet bowl, and that his Aussie hat, with his last few dollars tucked inside was also on the peg behind the cubicle door.

It had been as close as that.

PART THREE

Chapter 1

It came as no surprise to Bill as he stepped out of terminal three at Heathrow Airport to find that it was raining. There wasn't that much in his suitcase, just another pair of trousers, couple of shirts, some underwear, three or four pairs of socks and his wash bag, but as he went in search of a taxi, he looked enviously at fellow travellers moving easily along with the extending handles and built in wheels of their luggage. Still he gritted his teeth and with his bag bumping against his thigh squelched on until he found a cab. Bill sank gratefully into the rear seat and left the driver to load up. He gave Tina's Wandsworth address and settled back. England sure smelt different he thought as his nose wrinkled at the unpleasant mixture of car fumes and things that had got damp in the rain.

London was a complete culture shock for Bill. He had never seen so many people crammed into such narrow streets. Noise assailed him from all sides, whistles, horns, car doors and beneath it all the throb of engines. The buildings pressed in on him until he felt that he couldn't breathe. His taxi seemed to take forever, inching forward. He'd heard of gridlock but had never experienced it before. The pavements teemed with people, they milled at every crossing, jostling beneath umbrellas or hurrying along without trying to avoid the extra water that dripped from awnings over the shops. The young, old, tall, short, fat and slim wearing clothes that reflected their race and the cosmopolitan nature of the capital, and hardly any of them were smiling. Bill wondered how people could live like that, without space or sunshine, perpetually in the shadows; but clearly they did for they obviously knew nothing else. To them this was normal and already he hated it.

They crossed Hammersmith Bridge resplendent in its leaf green paintwork picked out with gold and trailed slowly in the rain through Mortlake and Putney towards Wandsworth. Bill paid the fare and standing under a tree and with his back to a shop, looked across to the small block of flats on the corner of Elmtree Close. Bill checked his watch, it was almost two o'clock. He looked down at his suitcase; knowing his luck Tina's flat would probably be on the top floor. He picked up his luggage and went into the shop. An Asian shop assistant looked up as Bill approached the counter.

"G'day mate, tell me, the flats across the road, do you know which floor Tina Rawlings lives on? It's just if it's the top floor I don't really fancy trailing up there with my luggage only to find she is out."

"Yeah she lives on the top floor."

"Wouldn't you know it. Do you think I could leave my bag with you, while I nip across?"

"Yeah, why not, give it here, but not too long eh."

"Thanks mate, I'll be about five minutes, ten tops." Bill limped across the road trying to avoid the puddles just as man in overalls and carrying a tool bag came out the front door.

"Thanks mate, save me using my key," and without waiting for a reply eased past him and climbed the staircase. Now it was not until he was outside the door with his hand poised to knock that Bill paused. He stuck his hand back in his coat pocket and frowned. How was he going to explain to Emily what he was doing there? What could he possibly say to her? He hadn't come to make her scared or more upset and now that he thought about it, if he told her everything he knew, she most certainly would be. No, he hadn't thought it through. He'd got it wrong. Frustrated by the impasse Bill was turning towards the stairs when he heard a telephone ring behind the door to the flat. Well one thing for sure if it was picked up, at least he would know someone was in. But no one did, it rang five times and then clicked as the answer machine cut in and a woman's voice apologized for being absent and to leave a message. Bill turned to go, then froze. Someone was leaving a message, a man's voice that Bill instantly recognized . It was the same voice he'd heard on Max's mobile. He quickly put his ear to the door.

"- it's Harrington. Meet me under the clock, Waterloo station at three o'clock. It's urgent don't be late. I'll try your mobile as well." Bill glanced at his watch and made for the stairs. He hurried into the shop.

"Here, do ya know where Waterloo station is? Is it far?"

"Na, not really, you want the A3 round the corner, it's about 12 miles. Head for Lambeth, number 28 bus I think. Take you about an hour in this traffic."

"Good on ya, have a drink." Bill shoved a fiver onto the counter and grabbing his bag swung it up and left. He got to a stop just as a red double-decker bus drew up. The doors unfolded and Bill stuck his head in.

"Waterloo Station?"

"You want the one behind cock, number 53. Mind the doors." Bill stepped back and peered down the road. No sign. His watch told him he had fifty five minutes.

Bill finally alighted at Waterloo Coach and Bus Terminus at 2.58pm. He limped as quickly as he could, down the connecting corridors towards the rail station, cursing his bag, that bumped his thigh with every stride. As he strode into the vast station foyer he could see the clock tower in the middle and the time. It was 3.05pm. He threaded his way towards it and twenty yards shy slid onto a bar seat and ordered a coffee. The noise was incredible. The public address frequently opened with a couple of bells and then delivered an unintelligible message. Everywhere people were crossing and re-crossing towards ticket booths, shops, coffee bars and eventually, away to his right, platform gates.

Bill peered over the rim of his coffee cup at the clock tower. A schoolgirl with a satchel over her shoulder and carrying a violin, two back-packers with their heads together looking at a map, a cleaner - a large coloured lady - who was moving slowly past ignoring the detritus she was suppose to be clearing up and that was that. No one that looked remotely like, or what Bill thought would look like, a Harrington. He took out the photograph of Tina and Theresa and scanned the crowd. He looked at the clock again twelve minutes past and scratched his chin. Finally he eased himself off the stool and picking up his bag made his way through the weaving travellers to the foot of the clock tower. He started to amble round it and suddenly bumped into a woman talking to a tall man on the other side. He mumbled an apology and turning, moved back the way he'd come until he'd rounded the corner of the clock base; then he abruptly stopped. He had just bumped into Theresa. There was no mistaking her, they had been there all the time, on the blind side of the clock. Bill pressed his back to the tower and moved as close as he dare to the corner and tried to listen. Well it was evident they were having some sort of row, but with all the surrounding noise of the station echoing around it was difficult to make out exactly what they were saying. One word however is universal in just about any language and he heard them both use that more than once, and often vehemently. "No." Then, as Bill tried to inch closer, he heard the unmistakeable sound of someone being slapped. Just once, but to Bill as he pulled back it seemed to reverberate right round the station. A dozen pigeons on top of the clock tower were startled into a circuit of the station, then there was the sound of high heels as someone, clearly very upset, ran off.

Bill's initial reaction was to follow Theresa, but he quickly realized that that would only take him back to the impasse of the flat. So Bill waited until the tall man that he had only glimpsed walked past. He was clearly furious and even without the clarity lost to Bill's peripheral vision the livid mark of the slap was evident. Bill pretended to study the rail network map, that adorned each face of the clock tower until the distance was discreet enough for him to follow the man he now knew to be Harrington.

Chapter 2

Through a veil of tears Theresa bumped into several people as she ran from the station. Eventually as she slowed to a walk and with a tissue to hand she found herself in the Jubilee Gardens beneath the vast London Eye. She stared out over the Thames, her earlier distress calmed to the occasional involuntary sob. She tried desperately to blot out the row in the station. To bury the memory and hurt, but cruelly her mind would not let it go as like a hungry dog it returned to retrieve it. For almost twenty years the great love she felt for Harrington, her most hopeful of secrets, had lain concealed. When Felicity had died so tragically she had wept for him as only someone with true love could. Everything he had asked her to do and more she had done willingly, forever harbouring the hope that one day he would see her for what she really was the beautiful, intelligent and passionate woman with whom he could rebuild his life. But it had all been in vain, her hopes dashed in a few moments under the station clock when she realized how she had been used. She had no idea what Harrington had really been up to during those years, but when a few days earlier she had opened the door of her flat to Emily, she was for several seconds absolutely speechless. It was as though Felicity had returned from the grave and as she took in the lovely oval face, the glorious mane of golden hair but above all the familiar laughing blue grey eyes, the candle of hope that Theresa had carried for so long finally spluttered out.

That same night as Tina and Emily chatted excitedly in the lounge, Theresa had taken to her bedroom and in the darkness sat by her window and looked out at her life, thinking what might have been and resigned to what she knew was to come. In the early hours, emotionally drained, unhappier than she been at any time in her life, she lay fully clothed on her bed and eventually fell into an exhausted sleep, but not before she had come to a most desperate decision. For her own sanity she would have to tell Harrington, just once, of her undying love for him.

Harrington was furious. As he stalked away from the clock tower towards number 8 platform, his hands thrust deep in the pockets of his trench coat, he was seething. Who did she think she was? He'd asked her there and given her the money to collect the pale blue Versaci dress that he wanted Emily to wear at Michael's twenty first in two days time. Then this. How dare she make a spectacle of him in such a public place. All that rubbish about being in love with him. She must be joking. She meant nothing to him and he told her so. Sure he'd occasionally slept with her. She was a good fuck. But that was all she was. In fact she was bloody ungrateful. For years since her marriage broke up he had helped her out, given her money and found her some escort work. Even the things he had asked her to do for him, like temping at the Ishmael Clinic and arranging for Tina to write regularly to Emily in Tasmania, she had been well paid. No, there was absolutely no excuse for her behaviour, and once she and Tina had brought Emily as their guest to the party at Langbourne and she was his, then he would cut all ties with Theresa. She was history. Harrington headed out to find a taxi unaware that Bill was close behind.

Tina was so excited that Emily was staying with her after more than ten years of writing to each other. They hardly knew where to begin and for Emily it was just what she needed. She needed to be away from the things and places that reminded her of the accident to the parents she loved so much. If her hours, particularly her waking hours, could be filled it would help her to forget and in Tina she found that instrument. There wasn't too much they didn't know about each other and about which they had not written. Tina was a great party girl so when Theresa suggested a sort of welcome party for Emily, she threw herself into organizing that with infectious enthusiasm. Her laughter, spontaneity and seemingly boundless energy was so overwhelming, that momentarily Emily was able to forget her own personal sadness as she too helped in its preparation. Whilst they were excitedly drawing up a list of friends to invite, Theresa looked up from her magazine and reminded Tina of a few names she'd forgotten and, as an afterthought, suggested she ought to invite Michael and Amanda. Pointing out that they'd probably appreciate time to relax with people their own age, particularly as the next day was Michael's twenty-first, to which they had all been invited and that would be a much more formal affair. Tina and Emily spent the next hour ringing round and leaving messages on land and mobile phones to everyone on the list.

It wasn't long before dozens of acceptances flooded in, including one from Michael apologizing that he would be coming on his own as his girlfriend's mother had had an accident.

Bill followed Harrington to the taxi rank and watched as Harrington added frustration to his anger by the absence, due to the increasingly heavy rain, of any waiting taxis. Turning sharply on his heel Harrington made his way back into the station and towards the tubes. Although not yet the rush hour, it was still very busy but Bill managed to keep track of Harrington selecting a carriage behind him and a seat from where he would be able to monitor his movements through the connecting doors. Tube stations seem to come up every two or three minutes and each time they slowed down, Bill was obliged to stand up or lose sight of Harrington. Eventually he stood by the doors for the rest of the journey and quite simply waited to see when Harrington left the next carriage, which he did at Marylebone. He followed him up the escalator, grateful for the respite that afforded him of carrying his bag, to one of the capital's most famous railway stations. As he pushed through the crowds, trying to keep Harrington in sight, Bill tried to remember on which side of the Monopoly board Marylebone was and if, indeed, it was one of the four stations. As they pushed further into the huge waiting hall of the station, the now familiar noises and smells assailed Bill. Tannoys, whose echoes garbled the announcements, laughter, a child crying, scuffling feet, the staccato of heels and many perfumes, coffee, hamburgers and the underlying diesel fumes with that burnt electricity smell peculiar to railways.

Harrington having glanced at his watch looked at the departure and arrivals board, as new times and destinations endlessly rippled into view. Eventually Bill noticed from his vantage point no more than five yards away that Harrington paid particular attention to one and then started off toward the entrance to the platforms. Bill watched Harrington until he saw which number platform he turned down then ran back to the board. Platform 6. Gerrards Cross, Princes Risborough, Hadenham, Bicester, Banbury, Warwick, Coventry. Bill noted that it would leave in four minutes. He quickly bought a single ticket to Coventry and ran as fast as his leg and luggage would permit. The train was just pulling out as he opened a door threw in his bag and gasping for breath hauled himself into the last carriage.

Bill worked his way slowly up the aisle moving from carriage to carriage, nonchalantly looking around as though trying to find a seat. Finally he came to the buffet bar and realized as the smell of coffee reached him that he hadn't eaten for almost fifteen hours. He bought three packs of ham and tomato sandwiches and two polystyrene cups of coffee and bracing himself against the swaying carriage, with his luggage between his feet, made short work of them. His plan, if he was unable to find Harrington immediately, was to get to roughly the middle of the train and at every stop it made on the way to Coventry stand at the door and try to spot him amongst the descending passengers. As it turned out that proved to be unnecessary because, needing to use the toilet, he made his way to the end of the carriage and literally barged into Harrington as he came out.

"Sorry mate." As he tried to duck past into the toilet Harrington grabbed his sleeve.

"Haven't I seen you before?" Bill screwed up his face in a goofy expression and peered up.

"I dunno, have ya?" Puzzled, Harrington looked at Bill for a long moment, then shrugged his shoulders and turning away from the buffet car headed forward to first class. Bill relaxed his face, but the palms of his hands were sweating and his mouth felt very dry.

Harrington alighted at Bicester and so did Bill, but now he was aware that he would have to be extra careful not to be spotted. For a change one thing was in his favour, it was nightfall. They both passed through the barrier with perhaps a dozen other travellers between them, but as they fanned out of the station entrance, Bill noticed a hesitancy in Harrington's step, and on instinct he ducked back in and stood behind the expandable steel grill partially closing off the entrance. As the last passenger exited the station and the sound of the departing train grew ever fainter there was just for a moment in that deserted place an eerie silence. Harrington had stopped, no more than a dozen paces away, his back to the station. The street lamp down and across the road casting his long shadow back towards the station entrance, where it just touched Bill's shoes. He held his breath and shrank back. Standing behind the grill Bill felt like a trapped animal, he glanced behind him but there was only the passage to the platform and if he moved now he knew Harrington would hear him. All Bill could see was the mesmerising shadow and even as he watched he saw it thin and a great hawk like nose appear. Panic surged through him. Harrington was turning back. He looked frantically around for somewhere to hide, then just as he decided that there was nothing else for it but to break cover a car horn sounded and a great black limousine slowed past the entrance, its headlights flickering through the grill as it passed and stopped. Then Bill heard a door close and the car pull away. When he looked down again the sinister shadow had gone, but snakelike through the tips of his toes the clamminess had returned.

Bill realized that he had not a moment to lose and ran out of the station and across the road to the first of three taxis at the rank. He piled in.

"Follow that car, mate."

"Come again."

"I said follow that car and make it snappy. There's a twenty quid tip in it, and don't be seen."

"Right. Bloody hell just like the movies." The faceless cabbie jolted it into gear and they squealed down the road. "Follow that car. Yes Siree."

They had been following the tail lights for no more than two miles when the cabbie indicated, slowed and turned into a garage. Bill shot forward with alarm and grabbed the driver by the shoulder.

"Hey, what you doing, we're going to lose him -"

"No we're not."

"Wadayamean, we're not? Look he's gone already."

"Trust me. I know who it is. I just remembered. That car belongs to the Blaines, Langbourne House - stately home just outside Middleton Stoney."

"You sure?" The driver turned and smiling displayed a row of crooked teeth.

"Twenty quid sure."

As Harrington sat in the back of the limousine and it pulled away he suddenly remembered where he had seen the man on the train before. It was the same person that had bumped into Theresa under the clock. Now wasn't that just a little bit strange that he should be on the same train half an hour later, particularly as it left not from Waterloo but Marylebone. To have done that he would have had to get on the tube at the same time he did. He must have been following me thought Harrington. He swivelled round and looked out of the rear window, just as the car following, a taxi, slowed and turned into the garage they had just passed. Behind them the road was empty. Harrington pursed his lips and there was something else. He glanced backwards again at the deserted road. What was it? Was it something the man on the train said? No, something else. Then Harrington had it. It wasn't what the stranger had said, it was how he had said it. It was his Australian accent. Harrington visibly paled. The police, were they on to him? No they couldn't be, what clues had he left them. He rattled the possibilities around in his mind and flung them along the baize of reason in search of sevens. No, he had left them none. He flung the dice out again, but with the same result. Harrington started to relax as the road behind continued to remain clear. By the time the great limousine turned through the vast gateway of Langbourne, his mind was occupied once more with his son's twenty-first. The time was 7.25pm. The date was January 16th, 2011 and the party was now only two days away.

The cabbie dropped Bill off at a small hotel in Middleton Stoney. After a much needed hot shower, Bill ambled down to the bar and perching himself on a stool ordered a beer and looked at the menu card.

"How big's the steak mate?"

"About 8 ounces, I think, Do want me to check?"

"Na, I'll have two of them, medium rare with French fries and a side order of salad. What wines you got. Any Australian whites?"

"No, I'm sorry Sir."

"So you should be! Alright then, what have you got?"

"I've got an Italian Frascati."

"Right I'll have that one, cold mind. Now tell me, there's a big mansion aways back behind some massive gates. Do you know anything about it? I'm a bit of a sucker for old buildings, and as I'm only over here for a month, want to see as many as possible. What can you tell me about it? Oh yeah, and what you drinking?"

"Thank you, just a half. Well you'll be talking about Langbourne House, the Blaine family. Been there for centuries. Harrington Blaine inherited it and the publishing business from his father about twenty five years ago. In fact there is a big party there the day after tomorrow to celebrate his son's twenty-first. Just about anybody who is anybody will be there. How the other half live eh?" Bill nodded in agreement.

"Well I guess that puts the kibosh on any chance I might have had to look round."

"Mind you," said the barman warming to his story, "not that money brings you happiness. The Blaine family have been beset with tragedy over the years. Harrington's parents died in a light aircraft crash, and about twenty years ago his own wife died when she plunged to her death from a balcony at the big house. She was an Australian like you funnily enough." Bill stopped drinking and peered over his glass at the barman as he dried glasses.

"Aussie you say?"

"Yeah, I'm pretty sure that's right. Anyway the bloke you should be talking to is old Dan. You'll find him by the fire in the public bar. Worked on the estate most of his life. Retired now. You'll have to speak up a bit, he's a bit hard of hearing, but likes a wee dram. Put a Bells in front of him and he'll talk all night," and with that the barman winked at Bill before moving off down the counter.

Bill carried his drink into the adjacent bar and looked round the smokey room with its half panelling and red flock wallpaper. Old black beams with hundreds of horse brasses traversed the ceiling and pierced the chimney breast below which the embers of a log glowed. Sitting to the right of the chimney an old man wearing a faded tweed jacket with leather elbows and a muffler was half asleep . Before him, on the little round table, a tankard and next to that an old briar pipe on its side in the glass ashtray. Bill drew a chair up to the table and reaching across gently shook the old man by the sleeve.

"Are you Dan?" The old man's head came off his chest, and he blinked several times and smacked his lips.

"Is it time to go?"

"No Dan, do you want a drink?"

"Who are you?"

"I'm Bill. I'm an Aussie and the barman said you used to work at Langbourne. You know the big house." Dan heaved himself upright in his chair, and reached for his pipe. Bill waited patiently while he retrieved some very black tobacco from an old leather pouch, filled the bowl, struck a match and using his thumb as a tamper finally got it alight. From beneath very bushy eyebrows a pair of faded blue eyes twinkled at Bill through the smoke of his pipe.

"Aye, I worked at Langbourne, all me life. Star'ed as a stable boy when I were thir'een and retired as 'ead gardener a year shy o'me seven'ieth. I'm eigh'y-six next summer yo' know." Bill drew his chair closer and pointed to the tankard.

"Well I'd rather have a Bells if that's alright with ee?" It was and Bill brought him one from the bar.

"The barman said that Mr Blaine's wife originally came from Australia like me. Do you remember her?"

"Remember her. You couldn't forget her. She was the most beau'iful woman you'd ever clap eyes on. Like a princess. Blonde, amazin' eyes. Actually came from Tasmania. I remember her telling me tha'. She used to walk round the gardens wi' me as I were head gardener and tell me about the plants from down under. I found 'er you know."

"How d'ya mean found her?" Dan cleared his throat and took another long sip of his whisky, then he sighed long and deep.

"The night she died. Fell over balcony, back o' big house. She and Mister 'arrington had gone up there after a party. She loved it up there. I would often see 'er sitting high up on balcony with 'er sketch pad. Anyway that night, I was on me way up to me room, in servants' quarters by park gates, when I 'ears this awful scream. I knew it were 'er. Well me and some others ran out with torches and there she were, lying in courtyard. Must have fallen thir'y feet if not more. It were never the same after that. She were such a 'appy soul. That's what 'er name meant you know, 'appiness." Bill looked puzzled,

"Happiness?" Dan scoffed, and shook his head,

"Don't they teach you younguns anyfing these days? Yes, latin for 'appiness." Bill looked blankly back.

"Felicity, you fool."

When Bill came round he was lying on the floor of the bar. Someone had put a cushion under his head. Dan was talking.

"- Well 'is mouth dropped open like sumun 'ad hit 'im in guts, dropped 'is beer and keeled o'er. Ee alrigh'?" Bill sat up and put his head between his knees and then getting slowly to his feet, felt for a chair behind him and sat down. The barman stood anxiously over him.

"Do you want me to phone for a doctor?" Bill managed a weak smile, and shakily got to his feet, his face as white as chalk.

"Na mate, I'll be alright. Must be jet lag. Whew. I think I'll just go to my room." He leaned momentarily, both hands on the back of a chair and took a deep breath. "Sorry about that."

"I guess your steak's about ready. Do you still want that?" Bill shook his head and fished out a twenty pound note.

"Na, I couldn't face that right now. Give it to Dan."

Chapter 3

The next day, Bill got a lift from one of the other guests into Bicester and from there caught a train that would take him the fifteen miles into Oxford. It was a cold but sunny morning and the sky was that pale blue peculiar to winter, but Bill saw none of it. He'd not slept well that night and not just because it was a strange bed. The proximity to Harrington disturbed him but not as much as the realization that he had stumbled upon the one missing fact, that made some sense of much that had gone before. Felicity the girl that had lived at Windermere House all those years before was Harrington's dead wife. But what was Emily's role in all this. Obviously Harrington was somehow involved in her life but why and how. The most logical conclusion was that Emily was his daughter. But why then was she living in Tasmania, without any contact with him, and what about the Beresfords? Had they adopted her? Then she looked so completely like Felicity. Then there was the accident.

Bill gazed out of the window at the passing landscape of hedges, great swathes of farmland and isolated houses. But his thoughts were twelve thousand miles away, reliving the moments when twice, twenty odd years apart, he had stood on the same bend of the cliff road looking down over the same precipice. Sandra's face, not entirely in focus floated before him, and as his throat closed, tears brimmed and one stole down his cheek. Just for a moment Bill wished he had his tablets with him, the strength of the medicines had mercifully blocked out the memory of her. All the tears he hadn't shed for Sandra and the life he would never know with her suddenly welled up. He stumbled to the end of the carriage and there by the door, with the wind blowing through his hair, William Rodgers, simple, honest and desperately alone, sank to his haunches and quite simply sobbed his heart out.

For more than an hour Harrington had been trying to reach Michael on his mobile, but without success. If nothing else his son was running true to form. He rarely contacted his father unless it was for money. Harrington could not open a magazine or a newspaper without seeing a photograph of Michael Blaine, heir to a publishing fortune, with his beautiful debutante girlfriend Amanda on his arm at some society bash or other. Harrington put up with his son's jet-setting ways, but had made it clear on numerous occasions that all that would change once he reached twenty one. Then he would be expected to join the family firm and learn everything there was to know about publishing and more. A new era for both of them was dawning. Harrington looked at Michael's photograph on the desk in front of him. He rang Amanda's parents.

"Hello Richard, Harrington here. I'm sorry to -"

"Harrington! My word you must be psychic, I was just about to ring you. Amanda's mother had a pretty nasty riding accident a few days ago, some dog off its lead, spooked her mount, and I'm afraid she's unconscious in the local hospital."

"Jesus, Richard, I'm so sorry. How is Jacintha, is there anything I can do?"

"That's kind old boy, but no it's really a question of waiting. The doctors are doing a great job, just a question of time really." There was a slight pause. "Anyway, managed to contact Amanda a couple of days ago through a friend. Did you know they were in California? I had no idea, boy do those two get around, and she got on the first plane back. There was only one seat available, so Michael took the next one out. We are expecting Amanda about now. I think she said Michael would be collecting some clothes from their flat in London tonight, staying there overnight and picking her up the next day and down to yours for the big night tomorrow."

"Well that's a relief, I had no contact and obviously with Michael's twenty first tomorrow -"

"Yes of course, but he'll be there. Don't worry old boy, probably one last fling with his friends before the big day and he has to knuckle down to earning a real living. Seem to remember you saying that your Dad had to practically drag you back kicking and screaming to start University when you were back-packing in Australia. He's a fine young man and we like him a lot. I just know he'll be a credit to you. Now, depending on how her mother is, Amanda will be there at the party as well, but on a personal note, you understand I'm sorry we won't be there now. Rotten luck, been looking forward to it for months and so was Jacintha."

"I'm so, so sorry, Richard . Which hospital is it? I would like to send her a little something. Give her my love." Harrington scribbled down the name and hung up. He sat there for a moment, then he picked up the phone just one more time and rang Chantelle's the local florists.

Calmer now he knew where Michael was, Harrington got to his feet and looked for the last time at the twin clocks on the wall. Then he walked across and reaching up lifted one of them down and placed it face down behind a computer alongside one of the two wristwatches he had worn simultaneously for the last 19 years. The obsession with parallel time was over. He glanced at the single clock on the wall and checked his remaining wristwatch against it. It was 6.30pm. Harrington walked slowly to the door and took one last look around at a room, within which he had spent so many years. He opened the door, stepped through and locked it for the last time. As he pocketed the keys and walked away towards that great staircase Harrington knew that in less than thirty hours, nineteen years of meticulous planning would come to fruition. He would meet Emily and life with Felicity could begin again.

At 10.30pm Michael stood out on the hotel balcony and looked out across the skyscrapers to the sea beyond. It was a beautiful day, but he was tired. They had got back very late from a private beach party. He glanced back through the open glass doors to the bedroom. Amanda was still sleeping, the bedclothes strewn around the bed. She was nude. He smiled tenderly and putting down his coffee went to her bedside. He loosened his bath robe, letting it slip to the floor and snuggled up to her back. She murmured and settled her bottom against him. He wondered how she would like life at Langbourne. In just a few days he would be twenty-one. He looked beyond Amanda's shoulder to where their luggage rested by the door. Tomorrow they would be flying back to England and a new life. In the east wing of Langbourne there was a lovely apartment waiting for them, also a flat in Chelsea, close to the publishing business, which would be theirs to use. Michael was philosophical about going into the family firm. He knew it was going to happen sooner or later, so the occasion of his twenty-first was as good a time as any. Still there was another day yet to enjoy. Amanda must have guessed what was on his mind, because she turned round in his arms and pressed against him. The phone rang. Amanda reached for it.

"Hi Dad. How did you find us? Is there anything wrong?"

Chapter 4

When Bill drew back the curtains on the morning of the 18th of January he was not surprised to discover a blanket of snow cloaking the landscape. On his way back from Oxford, where he had managed to buy a black suit, bow tie, white shirt and patent leather shoes, he had noticed the air temperature noticeably dropping. He glanced at his watch and as there was still an hour before noon and perhaps an early lunch downstairs, he decided he would take a walk. Anyway he had a letter to post to Maldini.

The night before, he had written to his friend long into the early hours. He recounted in detail all that had happened since he'd landed, including the discovery that the same Felicity of the photograph was the wife of a Harrington Blaine who had just flown back from Oz and that he was probably mixed up in the events surrounding Windermere. He explained that he found out from a retired Langbourne gardener that Harrington did actually know Max, and had employed him as his chauffeur for many years. This was the same Max who was the gardener and handyman to Emily's parents, and that following what now looked like a clandestine visit by Harrington, both Max and the parents had died in very suspicious circumstances. He also confirmed to Maldini that Emily was staying with Tina and her mother Teresa and recounted the incident with the answer phone and the events he witnessed at the station. He closed his letter saying that he would be gate crashing the twenty-first birthday party of Harrington's son but really had no other plans or ideas beyond that other than he was absolutely convinced that Emily would also be there. He signed off, apologising for losing his address, but hoped he would see this in the farm's post box. Anyway he wished him well and that one way or another he would hear from him in the days to come but should things go badly, well, maybe he would know what to do.

As he dressed Bill pulled out from another bag he'd brought back from his shopping expedition, a heavy knit pullover, a thick pair of socks, a scarf and some woollen gloves. In his hurry to get to the airport and everything else on his mind, he had completely forgotten that whilst it was summer in Tasmania it would be winter in England. Thus attired, Bill trudged through the snow towards the great gates of Langbourne. A hundred yards from those vast portals it was evident by the comings and goings of countless small vans and bigger trucks that preparations for the big night were well under way.

He walked casually past, noting that each vehicle was checked in by a man dressed in a sort of chauffeur's uniform, who would briefly talk with the driver, point down the long drive, indicate that they should then turn right, and then using a remote, raise a red and white canti-levered pole some thirty yards further down the drive. He would then lower the pole and turning, enter the gate house through an arched oak door and await the next arrival.

Bill carried on walking alongside the immense brick wall that seemed to go on forever. He occasionally passed the odd door set in the wall and, casually glancing over his shoulder to ensure he was not being observed, would lean his shoulder against them to see if they would open. None did, although one gave considerably but insufficiently for him to get through. Eventually, some twenty minutes later, by crossing the lane and mounting the adjacent bank he found himself with an excellent though distant side and partial rear view of the fine house. Obliquely he could just make out an imposing archway with parallel outbuildings leading to the rear of the main house. The two impressive wings, divided by a high open balustraded terrace were magnificently framed by towering Lebanese firs which Bill guessed must be better than two hundred years old. Satisfied that there was little to be gained by continuing any further, he leisurely returned the way he had come, walking once again past the gates, trying to get a better view of the house at the end of the tree lined drive, before gaining the hotel and a much needed lunch.

As Bill tucked into his meal, he weighed up his options for gate-crashing the party. He had to assume that each guest would be carrying an invitation that they would present at the gate house. In addition they would be passing through that point with their cars. The more he looked at it the more he realized that he would not be able to enter that way. Even if he managed to arrive by car and with an apology for forgetting his invitation, he couldn't be sure that security at the gate wouldn't check his name against a guest list. He could, of course, try the side gate about two hundred yards further down, but he had no idea of the terrain behind the high wall.

Then, even if he managed to get to the porticoed front door of the mansion itself, he had to assume that there would be a second rank of security there and very probably each guest who entered would be announced. That left him with rather less options than he hoped. Perhaps he could create some sort of diversion at the front door. Bill thought about that for a moment but couldn't think of anything that might work.

The big problem was that whilst there was anonymity within the mass of the guests arriving, that was also when the security was at its most impenetrable. Bill mused over the problem and searched for a solution laterally. So if the security is there when the guests arrive, is it there before? Apart from the gate security Bill doubted whether there was much at the house itself other than the staff of Langbourne and doubtless they would be more than occupied with their own duties. Then Bill had an idea, it was a bit of a long shot, but in the absence of anything better he thought it worth a try. He went to the bar, ordered a beer and a whisky and went into the public bar in search of Dan.

"Looks pretty busy at the big house today, Dan."

"Oh aye, that'll be young Michael's twen'y first."

"I suppose they decorate the house when it's a big do. Did you as head garden supply the flowers from the estate's nurseries?"

"Oh aye, but not in the winter, they always used the flower shop in Bicester, Chantelle's. Cousin of mine works there."

"Really, what's his name? I need to get some flowers, might do me a deal if I say I know you."

"Well he might at that. Ask for Ronnie."

Bill checked his watch. It was 1.50pm. He went to the public bar and got the barman to ring for a taxi. Outside the flower shop, a harassed looking man in his forties, was loading a transit with flower displays that were spread out all over the pavement. Bill put down his bag, picked one up and approached the van.

"Are you Ronnie?"

"Yeah what I can I do for you?" he took the display from Bill who promptly picked up another and handed it to him.

"Well, I'm trying to get into the party at Langbourne House. Problem is I haven't got an invitation and I wanted to surprise Harrington because we used to back-pack together when he was a student in Australia. If I present myself at the gate, they'll ring through and it won't be a surprise and that would be a pisser having travelled twelve thousand miles just to do that. So when I told Dan, he said you worked here and was a sport and could probably help out. So what do you think mate?" Ronnie raised his eyebrows and wiped his hands.

"Well, I don't know, what have you got in mind?" Bill handed him another flower display.

"How about I help you carry the flower displays in this afternoon? If you've got a spare white coat, I could wear me duds for the party under that." Ronnie looked unsure. Bill continued. "Go on Ronnie, it's worth fifty quid to me just to see Harrington's face tonight, he still thinks I'm down under."

Chapter 5

As the transit drew up by the lodge gates, Ronnie leaned out of the driver's window.

"Alright Bert this is the last of the flowers. This here's Bill and he's going to give me a lift. Right short-handed this week." The gateman looked briefly at Bill, nodded, waved them through and then raised the barrier. Bill watched fascinated as they followed the drive and the immense mansion with its impressive porticoed entrance came into view. They turned round the great fountain and came to rest before the dozen wide stone steps, guarded by life size sculptured lions, that ascended to a huge pair of panelled doors, one of which was open. They each carried a flower display into the magnificent oval foyer and working to a plan that Ronnie had on a clip board, placed them by number on elegant jardinières and arranged others in beautiful vases in arched niches in the wall. It was hot work and it was not helped by the bizarre rise in air temperature. Several times as Bill descended the steps for yet another great spray of flowers, he would look curiously up at a sky that whilst clear above him had a great wall of almost black clouds far off in the west. When the van was about half empty, Bill whispered that he thought that it was about time to slope off. He picked up one more display and holding it high enough to see, but not be seen, he walked across the foyer, beneath the enormous chandelier, and down a long oak panelled corridor in search of somewhere to hide. Eventually he came to the great ivory tusks that guarded the museum. He quietly opened the door to find it empty, then he turned back, crossed to a Japanese lacquered table standing against the wall. Quickly and rather inexpertly, he arranged the flowers in a vase there and, glancing down the hallway, slipped back into the museum. For several moments he looked around with great awe at his surroundings but conscious of his vulnerability should anyone enter, started looking for a discreet corner to hide. To the right of the far doors, that, unknown to Bill, led to the library, he found a nine foot brown bear on a pedestal. With some effort he moved it slightly forward, squeezed into the enlarged corner behind and settled down to wait. His watch told him he had better than three hours to go. Anxiously Bill tried to remember how many beers he had had that lunchtime.

Unusually for Harrington he was nervous. Normally, once he had decided on the theme for one of his evenings, he was quite happy to leave it to others to carry out his instructions, but today if he'd been down once, he'd done so half a dozen times. He'd consulted twice already with the caterers over where, when and by how many the canapés should be served. He had personally inspected the great silver ice bucket with its thirty bottles of champagne and descended into the wine cellars to satisfy himself that at least another five hundred were racked in addition to the fifty waiting to be brought up that were sitting in huge barrels filled with ice. For tonight, in honour of the occasion, there would be no other wine, only champagne. With an hour to go as he ascended the great staircase, he looked back at the great foyer. At the hundreds of candles in their silver branched holders. To the six wine waiters standing behind the table on which rested the champagne, surrounded by hundreds of flutes, each ready as required to discreetly pass amongst the guests ensuring no glass was empty. At the elegant gilded mirrors that adorned the silk panelled walls and the dozens of candle-sticks. The whole opulent scene illuminated by hundreds of tiny lamps and over a thousand crystals that made up the fabulous Langbourne chandelier hanging from an intricate gilt chain that descended more than forty feet from the domed frescoed ceiling.

As his eyes swept round the magnificent foyer he took in the mass of cut flowers beautifully displayed in the sculptured wall niches and mounted on the marble jardinières. Harrington turned to continue up the staircase, when he paused. There was something wrong with the symmetry. He looked swiftly round again and discovering what it was, descended the last few steps and walked across the marble floor of the foyer. On the far side, just before the wide corridor that led down to the museum and library, one niche was without flowers.

Puzzled Harrington looked round to see if it had been misplaced elsewhere, but everything else was as it should be. With one hand in his pocket he noticed one of the servants dusting further along the corridor and approached him. Harrington was about to address him when something caught his eye further along. He walked down and stood before the lacquered table and gazed down at the missing flowers.

Up until then the impression that someone had followed him on the train had slipped from his mind in the distraction of the frenetic activity of preparing Langbourne for the party. But as he stood there all that changed and Harrington slowly drew in his breath and his eyes narrowed. He glanced back down the hallway to the two other matching wall tables. No flowers. Then by his feet he noticed several chrysanthemum petals and turning three more behind him and in front of the museum doors, one more. From where he stood he could see that one of the great arched doors was very slightly open. Without making a sound Harrington stole across and very slowly pushed it open and stood silhouetted in the doorway. The faintly musty smell of hundreds of artefacts filled the darkened room. Motionless he stood there in the entrance. He was listening. But he was listening with all the cunning of a big cat stalking its prey. He held his breath and amplified his hearing, stretching out his senses so tightly that the slightest movement or sound would vibrate against them. So like a spider with one tiny hook round a strand of its web, with infinite patience he waited for the almost undetectable mistake that must surely come. For almost five minutes he duelled in the dark until with a grim smile he reached round, removed the key and stepping back closed and locked the museum door. He then punched in a number on the wall panel and the priceless collection was crisscrossed with invisible laser beams. Whoever was in that room was for all intents and purposes a prisoner. If he batted an eyelid the alarm would sound. Without a backward glance Harrington walked confidently towards the foyer, pocketing the key as he did so. He glanced at his watch, it was time, and the forces of evil fell in step with him.

Bill too held his breath as Harrington stood motionless in the doorway. He was convinced that his pounding heart beat would give him away, so he kept incredibly still and tried to calm it. He instinctively knew what Harrington was trying to do. He realized it was a duel, a battle of wills. It was, in its simplest terms, a battle between good and evil and one that could not be lost. As Harrington finally walked away, having locked the door and immobilised anyone and anything in the museum, he must have thought he had won. But he hadn't, for Bill was no longer in the corner behind the bear, for in search of somewhere to relieve himself he was now standing just ten feet behind Harrington, watching the drama unfold through a tiny slit in the cellar door.

Chapter 6

When the cellar door was thrown open and light from the corridor streamed down the wooden staircase, Bill shrank back behind a cobweb and dust laden wine rack. From the noise that filtered down it was evident that the party was in full swing. A wine waiter in a white jacket hurried down and picking up six bottles of champagne from the great barrels of crushed ice, rapidly ascended. As the waiter turned into the corridor and slammed the door shut, Bill stepped from his hiding place, and with his heart in his mouth, searched round in the dark for the bottles of champagne. He grabbed four and realizing this might be his best chance raced up the stairs and without hesitation opened the cellar door and turning to his right moved smartly down the long corridor until he was undetected just a few yards behind the hurrying waiter.

To his relief as they arrived Bill found that such was the press of guests that they filled the exit of the corridor and he was easily able to make his way inconspicuously to the table of champagne, unobtrusively deposit his bottles in the enormous ice bucket with the others and melt in with the guests.

Bill helped himself to a passing flute of champagne and, with the glass pressed to his lips, edged towards one of the great marble pillars of the foyer and from that vantage point looked casually around. He spotted Harrington immediately, he was no more than five yards away, standing amongst a dozen guests, exchanging pleasantries and occasionally throwing back his head and laughing. But Bill also noticed that Harrington frequently glanced at his watch and nervously at the double doors of the entrance.

The foyer was straight from a film set. Beautiful women in extraordinarily revealing dresses stood with groomed and urbane gentlemen immaculate in their evening dress suits. Glasses tinkled to group toasts as friends and acquaintances greeted each other. The hub-hub of conversation was frequently broken by shrill peals of laughter. A small orchestra played from a balcony that headed the magnificent spiral staircase, the sounds of the musicians competing with the great throng assembled below. Bill waited and watched and drank sparingly and could frequently hear Harrington apologising for the late arrival of Michael.

Harrington fixed a smile on his face, but inwardly he was seething at the bad manners of his son. They were already well into the party and still no sign of him. He paused as the barker announced the arrival of yet more guests.

"Lord and Lady Hamilton-Smythe. The Right Honourable Mr. Justin Feinnes, The Marquis of Devonshire, Sir Nigel Armstrong Brookes and guest, Mr and Mrs Richard Wentworth." Harrington strode across to greet them.

"Hello Lydia, you look absolutely stunning, and Richard, very suave. Glad you could come."

"Harrington so pleased you invited us, wouldn't have missed this for the world. I must say, old boy, you look better than ever. Doesn't he Lydia?"

"Yes Harrington, you do. Must be love. Now where's that handsome son of yours, you must be so proud."

"Well it's very kind of you to say so, but when did you realize Lydia you needed glasses? As for Michael we are expecting him any minute, and yes of course I am very proud of him." Harrington raised his arm towards the champagne table. "Can we have two glasses over here." Harrington passed them each a glass, and after introducing them to the party behind, excused himself, and glancing yet again at his watch, moved forward to greet more latecomers as they were announced. From his position slightly behind the column, Bill watched as Harrington circulated. Then suddenly the Barker announced Mr Michael Blaine and the entire ensemble pressed towards the main door to catch a glimpse. As Harrington excused himself and the crowd parted to let him through, Bill crossed behind and mounting the spiral staircase, from four steps up found himself with a perfect view of the entrance.

Standing in the doorway Bill could see a tall, dark very handsome young man. Even from where he was standing, it was evident that if you knew Harrington then you knew this was his son. The likeness was there for all to see. The slightly unruly hair, the strong jaw line and long straight nose, the easy smile and the laughing brown eyes. It was easy to see why he was the darling of the tabloids and magazines. Michael laughed at some of the pleasantries of the guests in a semi circle behind Harrington, who was looking very relieved and smiling at his son. Numerous camera flashes flickered the scene. Then from his slightly elevated position at the threshold of the great doorway, Michael held up his hands and the buzz of conversation and laughter died away. From the doorway Michael addressed his father.

"Sorry I'm late Dad, but I had reason. You will remember on the occasion of your own twenty-first, how you met mother for the first time here at Langbourne. Well I intend to go one better and on my twenty first I wish to announce that I am to be married." A little gasp went up from the crowd as Michael stepped to one side. "This Father is my future bride."

For perhaps half a dozen seconds there was complete and absolute silence as a devastatingly beautiful young woman, wearing a pale blue strapless silk evening dress, with long shimmering blonde hair tumbling to her shoulders and the most arresting blue eyes stepped into view and shyly sought Michael's hand.

"This, Ladies and Gentlemen, is Emily." He turned and looked at her. "I'm afraid it was just love at first sight."

Chapter 7

Harrington staggered back dumfounded at the image of Emily and Michael together. It took several seconds for its significance to sink in. A great wall of darkness all but engulfed him, but with a supreme effort of self control Harrington recovered and stepping forward embraced the young couple. As the guests burst into spontaneous applause and shouted their congratulations, Harrington briefly closed his eyes. When, moments later, he opened them he found himself looking straight into the eyes of Theresa standing just behind in the doorway. She was regarding him with a faintly amused but triumphant air, and in that moment he realised that it was she that had dealt the mortal blow. As Harrington stepped wearily back, pandemonium broke out as photographers crowded in to take the pictures that would appear in magazines and newspapers around the world.

From the staircase, Bill watched as a dazed Harrington wandered back through the milling excited guests across the foyer and into a room that led off the corridor to the museum. Heartbroken, Harrington leaned over the wash basin and splashed water over his face. He was still reeling from the shock of what had happened not five minutes before. All the years of planning, all the agonizing, all his hopes, dashed in a single heart stopping moment. He lifted his head and looked with great loathing at his reflection and questioned the image reflected there. But there were no answers, how could there be. He saw only a maniac with wicked eyes glaring back and then the great realization of what he had done, of where his obsession had taken him, to the brink of damnation and beyond, hit him like a thunderbolt. He closed his eyes and let the thunder of it reverberate around his mind until it was spent.

When he opened his eyes, only the old Harrington was there to look back at him and those eyes were full of remorse. Everything that he'd planned during the last nineteen years had been for nothing. But worse he had done some terrible things. He thought of Max, the Beresfords and the awful cruel manipulation of Emily, and the guilt of it all settled on him like a mantle, practically suffocating him. Too late Harrington realized that his great love for Felicity and the nightmare part he had played in her death had driven him to sell himself to the devil and this was the terrible price he had to pay. His one thought now was to hide, to get away from the party and back into the room where he had tried to realize his dream. Whilst reason told him that it was futile, a part of him couldn't let it go, if he did he knew his loss the second time round would send him insane. If he got there, surrounded by all that had made the last nineteen years bearable, perhaps there would be something he could do. More than anything now he needed time to think. Desperately for his own sanity he refused to accept that it was over. There must be something he could do.

Bill returned to the protection that the column afforded him and whilst the guests regrouped in various areas the main part of the foyer, watched as Harrington moved through them towards the staircase. Bill had mixed emotions about what he had witnessed. For Harrington, Bill felt nothing, but for Emily he was happy, she was evidently head over heels in love, and Michael looked no less than she deserved. But he was still a Blaine, and knowing what he did about Harrington and because he felt so protective of Emily, Bill harboured just one or two misgivings. But he didn't know Michael and reluctantly decided he should give him the benefit of the doubt. He looked across to where the young couple were sharing a joke with others their own age and as he raised his glass to his lips, afforded himself a half smile. He nostalgically remembered himself what it was to be young, with your whole life before you, and how nothing seemed impossible. He supposed it was the supreme optimism of youth, and, as he reflected on that, decided that was exactly how it should be. The future would most certainly blunt that particular sword. But for now future cares were not in the equation for them, it was the golden age of romance. They were in love.

As Harrington slowly reached the top of the great staircase, he turned and gripping the banister took one last look down to where Emily and Michael were moving from one group of congratulating guests to the other noting, with an ashen face, how they stole kisses as they did so. Then with his shoulders slumped he trudged away, alone, confused, disorientated and suddenly feeling his age.

Bill threaded his way across the foyer, keeping his back to Emily and Michael, and quickly mounted the stairs in time to see Harrington unlock a door in the corridor, step slowly through and close it behind him. Bill had no way of knowing that it was the first time in nineteen years that Harrington had left the keys behind in the lock. He casually walked along the carpeted hallway, until he found to his right a bedroom just beyond and opposite the door Harrington had entered. He slipped inside and by leaving the door an inch open found himself with an admirable view of not only the room across the corridor with its keys still in the lock, but of a large part of the hallway that stretched away towards the stairwell.

Encircled by the guests and standing before an oval table, Michael, with the help of Emily was unwrapping his presents. There was much ribbing, gaiety and frequent applause as each gift was held up. Discreetly the staff removed the wrapping paper and ribbons and then accompanied by a drum roll, an elaborate birthday cake in the shape of an open book was wheeled in and as the guests recharged their flutes, Michael looked round for Harrington.

"Has anyone seen my father? We shall need him for the toast." Some of the guests closest to him shrugged their shoulders and looked around the foyer. Then the ever present Brooks, the butler, approached and leaned his head confidentially to the side of Michael.

"I believe I saw the Master go upstairs Mr Michael, about twenty minutes ago."

Harrington automatically switched on his computers and stood as he had so many times over the intervening years before the window behind his desk, looking over the floodlit courtyard to the velvet shadows of the park beyond the gates. Hidden by the night, the great thunderheads that had been building all day fizzed and flashed in the far west and even as he watched a sudden solitary gust of wind whipped the branches of the sycamore above the stable roof, heralding the storm to come. In reality he saw none of it for he had turned his eyes inward in a fruitless search of a solution for his despair. His mind was still reeling from the enormity of it all. As the lightning inexorably approached, silhouetting the hills beyond the dark woods, Harrington desperately tried to marshal his thoughts, to reel in the sudden bursts of anger, and support the lethargy of his despair. What he needed more than anything at that moment was a cool head, but just as he believed he could achieve that, he would immediately be destabilized by a sudden flashback to Emily standing in the doorway. So close. He had been that close to bringing Felicity back into his life. But gradually he did calm down and, as his hands stopped shaking and his erratic pulse evened out, a great brooding blackness settled on him. For in that abyss there floated from the depths towards him a beautiful spirit that as it ascended dissolved into a wraith like phantom with a faceless skull.

In that moment Harrington knew that the past had caught up with him and he had nothing to offer in his defence. For by his own hand he had turned all that was beautiful into everything that was ugly. In the cold light of his failure he tried desperately to commune with his dead wife, but over eighteen years as the diaries had unfolded, he had sold her line by line, used her word by word until finally there was nothing left to share. By prying and poking into her most private and personal life he had stolen her mystery and by so doing debased his most precious memories of her. There could be no going back, because he could not undo the knowledge of what he had done. As his bruised mind stumbled about in the maze of his stupidity, a second thunderbolt hit him and he spun round from the window, and was suddenly drenched in sweat from the searing realization of it. Emily was Felicity's clone, and Michael had fallen in love with her.

Michael was in love with his mother!

Chapter 8

Michael stood uncertainly at the top of the staircase and looked down the long deserted corridor. He called out and waited several seconds, then started along the hallway. Ignoring the first bedroom, which he knew to be his mother's, he continued to the next and was about to knock when he noticed the keys in the lock of the room one along. He gently tapped on that door.

"Dad are you in there? We are about to cut the cake, and we need you there. Are you alright?" He waited for almost a minute and was about to knock once more, when the door opened perhaps six inches, and a drained Harrington appeared around its edge. Michael looked anxiously at his father. "Are you alright Dad? You don't look well at all, do you want me to call Dr Bellamy? He's downstairs, arrived about ten minutes ago." Harrington gazed sadly at his son, and imperceptivly shook his head, then he opened the door enough to slip through into the hallway, and put an arm round Michael's shoulder.

"Son, walk down to the terrace with me, I have to talk to you."

"But Dad, everyone's waiting downstairs, we -"

"I'm sorry my boy, but it must be now." Michael took another close look at his father and realized instantly that it must be of the utmost importance for his father to break with protocol, particularly at Langbourne.

"Yes alright Dad, of course."

From across the hallway, Bill watched and listened to everything that unfolded before him and by shifting his viewpoint fractionally was able to watch Harrington and Michael walk slowly away along the hallway and turn left through a pair of ornate double doors, which he guessed brought them onto the upper open terrace he'd seen when walking earlier that morning. Bill waited for a good five minutes. Without knowing why he was convinced that Harrington's room opposite, now slightly ajar, and with the keys still in the lock, held some dark secret. Determined to see for himself, he grasped the door handle and was about to step across, when he heard a woman's voice away to his left, calling for Michael. He instantly recognized it as Emily's. Once again Bill pulled the door almost shut and waited. He could hear the approaching fall of her steps as she wandered hesitantly along the hallway. Bill softly closed the door and put his ear to it and with bated breath waited. He sensed rather than heard her breathing, for she had stopped. He could imagine her glancing slowly round, then suddenly he felt the door handle move beneath his grasp. Quickly letting go, Bill silently placed his foot against the bottom of the door and braced himself. He felt the door give very slightly as Emily tried to push it open, then as suddenly as the pressure had been there, it was gone. He counted to ten and opened the door minutely to see Emily with her back to him walk obliquely across to Harrington's unlocked room and after calling without answer, push open the door.

For several seconds Emily stood perfectly still bathed in the pale blue light that flooded out from the open doorway. Then ghostly and with Bill powerless to stop her, she slowly entered.

In an agony of indecision Bill waited. For what seemed an age he waited, then almost before he realized it she materialized. As she stepped through the ethereal light that poured from the room, Bill took a sharp intake of breath and involuntarily his hand hovered before his mouth. She was deathly white. Her trembling hands sought and then fiercely gripped the architrave on either side and like a crucifix she hung her head as though in the greatest of pain, before closing her eyes. Then Emily gave a sigh of such absolute despair that for a fleeting moment Bill thought her desolation was such that she must surely expire. But even as he watched and the tears brimmed, she raised her head and slowly opened her eyes and Bill could see that all life was extinguished in them. Her chest fluttered with her ragged breath as in a trance she slowly turned and falteringly walked along the hallway. She sensed rather than saw Michael and his father through the oval windows of the double doors, but as she entered, unseen, she leaned back against them and with the key she'd taken from within, silently locked them.

The moment Emily had turned through the balcony doors, Bill, with his heart pounding and with a terrible sense of foreboding, crossed to Harrington's room.

For several moments Harrington said nothing to Michael as they reached the balcony. He simply stood by the balustrade and stared out over the dimly illuminated courtyard to the darkness beyond. Then glancing down into the courtyard momentarily seeing Felicity lying there, he sighed and turned back to where his son was waiting patiently.

"It's difficult to know where to start, Son, so I guess if I start at the beginning it will soon become clear to you why I am telling you all this at this moment in time. When your mother died, you were only two and it almost destroyed me. She fell from this very balcony you know." Harrington bent his head and breathed very deeply several times. "But the worst part of it all was that it was my fault. I tripped and collided with her.... and...." Michael put his hand on his father's shoulder.

"I know Dad, Dr Bellamy told me. But it was an accident. You cannot go on blaming yourself like this -"

"No, you don't understand Michael, it's not the accident. It's what has happened after that is unforgivable. I understand that the accident was a matter of fate. But what I did afterwards was by my own hand and I could have stopped that at any time if I had so wished, but I didn't." Harrington paused as another great flash of lightning rent the sky. Then hard on its heels the thunder growled.

"Your mother was a wonderful woman, you know. I loved her more than life itself. But she was gone and whilst it was difficult to accept, that all that was left were the memories, I did. Just five years of memories. So little for so much. What a waste. But I finally accepted that was the way it was and decided to return to work. After all I had you, and you are fifty percent of her, so in that sense she was still alive, but still I missed her. Oh how I missed her. But as I said she was gone. Then I found a lock of her hair." Harrington paused then gently shaking his head continued. "Now in the normal course of events it would have finished there. I would have tucked that away somewhere like the memories in my heart. But fate hadn't quite finished with me. It had given me one nightmare, but then decided to step in and lay the seeds of one even worse. While driving into the office for the first time since your mother's death, by chance I read about a Professor McGregor. That's all it took, one little article, which given another day I would have missed. A kind act by Max, my chauffeur, making sure I had something to read as we rode in, but one which would sow the seeds of a nightmare." Harrington stopped momentarily, then cleared his throat. "McGregor is a famous geneticist. At the time he went on record as saying that it was possible to clone someone from something as small as a single hair. So he did. I blackmailed him into putting his theory into practice. He took your mother's hair, extracted the DNA, placed it in an embryo, and implanted it into a woman undergoing IVF treatment. The child, a girl, was born eighteen years ago. She was brought up in Tasmania by the woman and her husband unaware that she was not from their own DNA." Harrington couldn't look Michael in the eye. He realized as the story unfolded it had overtones of Frankenstein about it.

"So let me get this right Dad. Somewhere out there is a girl, a young woman, that is a clone of my mother? You mean she's the same?" Harrington nodded numbly. Michael took a deep breath. "Does she know?" Puzzled Harrington turned and looked at his son.

"Know what, that for all intents and purposes she is your mother?"

"No, that she is a clone?"

"No of course not. You'd better let me finish. With her parents she moved to Tasmania and they lived in the same house that your mother used to live in before she came to England and met me. I think before I go any further with this story, you will have to understand why I was doing this -"

"I know Dad, you wanted to bring her back. I can understand that. But maybe she wouldn't be the same, might not ...er .. well want to be with you."

"You're right, but I had one thing that would guarantee that she would." Harrington looked uneasily at Michael, then said simply "I had your mother's diaries." Michael looked blankly at his father.

"I don't understand Dad, how would that make any difference?"

"Well at it's simplest level, from your mother's diaries I would know what schools she went to. What she liked to do. What her hobbies were. At its most complicated what happened to her. In other words everything that influenced and shaped her from the age of seven."

"Still I don't see how going to the same school would make that much difference-"

"No Michael, it's more complicated than that. How can I explain it?" Harrington looked away and chewed on his lip. "You remember when you fell off your pony and broke your arm?" Michael grinned,

"Sure did. Hurt like hell."

"Yes I know, I took you to the hospital, you were six and screaming blue murder. The point of that was that you wouldn't ride again after that."

"Yes....."

"Well actually that happened to your mother when she was eleven, and she was the same, she wouldn't ride after that either."

"Oh I see what you are getting at. But it doesn't happen to everyone that rides. If the clone didn't fall off a horse, she would just carry on riding -" Michael broke off and startled looked at Harrington. "She did fall off didn't she?" Are you telling me it wasn't an accident?"

"No, actually that was a bad example, the clone did not fall off her horse, and I'm disappointed that you think I would endanger her life. The real relevance of your mother's accident was that she didn't ride again. Which for a different reason - her horse was very badly injured accidentally in its paddock and had to be put down - the clone didn't either. You see it was written in the diaries. Do you understand now what I mean when I say the clone would be shaped by everything that happened exactly as recorded in those diaries. Alright she didn't break her arm, but just like the entry in the diary, she never rode again. If everything that happened to your mother, happened to the clone it would shape her in exactly the same way. Particularly if it happened at exactly the same time. Do you see what I'm getting at?" Michael took a deep breath, and looked sharply at his father.

"Seems a bit unhinged if you ask me. Well what other sort of things happened to mother then. And anyway how did you arrange these diary events when she lived out there and you were here?"

"You've heard me talk about Max haven't you?"

"Yes I have, he was your chauffeur way back. You grew up together here at Langbourne."

"Quite right, that was Max. When the clone and her parents went to Tasmania, I sent Max out there ahead of them to do up the property and be the resident handyman-gardener. If I needed anything doing I would ring him on his mobile. When he wasn't gardening, he lived in a wood about four miles away from the house."

"Is he still out there?"

"Yes, I'll come to that. Well anyway there was quite a lot of things that happened to your mother while she grew up there. Her dog died when she was seven. So did the clone's -"

"Jesus! You didn't have the dog killed, did you Dad?" Harrington hung his head and nodded. Michael turned away,

"I don't think I want to hear any more. That's disgusting. Jesus." Harrington put out his hand and grasped Michael's arm.

"I'm not apologizing, Michael I'm just telling you what happened." He shook his hand away.

"Still, bloody disgusting! Anyway, what is the point of all this. Where is the clone now?" Harrington rounded on his son.

"Well I'll tell you if you give me a chance. It's hard enough for me already, without you making it more difficult." Harrington broke off as the flaring lightning followed almost immediately by thunder practically drowned out what he was saying. Michael sullenly thrust his hands in his pockets and looked grimly out into the night. Harrington steeled himself and continued.

"Well eventually she reached the age of eighteen."

"What else happened to her?"

"It's not important -"

"Yes it is, maybe not to you, but I bet it was to her." Michael glared at his father, staring him down.

"Well we altered some exam results to push her into the arts." Harrington paused, wondering how he was going to explain about Emily losing her virginity.

"And?" Harrington looked at his son, noting even in the poor light of the terrace, the heightened colour and the mounting anger.

"Well we arranged her first...... You know..." Harrington trailed off.

"Know what? Her first what?" then it dawned on Michael. "Jesus that's disgusting, Jesus, that's fucking terrible! Let me get this straight, not only do you pry into the private diaries of my mother, but then you arrange for that unsuspecting girl to get laid - I can't believe I'm hearing this. My own father. Jesus! Who did it? Max?"

"No of course not, it was some lad from the beach parties she used to go to."

"Just like that? I don't believe you. What really happened? I want to know." Harrington was beginning to wish he hadn't taken the decision to tell his son.

"We brought a lad in from the mainland, and he well basically got her a bit drunk at one of the beach parties-"

"Bastard! Paid him to do it, did you?" Michael turned away and walked up and down beside the balustrade, muttering and swearing under his breath. Finally he walked up and stood very close to his father.

"You know what that makes you, don't you?" Michael hissed. "Well let's hear the rest of it then." Harrington turned up his collar as the first few drops of rain started to fall. Neither of them saw Emily as she silently came through the terrace doors and stood in the darker shadows against the back wall.

Unblinking, Emily, watched with curious detachment as the two men argued. In her bruised and battered mind she was still trying to come to terms with all that she had seen in that room. It had taken her several seconds to realize that it was her own image that floated along the many screens. For a moment she had quite simply stood there mesmerized by them. But then as her eyes flickered to the upper bank and back to the lower, it slowly dawned on her what she was looking at. Parallel lives. But who was the other woman, her twin? As she moved closer out of the corner of her eye she noticed a row of hand written books open on a desk. She picked up the first and recognized it as a diary. She read the first entry and froze.

'Sandy found dead'.

She had written the very same words on the first page of her own diary. Then she saw the photographs on the desk. Michael's father with herself? She looked closer and found the inscription. Felicity and Harrington Blaine 1988. She drew back in confusion. Next was a photograph of Michael and alongside that, one of... well who? Was it Felicity or herself. Then she noticed the background. It was the upper hall in Windermere House. It was her, but how? Then it hit her and she took an involuntary step back.

"My God, the mirror!" She felt the blood drain from her face. "I've been photographed through the hall mirror. But why?" Totally confused she stood back and looked up at the screens with their twinned looping images. As one image appeared on the screen furthest to her left, it moved to the right from one screen to another with another image following. It was then that she saw an image of her and Wayne on the beach. She remembered the beach party, it was Saturday 23rd January, how could she forget. She tracked it right until it disappeared. Then her mouth went dry as a shocking thought crashed in on her. With trembling hands she picked up one of the diaries.

"Please God don't let it be in there," she whispered. She turned the pages until she reached the 23rd of January. With a cry of utter disbelief she dropped the diary and sank to her knees. It had been arranged! Hardly able to breath, her heart thumped wildly. The dismay she felt gave way to a terrible feeling of loathing and it engulfed her. Then an even more awful thought surfaced. With the blood draining from her face and with shaking hands she reached for the last diary.

Chapter 9

It took Bill several seconds to adjust to the wall of blue light that emanated from within. When his brain finally unscrambled the image before him, it sent a single message to a muscle in his jaw and his mouth dropped open with astonishment. Directly in front of him a double bank of computer screens, perhaps twenty in all, were arranged in a huge semicircle around a central desk, on which were three photographs. On the left, Harrington, with his arm round the waist of a beautiful young woman he presumed must be Felicity; central, a slightly serious Michael, hands in pockets, and to the right, Emily in what Bill thought looked a lot like the first floor hall of Windermere. Below Felicity's photograph there was a newspaper cutting beneath a small oval Victorian box with a lock of blond hair nestling within. Bill slid the box to one side and revealed an article with a photograph of two identical little boys headed 'Clones or Twins?' and written in the column below two lines underlined in red ink, 'Human cloning was possible using the smallest DNA sample such as that found in a single hair'. Bill's eyes flickered across to the lock of hair and then the picture of Felicity's above.

"Well bugger me! So that's how they did it." He drew in a deep breath, expelled it, and shook his head incredulously. In front of those photographs there was a computer keyboard, a notepad and to the right of that several telephones. Bill slowly sat down at the desk and looking up, rubbed his sweating hands on his thighs. The upper and lower banks of screens seemed to be synchronized, as though in parallel time. The top screens appeared to be of Felicity and the lower Emily. Bill watched in fascination as the twinned images continuously played out. Each showing their parallel lives unfolding and throughout it all the uncanny likeness. Same hairstyles, clothes, likes and dislikes all unfolding before him. Like a tape recorder he found the button to fast forward the real life movie that was being played out. Year by year, hundreds of images all telling the same chilling story. The scale of the manipulation raised the hairs on the back of Bill's neck and with a sinking heart he realized the nightmare that he had only been reading about just a few minutes before had been confirmed. Emily was Felicity's clone. Suddenly Bill spun round and faced the door as icy fingers closed round his heart and the clamminess instantly covered his body once more.

"Christ! She knows!"

Horrified Bill raced from the room, just as a flash of lightning illuminated the night sky. The booming thunder, chased him down the hallway to the double doors where it rattled them even as he arrived. Unable to get in he could see Emily through the oval windows walking very slowly across the open terrace towards Michael and Harrington standing by the balcony balustrade. Even from where Bill was standing and without the benefit of hearing them it was evident they were having a very heated argument. Yet more lightning lit up the night sky as the storm closed in and the first great drops of rain began to fall. Then more heavily as Bill grabbed the door handles and shook them violently. He pushed, pulled, and pounded but to no avail as Emily, heedless of the rain that soaked her silk dress to invisibility, inched inexorably away from him. Another great flash of light and with an instant ear-shattering roar the fearsome storm hunched its shoulders and circled its arms over Langbourne. Bill took one last despairing look as the rain flooded down on to the terrace, then he set off down the hall towards the stairs.

Harrington glanced up as yet more lightning flashed and turned to leave the terrace as the rain suddenly started to bucket it down. But Michael grabbed hold of him, his face furious.

"Oh no, you're not getting out of it that easily. I said what else?" Briefly Harrington squared up to his son, then just as suddenly all the fight went out of him as he stood there with the torrential rain pouring down his face, dripping in a steady stream from the end of his nose and streaming down his neck and soaking him beneath his dinner jacket. He'd never felt more miserable or less in control in his life.

"Your mother came to England when her parents..." Harrington couldn't say it. Michael grabbed him by the lapels.

"Spit it out, don't stop now, you bastard! When her parents what?" Emily's voice cut across them from the back of the terrace.

"When like mine her parents died in the same car accident." Both men spun round to face her. Emily advanced from the shelter of the back wall. She was already soaked, but as the rain caught her full on the blue silk dress clung like a transparent second skin. Her face was deathly pale, her sodden hair, dark on her shoulders, but it was her eyes that transfixed them. They were almost luminous in the half-light. The colour seemed to have diminished to the palest blue. They were huge but completely lifeless. She herself looked disturbingly unreal. With the tiny white lines of her underwear defined beneath the translucence of her dress, it was though they were looking through her. Michael was the first to react.

"Emily!" He made an involuntary movement towards her. Harrington sprang between them.

"Don't touch her!" Unsure Michael stopped and looked first at his father and then at the pale quivering creature beyond. Then the awful truth hit Michael, and the full horror of it sank in.

"The clone! It's Emily, isn't it!"

As Emily fell to the ground in a dead swoon, Michael's first punch caught Harrington high on his head, staggering him back against the balustrade. Then, before he could recover, Michael was on him. All the pent up fury and rage within him landed on Harrington in full measure. The blows rained down mercilessly and Harrington already bleeding from the onslaught sank to his knees. Instinctively he grabbed his son round the knees and pitched forward. Michael landed heavily on his back and was momentarily winded. Despite the beating he had received, it gave Harrington a precious moment to find himself and gather his senses. As Michael kicked himself free, Harrington was already half on his feet. He launched himself at his son, and with his extra weight forced him back. As they came up against the stone balustrade Harrington half-turned Michael and wrapped him in a suffocating neck lock. The struggle lasted perhaps another fifteen seconds then unable to breath, Michael started to sink.

Bill stumbled back along the corridor headlong down the staircase and into the main foyer. As he fought his way through the throng towards the front door, a massive thunderbolt grounded nearby and for a moment the great chandelier, dimmed and the crystal shards tinkled. He burst out through the huge entrance doors and leaping down the steps, oblivious to the pain in his knee, ran along the face of the mansion. As he rounded the corner a great gust of wind almost threw him against the wall, but with his head down against the driving rain he groped forward already soaked to the skin. For as he staggered forward only one thought filled his head. He must save her. For in a strange way, Bill knew that this was his last chance also. Splashing along he mentally added up the ledger of his life and realized there was only this. A chance to put behind him the vacuum of misery that was, in reality, his life. To be there for Emily when she so desperately needed someone. His last chance to make the difference between living and just existing. Should he fail then his whole life would have been for nothing.

But unknown to Bill, he was not alone. As he raced along the great facade of Langbourne, a thousand unseen hands pushed him. For with him at that moment, all the sadness, all the pain, all the unfulfilled lives and the unrequited love of the world willed him on. Rounding the final corner that took him to the great courtyard, the storm unleashed its full fury. Bill found himself running in several inches of swirling water, with stinging rain in his face and a violent wind tugging mercilessly at his clothes.

A clone! Suddenly for Emily as she got shakily to her feet, the missing pieces of the jigsaw fell in to place. Now she understood. Now all those strange premonitions, the frequent deja vu, suddenly had an explanation. A bitter smile played round her lips. A clone. A non-person. Someone made not in love but in a test tube with a stolen identity. A fake. A counterfeit. A fraud. As each noun came into her head so her anger mounted. One man, for reasons that only he would really know, had tried to play God. And here she was, a freak. An empty shell that over the years some madman had tried to fill with the life of another. Well he had filled it with everything but the most important thing. The soul. He had tried to bring a dead person back, by exposing her clone to the most awful manipulation and appalling acts of cruelty. He had murdered innocents in pursuit of his devilish and all consuming obsession. She thought of her parents and momentarily closed her eyes as she communed with them for the last time.

Out of control, Harrington pressed home his advantage. He could feel Michael starting to sag beneath the deadly neck lock when unaccountably he felt afraid. Puzzled he glanced over his shoulder and found Emily had fixed him with a look of such hatred and venom, that his grip slackened as he turned to face this new danger. Michael slipped to his knees gasping for breath.

With her hands before her like claws, Emily crouched and with her teeth bared, launched herself at Harrington. Like a coiled spring she leapt with all the force of the short life she'd had and that which she would never know. She flew at Harrington for all the misery he had caused and the lives he'd taken. She struck like an avenging angel. Powerless against the ferocious attack, Harrington staggered back towards the balustrade as Emily gripped his throat in a vice like grip. Small as she was her momentum propelled them unerringly towards and over the wet rail of the balcony. At that very moment Michael struggled to his feet and with his breath searingly painful in his lungs made a despairing lunge as they sailed past, and grabbed a handful of her hair.

As Bill approached the high balcony he heard a hoarse cry, and looking up watched horrified as Harrington and Emily, locked in a terrible embrace, fell struggling through the air. Without a thought for his own safety he threw himself forward. Harrington caught Bill a massive glancing blow then smacked fatally into the black rain soaked cobbles. As Bill buckled under the weight of the impact, Emily too hit him square on and collapsed to one side. On his back Bill lay there in comparative silence as the storm started to edge beyond Langbourne. The rain less heavy now was cool on his face. Very slowly he moved his head. Emily was lying on her side alongside him, her face just discernable in the dimly lit courtyard. She was looking wide-eyed at him. Blood was trickling from the corner of her mouth. He managed a painful smile. Her eyes glistened back at him and a single tear escaped. He knew his back was broken but he tried to move his hand anyway. It wouldn't. He looked again at her.

"Hand." His voice sounded strange and a little way off. She didn't say anything, but a moment later he felt her trembling fingers touch his, then weakly grip them. He managed to squeeze them back; to will what strength he had left into her. So in silence they lay there hand in hand and for a few precious moments, their fading hearts beat as one. Each had lost but each had won. Neither was alone. Despairingly Bill felt her grip gradually loosen and then her fingers slip from his. He didn't turn, not wanting to see the lights fade in those beautiful eyes.

"Bye little Ems, so, so sorry... safe journey girl," he whispered. He could feel his heart breaking. He looked up through his tears, just as a last flash of lightning lit up the balcony. Michael was hanging over it, staring down just as his father had twenty years before. There was a strange look in his eyes and he was clutching a handful of hair. Bill groaned despairingly. "Please God, not again."

His breath was very ragged now and he winced as the pain started to spread inexorably through his body. For a moment he was desperately lonely and afraid as he fought the blackness that was rising like a tide. The storm was over and where there had been nothing but a livid sky, silver edged clouds slowly drifted apart and, in the pallid light of the emerging moon, his failing heart started to race a little for he thought he could see his beloved Sandra reaching down to him, and through her tears she was smiling. For a moment Bill's eyes lit up. Then as the wave of darkness engulfed him, on a wet and lonely courtyard, twelve thousand miles from home, in that last precious moment a contented Bill closed his eyes, for he had finally found what he was looking for and the long wait was over.